☝ **W9-DET-660**

A Novel by Jerry Slauter

FINE LINE

Passion and Providence

Timmy, 11/7/205

God bless.

[signature]

Illustrations by Scott Wiley

ISBN (Print): 978-0-9860223-1-9
ISBN (Kindle): 978-0-9860223-2-6
ISBN (Electronic Ebook): 978-0-9860223-3-3

Library of Congress Control Number: 2015930472

Illustrations: Scott Wiley | www.wileystudio.com
Layout: Wendy K. Walters | www.palmtreeproductions.com

Prepared for Publication By

PALM TREE
PUBLICATIONS

Palm Tree Publications is a Division of Palm Tree Productions
WWW.PALMTREEPRODUCTIONS.COM
PO BOX 122 | KELLER, TX | 76244

Contact the Author:

www.WoodcuttersRevival.com
email: jerrysworldsavings@me.com

CONTENTS

Acknowledgements

A special thanks to my family for putting up with me through the research and writing process. Thanks to Barb who read the manuscript aloud while we were driving, a very effective supplemental means of proofing.

Thanks to Gayle Schloesser and Donna Hale for proof reading and offering editorial input. Thanks to Scott Wiley for his terrific illustrations. Thank you to Todd and Wendy Walters for their formatting, publishing and promotional expertise.

Special thanks to Chris Brown of the Williamsport Washington Township Public Library with the most extensive collection of Mudlavia artifacts and information. Chris is an enthusiastic and tireless researcher of the fascinating Mudlavia resort history.

Chapter One

NEW BEGINNINGS

aryl was running. He could hear the footsteps closing in behind him. His heart was racing and his chest was uncontrollably heaving in and out with huge gasps. This was not a rational fear. This was the instinctive fear of the animal – the hunted. There was no time to think. He was in survival mode. He saw the opening to an ally. Maybe he could elude his pursuers there. He began to realize how the entire situation seemed to be playing in slow motion. A thought flashed in his mind, "This is like déjà vu all over again!"

"Crack!" He felt a sharp pain across the back of his head and went down. He was dazed but not completely unconscious. Lying on the ground, he looked up and could see two shadowy faces. They were outlined by the dim backlight of a shaded lamp over the rear doorway to one of the buildings on the ally. One person was wearing a traditional police helmet, made of rigid fiber covered by cloth with a little round hump on the top. The other wore a bowler, a hat with a small rim and a rounded dome.

In spite of the angst and pain, Daryl found some amusement in the situation. "A bowler! Who wears a bowler anymore?"

"It's stylish and protects my head. Maybe you should be wearing one."

The other person interjected, "Don't talk to him!"

Turning to Daryl, he said, "Quiet Dailey, or you might meet Billie again."

Daryl exclaimed, "How do you know my name? You were watching for me. This is a set-up!"

The person with the police helmet said, "You're just delirious from your drinking and you must have hit your head when you fell."

"I fell because you hit my head."

"Well, there are two of us and we didn't see it that way." As the two assailants began cuffing him and hoisting him up, the man with the bowler asked, "Hey Dailey, do you know what an Irish setter is?"

Daryl stumbled, "What? Of course I do."

"Yeah, it's an Irishman who's too drunk to fight."

Daryl was brought to his feet. At eye level with the two men and seeing their faces in the dim light, he said, "Oh, Officer Nelson. And, you would be Julius or August Knapp, correct?"

Officer Nelson answered, "Don't worry about us. We're just doing our job. We're taking you in for disorderly conduct, inciting a riot, public intoxication and resisting arrest."

Julius Knapp stepped on something breaking it under his feet with a distinct crunch. As he bent over and pulled the film from a camera, holding it up to the light, he said, "Oh, here's your Kodak. Sorry, it appears to be broken. This film must be ruined, too"

Daryl said, "Yeah, you made sure of that. Have something to hide?"

Officer Nelson interjected, "Save it for the judge."

They walked Daryl back to the Wellspring town square and placed him into the police wagon. Once secured inside, they proceeded to the local precinct. They processed Daryl, told him he would get a bail hearing in the morning and placed him in his cell. Even though he was distressed, he soon drifted off to sleep.

The next morning Stewart was in the office, bright and early. James leaned in from the hallway. "Hey, we have a bail hearing in an hour."

Stewart acknowledged and went back to his work. He was preparing for a meeting, scheduled for the following morning with Victoria, Michael and Robert Conner. They intended to discuss the future of Thomas Mines. Conner called the meeting since he was the only investor outside of Edward. Victoria also wanted to resolve concerns about the transfer of ownership into her sole possession, following her father's death.

Stewart was extremely happy with his work, especially since the previous week when James called him into his office for the usual weekly meeting. At that meeting, James tossed a thick book across the desk, letting it a bang down under the heavy weight. Here's your manual for the Colorado Bar Association exam. Study it. Answer the questions. When you feel confident, we'll schedule your exam."

Stewart asked, "The test is voluntary, isn't it?"

"Yes, and with all the practical work you're doing, it should be no problem. I'm having you study for it and take it just so we don't miss anything in your training. I want you to be prepared for whatever the job throws at you, not just some prescribed arbitrary and voluntary standards."

After the discussion with James, Stewart thought about Michael and Victoria. He mused over the memories of the winter spent in the cabin, helping Michael recover. He had been working so hard that he had not taken much time to think about home, the previous winter and Victoria. How was Michael adjusting to life in Discovery? How was he doing with the loss of his brother?

How was Victoria handling the grief of losing her young husband after just one week of marriage, only to lose her father a week later? He assured himself that Victoria's Uncle Michael would probably be the one she most needed to help her work through the grieving process. He remembered how much sustained family support helped him adjust to the death of his Gramps.

They planned to board the train in a couple of hours. He was scheduled to meet them for supper and help them get settled in to their rooms at the hotel. They would discuss the situation after supper, as Victoria promised to bring any files she deemed pertinent to the scheduled meeting with Conner.

It was nearing time for the bail hearing, so Stewart stopped by James's office as they made their way to the court house. As they were waiting for the defendant to be brought in, he reminisced over the time he was in this same court, not knowing if he would be labeled as a criminal for something he did not do. At that time, even with that heavy consideration hanging over his head, he was more concerned for the recovery of the man he allegedly attacked. He had not seen Sven since the trial and wondered how he might be now.

A policeman came in and asked, "Are you James Peterson?"

"Yes, I am."

"Come this way. The defendant has been brought it."

As Stewart and James entered the small closet sized meeting room, Stewart was shocked to see a familiar face. It took him a few seconds to remember why Daryl looked familiar. He had only been with Daryl a few days on the trail before Daryl and Raymond took the route into Discovery. Since the only previous time they met, both Stewart and Daryl had grown mustaches. After a few seconds, Daryl's face brightened as he recognized Stewart.

Daryl relayed the story of the arrest. "I was attending the labor rally for the Gazette. I took some photos and listened to some speeches. I've been covering the rallies for a few weeks now. Last week, I took some Kodaks of some police roughing-up the participants. I also published a column about the Pinkertons and police brutality.

"When Julius Knapp and Kevin Nelson cracked me on the head with a Billie club and arrested me, they called me by name. I knew their names since they were the primary objects of focus in my story and investigations."

Stewart formed a knowing smile and replied, "I've had similar dealings with those two. I was arrested for being involved in labor problems and framed for assaulting one of my co-workers. Ironically, I saw Julius strike Sven Erickson and Kevin Nelson arrested me within minutes. He had to be standing by as a lookout and damage control should their premeditated scheme go bad.

"The Knapp brothers were the witnesses at the trial. We'll see what they offer, but I'm afraid we might not get a fair hearing as the prosecutor is in cahoots with August and Julius Knapp, Pinkerton agents and Officer Nelson. We even caught them in the act and appealed to Governor Mitchell. In his response, he stated that the Pinkertons might be unconventional, but were necessary to assist in establishing law and order in labor disputes."

Daryl added, "And to suppress the rights to assemble and organize!"

Stewart acknowledged, "I'm afraid you're right."A police officer tapped on the door from the hallway and stuck his head in, "Time for court."

James replied, "We're ready."

As Stewart, James and Daryl entered the courtroom, swinging the waist high walnut gate that separated the tables and benches from the galley, Stewart looked over at the prosecutor's table. He figured Connor, and not one of his assistants, would be there when it was Pinkerton business. Stewart nodded and offered a reluctant smile to Robert Connor. Conner returned a half smile, half smirk in Stewart's direction and boomed, "So, we meet again."

Stewart did not acknowledge. He directed Daryl to the defendant's table.

The bailiff stated, "All rise for Judge Baldini."

Judge Baldini entered and stated, "You may be seated."

The bailiff read the docket, "Bail hearing for the People verses Dailey."

"Prosecution, you may proceed."

Connor stood up and said, "We request bail to be set at one-thousand dollars, and for Daryl Dailey to be held over for trial for drunk and disorderly conduct, inciting a riot, resisting arrest and assaulting an officer."

"Defense?"

Stewart had been directed to present at the hearing, "Your honor, we request that Daryl Dailey be released on his own recognizance. He was doing his job as a reporter and photographer, covering a peaceful rally. He was signaled out by Julius Knapp and Officer Kevin Nelson, as they had been subjects in his previous investigations."

Connor retorted, "Objection, this is not a trial. This is a hearing simply to determine bail, and the determination to continue to trial."

Judge Baldini responded, "Sustained."

Stewart concluded, "Your honor, Mr. Dailey has no prior arrests and should not be considered to be a flight risk."

Mr. Connor asked, "Your honor, may we approach?"

Judge Baldini confirmed, "Approach."

Connor stated, "Your honor, we have a plea deal to offer. If Daryl Dailey finds other meaningful employment and does not get into any trouble, the State would consider one years' probation."

James asked, "How long is this offer on the table?"

Connor responded, "Until the date of the hearing."

"I will discuss this with Mr. Dailey."

Stewart, James and Connor returned to their tables. Judge Baldini stated, "A preliminary hearing is set for Wednesday, August Fifteenth, Nineteen and Six to determine if Mr. Dailey should proceed to trial. Bail is set at one hundred dollars. The defendant is released on his own recognizance."

Stewart shook Daryl's hand and asked, "Are you busy Wednesday morning? If not, would you be at the office about eight?

Daryl smiled his usual charming smile and said, "I'll see you then."

Stewart changed his smile from friend to attorney as he stated, "You know, you're going to need more than charm to get through this."

Daryl took on a more serious expression and stated, "I know, but I have competent counsel."

Wellspring Jail

Chapter Two

THE PAST DIES HARD

Victoria and Michael caught the Ten Fifty-Five in Discovery. As Victoria stepped from the platform onto the train, she remembered the last time she boarded in Junction. She and Raymond were on their honeymoon. Her father was also aboard that train and discerned that she and Raymond were returning to Discovery from their elopement. Now, she would never see her husband or father again, at least on this side of heaven.

With that realization, she turned her face to the window. Michael, sitting beside her could tell she was not just gazing at the scenery. Rather, she was attempting to conceal the tears welling in her eyes. The numbness and shock were wearing off. She offered, "I feel like I'm attempting to cope with the day to day survival. Some days are tolerable. Some seem not to be."

"That's right, Princess. We all mourn in our own way."

Sniffing, Victoria responded, "When Mother died, I was sent off to live with Aunt Whitney. Children don't grasp the full significance of death, not that adults get it much better. I was numb. Father attempted to comfort me. He was at such a loss, that he didn't know what to do. Aunt Whitney had been in my situation and understood. She also lost her sister in the loss of my mother. She listened to my grief. She didn't have to offer any answers. I just knew she would always listen.

"We went to see the *Wonderful Wizard of Oz* on Broadway. Dorothy told Glinda that she had to get back to Kansas, because it was too expensive for her aunt and uncle to go into mourning. Whitney laughed, but I didn't get the line. I had seen women dressed in black. She explained that in proper families, mourners usually buy a whole new wardrobe to be properly attired during the period of mourning. I was just fourteen and glad children weren't expected to abide by the custom."

Michael responded, "Princess, as you grow older, you'll realize that you don't have to do things that are expected of you as much as the things that you know are right verses wrong. I know you were hit doubly hard losing Raymond and your father a week apart. The loss of one is beyond comprehension, but both. Who can know you how to feel?"

"When Father died, I was already numb from possibly being a young widow. I was able to be with Father, knowing he was dying.

I told him that I forgave him since I felt that he caused Raymond's death by making him go back into that cavern. I was glad I made him feel better before he died, but I was not able to forgive him so quickly. I still blame him for causing Raymond's death. I blame him for leaving me, and I blame Raymond for cowering to my Father's demands. He would probably be here now if he had stood up to Father."

Michael responded, "I know, Princess. I think about how I could have dealt with your father differently. Maybe we wouldn't have had our quarrel. Then I realized we can't change the past and we're not responsible for the decisions of others."

As Victoria dabbed her eyes with her only white accessory, her lace handkerchief, she attempted a smile and said, "Oh, you're probably right."

They engaged in further conversation for the remainder of the two hour trip to Junction. As they switched from the spur line to the main line, Michael said, "I'm ready for the dining car, how about you?"

"Yes, but I have to be careful to not make eating my only source of comfort."

"I know Princess, but you have to keep your strength up, too."

Victoria continued, "I know some people in my situation can't eat. They have no appetite. Some people seem to find comfort in no other source than food. It might be vanity, but I feel that my clothes are getting tighter. My face is fuller. Maybe it's puffy from crying all the time. I don't know. I feel like I shouldn't be so hungry."

Michael listened. He did not attempt to offer any advice. They enjoyed a tasty lunch of baked ham, sweet potatoes, cranberry sauce and carrot cake. They drank a leisurely cup of coffee as they watched the scenery pass. Victoria said, "I haven't been on this section of track since I came back from staying with Whitney."

Michael smiled, as if he were caught up in fond memories and casually asked, "How is your Aunt Whitney?"

Victoria said, "I never told you. She was widowed about a year ago."

"I'm sorry to hear that. Is she alright?"

"You know Whitney. She's getting by. She had to hire a tenant farmer to manage the farms."

"Could I get her address from you before we get to Wellspring?"

"Sure," Victoria responded as she took a second inquisitive glance at Michael.

As they returned to their seat in the coach, Victoria said, "Uncle Michael, I sure appreciate the way you've pitched in to help with managing the mines. It seems in the years you were gone you haven't forgotten any of it."

"Oh, some of it has changed, but the basics remain the same. I rely strongly on your business savvy. I think you gained your father's strength in ability to think logically. From your mother, I think your perceptions are tempered by emotion and concern for others."

Victoria continued, "When the men walked off after attempting to rescue Raymond, I thought we would lose the mines. Then when most of them came back after... after Father died, I knew we would survive. The men seem to be willing to follow your lead."

"Oh, I just treat them the way I'd want to be treated in their situation. You know this uncertainty has got to be troubling for them, not knowing the future of the mine."

"I feel like I've not been carrying my responsibilities. I wish I didn't feel like I was walking around in a fog," Victoria confessed.

"Princess, you don't need to worry about doing any more or any less than you are. Your primary focus has to be to take care of you. I believe that's why I felt the strong leading to go back to Discovery. We don't always know those things when they happen, but we can see clearly looking back on them."

"I'm afraid I would have lost the mines without you."

Michael reassured her, "I think you'd have managed just fine."

They engaged in quiet conversation, taking breaks, just sitting and relaxing for the remainder of the four hour segment to Wellspring.

Victoria said, "This is so nice; just relaxing. The stress has been so overwhelming. I'm so glad we were able to schedule the entire two weeks here and not have to rush back."

As Victoria and Michael rode the train down, Stewart was working in his office, anticipating their arrival. He heard another knock on the door and looked up. There, standing in his doorway was Sven. Stewart jumped up to greet him.

"Stewart, I haf somevon I vant you to meet," he said with his big boyish grin and thick accent. "Dis ist Heidi Olsen. She ist from Olt Country. Ve are very serious."

Stewart smiled and shook Heidi's hand. "It is so good to meet you. We both have the greatest amount of respect for this man."

Heidi smiled and nodded in agreement. Stewart turned to Sven and said, "You big Swede! You always teased me about having a girlfriend. How long have you two known each other?"

"Oh, about fife monts now. She vas nurse at hospital, ven I stay," Sven answered, not able to conceal his pride and affection for Heidi.

"Stewart, I am still looking for a chob. Do you know of anybody who has verk?"

"I might know of somebody who needs a miner. You can do that, can't you?"

"Vit dese big hands like chovels, I can certainly try," he said holding up his hands as if for examination.

"Well, I'll see what I can do."

"Tank you, Stewart. I know you vill try. Ven vould you like me to check back vit you?'

"Check back in three days."

"Vill do," said Sven as he and Heidi turned to leave.

"I am extremely excited to meet you, Heidi." Stewart shouted as they were progressing down the hallway. "I look forward to seeing you in three days, Sven,"

"Oh, I better get to the depot!" Stewart blurted.

Stewart got there just as the train was pulling into the station.

Stewart could not conceal the excitement in his expression upon seeing Victoria and Michael finding their way down the steps of the train. He hugged Victoria and shook Michael's hand. Victoria was happy to see a familiar face she had not seen for the previous three months. She said, "I like your mustache. It makes you look so distinguished. Thank you for agreeing to meet with us and for making the so many arrangements. I want you to know how truly grateful I am to you for saving Michael's life up on the mountain. He talks about you constantly."

"I hope he exaggerates the strengths and downplays the shortcomings." Stewart chuckled.

Victoria smiled and replied, "He has mentioned no shortcomings."

Stewart attempted to hide the obvious blush on his cheeks as he led them into the hotel lobby and got them checked in. Victoria and Michael decided to get situated and freshen up before supper. Stewart took Victoria's files and went back to the office to peruse them. They agreed to meet back in the lobby at eight to venture out for a late supper.

While Victoria was resting and freshening up, Michael walked back to the Western Union Office. He typed a telegram to Whitney Marsh, paid for it and left.

Victoria and Michael had not eaten fresh western steaks for quite some time, so they decided to go to the steak house just a block and a half from the hotel. During supper, Stewart asked a few questions about items he found in the files. They decided to meet in the morning to go over the files together and prepare for the afternoon meeting scheduled with Robert Connor.

The next afternoon, as they entered the conference room of the law office, Robert Connor rose to greet Victoria and Michael. He looked at Stewart and said, "So, you don't need a real lawyer for this. I'm glad you are confident in our working relationship."

Stewart responded, "I might not be a real lawyer yet, but I soon will be. If we find something in which we need council, James has made himself available to step in. We trust that your concerns are for the welfare of Victoria and the future of Thomas Mines."

Connor replied, "That brings us to a significant point. I'm concerned that, with Edward being gone, the mines are left without proper attention."

Victoria interjected, "I've been running the business aspects of the mines for several years, now. I was always taking on more responsibility in the management and ownership as my father and I felt I was ready. Besides, Uncle Michael knows the process. He built and managed the first wood-fired smelter up there. He's also good at leading people."

Connor retorted, "That's all well and good, but I want to make you an offer. I own twenty five percent of the operation. I was thinking I might do us all a favor and buy your interests out. I know you have a lot on your mind at this time. Quite frankly, with the down time from the accident and ever changing conditions of the business, I was thinking the future of the mine might be better served under my control."

Victoria responded with a sarcastic grin, "Why, Mr. Connor, how thoughtful of you."

Connor replied, "I just want to help."

Victoria responded, "Oh, I'm sure you do. You realize that you only own twenty-five percent of the actual mine? The other assets in the town of Discovery were owned solely by my father. That leads us to another related matter. You were handling Father's estate too?"

Connor reluctantly responded, "Yes, I was."

Victoria continued, "Mr. Taylor found some receipts with your name on them for three life insurance policies. Two of the policies name me as the beneficiary, in case of death of Father or Raymond. You were going to mention these, weren't you? "

Connor reasoned, "Of course! I just thought we should discuss our plans with the mines, too. I am a partner."

Victoria stated, "Let's find out where I stand personally before we determine if I have the resources to maintain my position as the owner of the mine."

Connor explained Victoria's inheritance and monetary gains from the policies. He then offered her a document explaining his proposal to buy her interests of the mines.

Stewart said, "We'll spend some time going over these documents. Do you want to get back together the day after tomorrow, in the afternoon?

Connor agreed to meet in two days. After Connor left, Stewart brought James in and the four discussed the proposition. Michael and Stewart both commented how calm and strong Victoria had been in dealing with Mr. Connor.

Victoria stated, "I put up a strong front, but I'm not ready to do this by myself. I think I realized that I was living Father's dreams, not my own."

Michael said, "Princess, you don't have to decide now. You'll have the resources whether you keep the mines or not. I'll be there to help you, too."

Stewart interjected, "I'll be there, too."

Michael brought up another point, "You know Princess, everything I know and everything I hear tells me that you shouldn't make any major decisions for a year after becoming a widow. In your case you are an orphan as well. You also lost your business partner."

James and Stewart both agreed with Michael's statement. James said, "I've seen too many people make rash decisions during times like this, later regretting them."

Victoria said she would pray about her decision, but unless otherwise convicted, she would sell the mines and other assets. "To be honest, I don't think I can even do this for a year while making the decision. Besides, with the offer Mr. Connor made and the payment from the insurance policies, I'm sure I have an adequate buffer until I do decide what I want to do."

"That is all well and good, but I just don't trust Connor," replied Stewart.

James assured them, "From what I see, the offer is legal and appears to be fair. Stewart and I will study it all in detail this afternoon."

Michael stated, "I'd like to keep the tools and equipment in the woodshop and machine shop. I either brought or purchased most of those items when Edward and I were in business together. They would be expensive to replace. I'm sure Connor can afford to set up his own shops."

Victoria agreed, "Uncle Michael, you are certainly entitled to your property, and I don't see these things being a deal breaker for Connor. I'm sure they mean so much more to you than they would to him."

The four had lunch together in the diner where Stewart had eaten on the first morning that he went to work for Townsend. Michael and Victoria returned to the hotel, agreeing to meet Stewart for supper. Victoria went to her room and slept most of the afternoon.

Chapter Three

NEWSBOYS

On Wednesday morning, Daryl came to the law office and sat down in the waiting room. Shortly, Stewart and James came in and motioned him to join them in the conference room.

Stewart began, "We're glad to see you. I hope you haven't been worrying excessively about your situation. We'll do all we can for you."

Daryl responded, "Thank you. I'm glad you're helping."

Stewart and James both laid out legal pads and pencils on the table, as if they were preparing for a lengthy session. Stewart asked, "Have you been in any other legal trouble?"

Daryl said, "Nothing here, but I had a similar situation in New York. I'm not sure if there was an arrest record."

Stewart said, "Okay. Why don't you tell us about it? Remember, we're on your side and the more we know, the more we'll be able to help."

Daryl began, "Well, I was a newsboy on the streets of New York. I became orphaned and the Foundling Society took me in. They offered orphanages, industrial schools, boarding houses and jobs – mostly delivering papers on the street. They also ran orphan trails to help get the orphans out of the city and into homes in the country."

James asked, "Couldn't that system have been abused with children taken in for the wrong reasons? Couldn't they have been placed with families where they would become servants, or worse?"

Daryl answered, "Of course. The system was loose fitting and had room for abuse. The fact is, the kids who weren't able to make it out of the city faced far greater certainties of harm and neglect than those who were sent out. I met Dr. Herman D. Clark and other church and community leaders who oversaw and assisted all they could. Pastor Clark wrote to each of his children every year. He also took several trips from New York out into the countryside to make sure each child was placed in a home with a loving family. There were other pastors and workers who did the same thing."

Stewart asked, "So, what happened?"

Daryl continued, "We were getting the papers for sixty-five cents per bundle of one hundred. On a good day we made about thirty-five cents for long hours and hard work. We could not return unsold papers. The risk was all on us. We made enough to buy a day's lodging, if we were lucky along with two meals, a pair of shoes and a coat, and have a few cents for cigars or shooting craps."

James interjected, "Wait a minute! They allowed you to smoke cigars and play dice?"

Daryl said, "No, they didn't approve of that, but there were thirty thousand of us in the streets. They couldn't watch us every minute. When they could, they would get us into the industrial school to learn reading, writing, math, printing papers, woodworking and sewing for the girls.

"There wasn't always room in the classes for us, so we took what training we could when we had the chance. Since I was taken in as an older orphan, I earned part of my keep by watching out for and teaching some of the younger boys. Pastor Clark told me he was training me to be a leader, so I didn't have to work the streets as many hours as most Newsies."

"So in 'ninety-eight, the Spanish American War breaks out and papers sell. By July of 'ninety-nine, Joseph Pulitzer at the *New York Evening World* and William Randolph Hearst at the *New York Evening Journal* decide to charge us sixty cents per bundle. They were called the 'Sensationalists' because they knew how to turn tragedy into profit.

"The newsboys were outraged. We figured you couldn't starve us survivors. We were used to getting by on nothing. The fat cats could never be satisfied no matter the amount of surplus. No amount of wealth would ever be enough. During the strike, which lasted two weeks, Pulitzer's *New York World* circulation dropped from an estimated three hundred and sixty thousand to one hundred and twenty-five thousand copies a day.

"A few more cents a day for us was the difference between getting a hot meal and a cot or sleeping on a storm grate. A few more cents per paper for them or lower profits for us meant a second house upstate, another trip to Europe or an Ivy League education for the kids of Pulitzer and Hearst. They reasoned if they got together to form a monopoly or a trust to make sixty cents per bundle instead of fifty cents at proceeds of one million five hundred thousand dollars instead of one million, that's good for capital and the nation.

"If we got together to improve our miserable lot, they called it Socialism. They used tax dollars to break us up and tried to get our churches to make us feel guilty. They used their own papers to stir public opinion against us. There was pressure on Pastors Clark, Washington Gladden and others to lecture us from the pulpit. They wouldn't give in. They were even attacked by the paper moguls for not complying and were accused of preaching a 'Social Gospel.'

"Hearst and Pulitzer found a shill to spout their virtue and to condemn the collective actions of the newsboys. Gaylord

Lynchbaughm used to write independent editorials and sell them to the United Press International. He claimed he was independent and worked for himself. We were sure he was paid to specifically place his editor/owner favorable articles in the *World* and the *Journal*. Of course, he commented on enough other information to sell some articles to other papers. Funny thing, though, the other papers began to support the newsboys. As Hearst's circulation began to drop, he threatened to take Lynchbaughm off the dole."

Stewart injected, "Daryl, it's strange, but when I've talked to you in the past, hearing only a few words at a time, I could detect a slight accent. Now when you get excited, explaining your story, I detect some New England or New York accent. I only heard a few words from you until I came to Wellspring. It took me a while to learn to detect them."

"Oh, yeah! When I get excited, I'm not so careful to pronounce my words as deliberately as I am in easy, simple conversation."

Stewart asked, "Would anybody like some coffee of anything else to drink?"

After a short break, Stewart asked, "So how did you get into trouble?"

Daryl continued, "Lynchbaughm started in Chicago. Melville Stone, Associated Press manager kicked him out of the *Chicago News*, because the Associated Press upheld standards of accuracy, impartiality and integrity. He started in Scripps, which became United Press International in eighteen-ninety three. The UPI was competitive and scrappy. That was when he found his way to New York and linked with Pulitzer and Hearst.

"I knew a reporter, who had worked with my parents when they were alive. I'll tell you more about him later. At first, he was skeptical about the newsboys and their story. He thought we would either bring the papers down, or get ourselves fired or worse. Either way, he didn't think we had a chance. He asked how we could organize. The newsboys were too diverse and too scattered to hold together.

"Then, as I explained my story, much like I'm doing with you, he began to listen. He gave me some tips on writing and an old Kodak to take pictures. After I wrote some articles, he proofed them and I used my connections to get inside the print shop at the industrial school. He even found us some surplus paper from his paper's warehouse. So I printed a paper. We got it distributed and began to find unity among the various newsboy leaders from each burg.

"Since I was older and had built up some seniority, I was able to have a stand on Newspaper Row. Lynchbaughm strolled by every day about ten in the morning. He always bought a paper and opened it to his column. I think he liked to see his picture and read the column from the paper as he proceeded to his office.

"Before the strike, he used to lecture me about his views. Sometimes, he wore a big top hat and heavy wool coat with a fur collar. He smoked a huge cigar and brandished it as if it were a symbol of his importance. When he had no hat, his thinning gray hair was slicked back. As he began to talk, his fat cheeks would blubber. With his large protruding teeth, he looked like a big wood chuck attempting to clean an ear of corn as his head bobbed in a rhythmic nod, jabbing his cigar at us to emphasize a point.

"As I watched and listened, it was very difficult for me to keep a straight face. He always became indignant, as though I was mocking him. He would make a point raising his finger into the air and then, dramatically, pausing as if reaching an epiphany and placing his pointed finger on his lips in a moment of pregnant pause and reflection.

"He would talk to us as if we could not read and had no interest in the real world. If only he knew how hard our world was. He would tear up and say, 'Do you know I tell you this because I love this country?'

"We just let it go and baited him into discussion every day, as it drew a crowd, and crowds sold papers. The distraction was entertaining and useful in breaking the monotony from the long day. He would tell us we could not understand the big picture without his interpretation. He said he stayed up late at night studying so he could educate the common man. He was oblivious to the mocking and jeering expressions of the onlookers in the gathering crowds.

"He would go on a rant and state that Herman and Gladden should not be allowed to incite the youth. He said they preached a 'social gospel' because they sought social justice. He said anybody who hears their preacher say anything about a social gospel should flee.

"Then, during the strike, our tempers were at an edge. He was tense because he had already been threatened with his job if circulation did not return to normal. I told him I had no paper to sell him, but handed him one of mine. He started, 'If you could read...'

"I burst out, 'What makes you think I can't read? Do you think we just sell the papers and don't have time to study them? I wrote this one. I am a newsboy and proud of it. You're a views boy. You don't report the news. You attempt to create it. What's the matter, Lynchbaughm? You look as if somebody just stepped on your grave!'

"For the first time, he was speechless, as he looked at me with wide eyes and an open mouth. I think it was disgust, shock and awe. He left and stormed off toward the paper office. The next day, about ten o'clock, I see him from a distance, this time on the opposite side of the street. Suddenly, a police wagon pulls up. Two officers grab me and look over to Lynchbaughm. He nods and starts walking.

"They took me in and told me to contact Dr. Clarke. He came down for my arraignment. They were ready with a deal. Dr. Clarke agreed to put me on an orphan train that afternoon to avoid being put away. There were no funds for legal services and public defenders did not care about children's rights.

Stewart and James just sat there staring at Daryl, suddenly realizing he was done with his story. Stewart was the first to speak, "It sounds as if there will be no paper trail. They wanted the deal so quickly; they probably kept no record of the 'arrest.' Besides, you were a minor. "

James sat looking at the table with a reflective expression on his face. "I wonder how the leaders of the Foundling Society and the Orphan Trains had so much passion to devote to saving kids."

Daryl explained, "I remember Dr. Herman giving the same theme with variations in his teachings and sermons. He compared New York, and any large city to Babylonia. The sky scrapers and in the financial district were Towers of Babel. In Chapter eleven of Genesis, the people thought they could reach the heavens by making brick and using tar for mortar. They reasoned if they could reach heaven, they would not need God. They concentrated into the region and attempted to memorialize themselves. He diversified their language and scattered them throughout the earth.

"Since Dr. Herman and the others couldn't take care of every child in the city, they provided ways to scatter them throughout the country by means of the orphan train. He always came to the Great Commission in Matthew, 'Go out and make disciples of all nations.'"

Chapter Four

VICTORIA'S DECISION

Victoria and Michael had a suite with a living room. Through a door on each side was a private bedroom. The suite was a little more costly than a single room, yet less expensive than two single rooms. Besides, the suite afforded a common area for camaraderie with private rooms for privacy. The bathroom was off the main room.

Victoria had a rough night of sleep. Every time she drifted off, the realization returned that she would have to make her decision by the afternoon. Of course, she could put it off. She held the controlling interest. However, putting off the decision would only cause more sleepless nights.

When she could calm herself enough to drift back to sleep, she would see the light from the living room from under her door and hear Michael rattling around at the table. She knew he was having trouble sleeping, too. She knew that he would have stayed in his room and prayed quietly unless he had some ideas to write. If he had ideas to get on paper, there was no use attempting to suppress or control them.

She smiled and thought how having loving family members around could be so comforting, but sometimes came at a cost. How many nights had Michael been up in that cabin, with nobody to disturb or to share his thoughts? She thought of Stewart and how much she appreciated his sacrifice. Had she mentioned it to him? Oh yeah, at supper about four times the previous evening.

There was something else that bothered Victoria. She could not control her emotions. She knew it was from the mourning process, but was there more? What about these mood swings, from elation to sorrow, from feelings of strength and indomitable capability to doubts and fear. She also fluctuated from feelings of soundness of mind to uncertainty and indecision.

After the light in the dining room went off again, Victoria decided to go out and have some tea and toast brought up. As she was sitting at the table waiting for room service, she noticed a stack of papers. They were arranged on the table with the writing clearly visible, so she decided to peruse the top paper. In Michael's scribbling, she read:

Tides of Fortune or Providence?

Financial fortunes can be realized in an instant. They can vanish even quicker.

For all your learning of Economics, Industry and Science; for your desire to comprehend and control human nature; for your fretting and machinations, worrying about thieves breaking in and stealing, moths and rust corroding and deteriorating; you better leave a major portion to Divine Providence. Fail not to consider the role of God in our everyday lives. It is a fine line that distinguishes success due to Divine Intervention or human wisdom and effort. Present life is a thin veil through which we see dimly – a thick fog through which we proceed precariously.

He quoted Proverbs twenty-three, verses four and five:

"Weary not thyself to be rich; Cease from thine own wisdom. Wilt thou set thine eyes upon that which is not? For riches certainly make themselves wings, like an eagle that flyeth toward heaven."

As Victoria finished reading this and some other paragraphs, there was a knock at the door, "Room service."

She retrieved the tray, gave a tip and returned to the table. As she finished the tea and toast she suddenly felt nauseous. She ran to the bathroom and lost her breakfast. As she rinsed her face, she felt light headed and stumbled to a comfortable chair in the living room. She had never experienced this type of sensation.

Then, a movement was felt from inside her. The movement was not in her stomach. It was from somewhere below the stomach. Could she be? No, she did not have time. She had no husband. What if? What joy! What responsibility! What a health risk! "I'll get to the doctor as soon as I can. I need to get this mining situation behind me."

Just then Michael came out from his room. "Do I smell breakfast?"

"Yes, I was hungry, so I ordered a little something to eat. I knew you were up and down most of the night, so I didn't want to wake you."

Michael responded, "Oh, I hope I didn't keep you up."

"No, I was having trouble sleeping. Michael, I know I'm not supposed to make any major decisions when I'm so deep in mourning, but I think I have made up my mind."

"Princess, I'll support any decision you make. I just don't want you to regret anything later, wishing you'd done things differently."

"I know, Uncle Michael. I know. I read what you wrote. I hope you don't think I was being nosey. To me, it sounds like you believe we should do all we can to do right, but leave the decision up to God."

"Yes, we don't know all the answers. We don't even know all the variables. We're responsible to make our decision, stick with it and allow the grace of God to make it work.

Victoria added, "Maybe we can see a doctor tomorrow or the next day, at least before we go back to Discovery."

"I'll go down to the desk and see if they can recommend anybody. If the office isn't too far, maybe I can go schedule an appointment for you." Michael offered.

"Thank you, Uncle Michael. That would be great. Then we need to be ready to meet Stewart for lunch. I want to get these meetings with Connor over with."

Michael got ready. As he left, he told Victoria to rest and fret about nothing. He assured her things would work out.

Michael asked at the desk. There were two doctors' offices within a six block radius. He jotted down both addresses. As he found his way into the street, he enjoyed seeing people bustling around, taking care of business, sightseeing, visiting with friends and family, enjoying the cool dry mountain air. He wondered how he got by so long on his own up in the cabin. He also wondered if he might not have made his way to Discovery or Wellspring on his own, even if Stewart had not intervened into his life.

Anyway, he reasoned, the timing was perfect to be in Discovery; in time to forgive his brother, meet Raymond and be there for Victoria in her time of such extreme loss. He thought how Victoria was a strong person, but how much grieving could she bare? He was also concerned about her health and the reason she wanted to see a doctor. Could she take another burden in her life at this time?

Michael found the first doctor's office. As he inquired inside, he learned the doctor would be too busy to make an appointment for the remainder of the week, especially with a new patient. He found his way to the second office and discovered they had a cancellation for the next morning. Michael set an appointment. The receptionist assured Michael that if an emergency arose, the hospital had an emergency room. She told him how to get there from the hotel, if they should need to go.

Michael and Victoria spent the next hour resting and talking. They met Stewart for an early lunch so they would have time to discuss their strategy before proceeding to Conner's office to determine how the deal would progress. Stewart hugged Victoria and gave Michael a friendly handshake.

"Good morning, Stewart. Are you well?" Victoria asked.

"Yes, I am. Did you sleep well?"

Victoria answered, "Oh I was up and down all night. I was also nauseous this morning. I'll be glad to get this transaction behind us, whichever way it goes."

Michael answered, "I was getting up and writing most of the night. Victoria let me sleep in, but that is worse on me than getting up at a regular time."

Stewart said, with a knowing smile, "I understand."

They enjoyed a casual lunch with small talk. Finishing their lunch, Victoria started, "I wasn't sure I would like Irish food so well. I was also not sure what I could keep down after this morning, but I was definitely ready to eat. I'm glad you recommended this place, Stewart. Have you prepared the counteroffer as I directed?"

"Yes, here it is. There are some details I need to point out and discuss before we talk to Connor."

Victoria added, "I don't know if he'll accept this proposal, but I don't have to sell. If he wants it bad enough, he will accept. I don't feel like haggling every detail."

"That is a good attitude to project, Princess. If he sees that you aren't desperate, he'll be more motivated to take your offer and run," added Michael.

Stewart broached another aspect. "Victoria, I have two friends who need work. Do you need any miners at this time?"

Victoria thought and responded, "We could probably add some new people, but that depends on whether Connor accepts the offer, including keeping my present workers. Are they dependable?"

"One is extremely dependable, but he's had some trouble getting work in the community. The other can be dependable, but easily distracted. He needs a break. His name is Daryl."

Victoria brightened and said, "Not Daryl Dailey?

Stewart said, "Yes, it is Daryl Dailey!

Victoria continued, "He worked for us for a while. He came in …" Victoria faltered slightly as she attempted to finish her sentence. "He came into Discovery with Raymond. He left after the first indication that mining could be dangerous. I only wish Raymond had been that cautious. Maybe… "

Michael interjected, "Now Princess, you can't be living your life wondering, 'What if' all the time."

Stewart said, "We better move on to Connor's office."

At the meeting, Victoria regained some of her pluck and quick wit, although most of the fight was out of her. She handed Connor the proposal and stated her conditions. "I request that you agree to keep my employees for three months. That would get them through Thanksgiving. I also know you'll need some time for the transition, so we can include three months for you to find and train a manager to run the mine before you take possession."

Connor answered, "Let me look this over. I can give you an answer either way today. Would you like some coffee or tea while I take a few minutes and talk to some other interested people?"

After Connor left the room, Victoria told Stewart, "If he agrees to my counteroffer, I'll pretty much be out of the mining business in a few months. For a while, I thought he wouldn't be that interested when he saw the numbers. Now, I think he'll go for it without much further haggling."

Stewart and Michael agreed. Michael said, "Although you shouldn't be making major decisions you had to make a decision, one way or the other, in this case. Keeping the mines would be a decision. Selling the mines would be a decision. You have to place it into God's hands and trust He will guide you and the situation."

Connor came back into the room. "We have decided to accept your counter proposal. We'll have the agreement drawn up within two hours."

Stewart, Michael and Victoria spent the next two hours looking around the shops and book stores in the immediate area and getting some coffee and tea at the café. They went back to Connor's office. He came in and signed the papers. They spent an hour or so discussing the transition period. Victoria offered, "I will be out of the house by Thanksgiving. If you choose a general manager any time between now and then, he'll be welcome to train in any aspects of mining. At that time, Mr. Connor, you will have paid in full and resume full control of the mine and the town of Discovery."

Connor then told Victoria he would read the will and settle any loose ends from the estate. Stewart asked, "Why did you wait until you got what you wanted out of the deal before going into details about Victoria's inheritance or insurance policies?"

Connor responded, "Oh, I wanted to handle one issue at a time and not muddy the waters."

Stewart, getting a little heated under the collar and protective of Victoria said, "Did you want Victoria to feel she was worse off than she was so you could create a sense of urgency to sell?"

"Listen pup! When you get your license, talk to me about ethics and how to conduct my practice!"

Victoria stood up and said, "This is getting us nowhere. I sold because I decided to sell. If I had thought Mr. Connor was attempting to cheat me, I'd have dug in and drug my heels. I sold because I just don't want to raise a fam…, I mean be tied to Discovery and live under the constant stress of running the mine. I feel my life is taking a different direction. That's all."

With that, they gathered their papers, shook Connor's hand, and agreed to keep in contact through the transition period.

They went back to the hotel and had an early supper. After supper, Victoria excused herself, proceeded up to the room and went directly to sleep. Stewart and Michael stayed in the lounge and talked until midnight. Michael went up to the room twice during that period to determine if Victoria was alright. On his second return he brought his Bible. He opened it and quoted Proverbs sixteen, verses one through three:

"The plans of the heart belong to man, But the answer of the tongue is from Jehovah. All the ways of man are clean in his own eyes, but Jehovah weigheth the spirits. Commit your work to Jehovah, and the purposes shall be established."

He closed the Bible, looked at Stewart and both simultaneously said, "Amen!"

Chapter Five

FRIENDS AND FAMILY

Victoria was up early the next morning. Michael slept in after his long evening with Stewart and emerged from his room just as Victoria was coming out of the bathroom. "Are you feeling better this morning?"

"Yes, that full night of sleep made a big difference. I feel like I've had the weight of the whole world lifted from my shoulders. Would you like to call down for room service? We have two hours before the doctor's appointment. Were you going with me?"

"Of course, Princess, I wouldn't miss this for the world. Stewart is going to be here in an hour to get us situated with the bank."

Victoria, reading the room service menu, looked up and nonchalantly said, "Oh that's considerate. That'll be very helpful, but he doesn't have to do that. I'm sure he has work to do."

Michael smiled and said, "Oh, we're part of his work and I know he doesn't mind spending a little extra time with us while we're here. I'm sure he enjoys our company. Before setting out, he was always close to his family. He probably considers us to be family now. "

Victoria said, with a warm and thoughtful expression, "He's such a considerate man. I do appreciate all he's done for us. He does so much more than the legal work we pay him to do."

Victoria and Michael met Stewart in the lobby. Michael noticed each time Stewart and Victoria greeted one another, they each seemed to look a little more directly into the other's eyes. They kept their hands clasped a little longer in a handshake that was losing the appearance of a business handshake. They clasped both hands in front when neither offered a hug. Other times, one or the other offered a hug.

Stewart showed them the bank and asked if they wanted to go in and meet the teller and office manager, and open their accounts. They completed the bank work in just enough time to walk leisurely to the doctor's office. Victoria went into the exam room and met with the doctor. He told her to wait in the reception area, and he would get the test results as quick as possible.

Within thirty minutes, the receptionist told Victoria, Michael and Stewart the doctor wanted to talk to them. As they entered his office, he stood to meet Michael and Stewart. He looked at Stewart and said, "Congratulations, you are going to be a father!"

With a sheepish grin, Stewart said, "Oh, I am not...I don't...I'm just a friend. Victoria is a widow. Michael is her uncle."

The doctor with a red face and a silly grin said, "Oh, I'm so sorry. I just assumed. I have trouble getting most husbands to come in with the patient. She must be special."

Michael and Stewart said simultaneously, "Oh, she's special!"

The doctor went on, "This is going to be a very difficult pregnancy. She is going to need all the support she can get. How recently was she widowed?"

Victoria interjected, "I'm right here. You don't have to talk as if I'm absent."

The doctor said, "I'm so sorry! I just caught myself off guard by assuming."

Victoria said, "I've been widowed for about four months. I thought I'd lost my menses due to the grieving. It only occurred to me in the last two days or so, that I might be expecting a child. I also started having morning sickness and felt the quickening."

Obviously still embarrassed, Doctor Gilmore fumbled for a reply, "The grieving explains a lot. I should've asked you during the exam. That's why I like to follow up a visit with a discussion. I thought you were in a depressed state. Not knowing you, I had nothing to with which to compare your demeanor."

Turning to Michael and Stewart, he said, "She should try to eat small amounts, as often as she can. Find out what she can keep down. Hopefully, the morning sickness will not last. You make sure she gets plenty of rest. She should not be on her feet more than a couple of hours a day, total!"

Michael spoke for both, "I'll be with her most of the time. I'll see to it she follows your instructions."

Victoria protested, "I'm not a child."

The doctor retorted, "No, but you are with child."

After the visit to the doctor, Stewart made sure Michael and Victoria were safely escorted back to the hotel. They had lunch in the hotel dining room. Victoria asked, "Would you like to come up for a while, and maybe go to supper? We're not sure how long we'll be in town and uncertain about our plans for returning to Discovery."

Stewart smiled as he gazed into her eyes, smiling dreamily and said, "Sure!"

While they were sitting in the living room, they heard a knock at the door. Victoria said, "Who could that be?"

Michael got up from his seat with a strange grin and said, "We won't know until we check."

Victoria and Stewart looked at each other as they could only hear Michael's end of the conversation. The person in the hall asked, "Victoria needs me. I asked if anybody else needed me. You said, 'Yes.' Now who would that be?"

Michael said, "I need you."

At that, he turned and led Whitney into the living area. Victoria looked shocked. Stewart smiled pleasantly. Michael introduced Whitney to Stewart.

Whitney had wavy, shoulder length chestnut colored hair. Her piercing eyes were hazel. She wore a green plaid skirt with a matching frock jacket, fish net stockings and high laced shoes with high platform heels. Whitney looked Stewart straight in the eye and said, "He is a handsome one, Victoria!"

Stewart's smile turned to an openmouthed expression of shock, as he was taken aback by Whitney's beauty and directness. Victoria, who was attempting to get up from the sofa as quickly as she could, also had a look of shock. "Aunt Whitney, what are you doing here?"

Whitney answered, "Michael said you were in a motherly way and might need a feminine touch. I'm so sorry to hear about Raymond and your father."

Victoria looked even more perplexed." We just found out this morning! In fact, we just got back from the doctor's office"

They both turned and looked at Michael. He said, "I contacted Whitney as soon as we got into town. I guess she was on the next train out."

Victoria delved further into the mystery, "But you told her I was with child. How did you know?"

Michael said, "I guess I just had a feeling."

Whitney protested, "You mean you drug me all the way out here on a hunch? What if she had not been expecting?"

Michaels said, "Oh, relax. You probably needed to get away from the farm and Indiana. Besides, Princess needed you, even if she wasn't with child."

Whitney asked again, "And…?"

Michael protested, "Yes, I need you. Why do you keep making me say it?"

Whitney retorted, "Well, maybe if you weren't so darn bullheaded, things would've come out differently."

Michael said, in as calming a manner as he could, under the circumstances, "Maybe, we are too much alike, and that was the problem. I'm sure we don't need to air our past in front of these two. We need to dwell on the future."

Victoria and Stewart stood, observing the entire exchange with open-mouthed expressions of surprise and delight. Victoria said, "Oh, I find this very interesting. I never knew."

Stewart said jokingly, to break the tension, "I will call down for room service. Who wants coffee? Who wants tea? Who wants something stronger?"

Victoria opted for tea. The others ordered coffee. As they sat drinking coffee in the afternoon, with the cool mountain air wafting through the room, they engaged in a long, leisurely conversation. Victoria said, "I'm drowsy, but I don't want to miss this. So, it sounds like you two were an item at one time."

Whitney was first to respond, "When Edward and Patricia were falling in love and making plans to get married, Michael and I always had affection for each other. It constantly seemed the world was filled with Edward and Patricia's plans and arrangements. I hope talking about your parents doesn't make you feel uncomfortable, Victoria."

Victoria said, "Oh no. I knew they both demanded the attention of many others, especially later when I could recognize what was happening. They never really told me about how they met or their early years of courtship."

Glancing at Stewart, Victoria said, "When I lost Mother, I found that Aunt Whitney was the only person who understood my need to grieve. I was too young to realize that when I returned from her home to Discovery."

Addressing Whitney more directly she continued, "I deeply appreciate the patience and understanding you demonstrated during those very troubling years of my life."

Whitney, drying the tears from her eyes, said, "Oh, you were no bother. You were always more like a daughter to me than a niece. I might have been some help to you during those years, but you saved me. After Patricia came out here with Edward, you were the only family I had.

"Sure, I attempted to keep busy with arts and culture, books and theater, and women's rights. Those things mean nothing after a while unless you have somebody with whom to share them. I had hopes for Michael and me. I warned him. If he had to go west to find his future and fortune, I could not guarantee that I would wait forever. If only he would have told me how he felt.

Michael, unable to hold his temper, interjected, "You always wanted me to state how I felt. Even now, you want to know if I need you. Do you think I felt needed when you were so busy with all your activities and organizations? Finally, Patricia told me you were engaged. How did you think I felt? You always told me you were a city girl, and then getting engaged to a farmer? I couldn't picture you living on a farm. It was off to war for me."

The conversation went on through the afternoon. Finally, Victoria said, "Is anybody else getting hungry? I'm ready to get some supper."

They all agreed and decided to find a place close by. After supper, Victoria excused herself. Stewart went to the office to catch-up on any work that might have been neglected while entertaining guests and clients. As Victoria drifted-off into a deep and restful sleep, Michael and Whitney sat in the living room, talking about the past and missed dreams until the early hours of the morning.

Chapter Six

HUMAN TRAFFICKING AND INFANTICIDE

Stewart was talking to James in the conference room when Daryl came into the law office. They shook hands and offered cordial greetings. Stewart offered Daryl a cup of coffee. James and Stewart settled in to discuss Daryl's situation.

Stewart began, "What else can you tell us about your situation in New York? You were assisted by the Foundling Society. How were you orphaned?"

Daryl lowered his eyes and took on a pensive appearance, as if he had not been required to talk about this situation or think about it for some time. After several minutes of collecting his thoughts and his emotions, he said, "It is a long story. Are you sure you have time? Does it matter?"

James assured, "We won't know until we hear it. We have time."

After a few more moments of thought, Daryl began, "My parents were great! They were young when they had me, probably not even twenty yet. I'm telling through the reflections of their friend, the reporter, David Graham Phillips. He was the person who, later, helped me with my journalistic attempts to write the News Boy press releases. I'll tell you more about him later.

"They were free spirits. They met David down in the Village, where artists and journalists liked to hang out. Some called themselves 'Bohemians.' When I was born, Mom and Dad had to work all the time, so they were rarely able to hang out down at the village any more. From David's account they rarely had time for anything except working.

"When I was six, Mom discovered she was expecting a second child. They tried to make ends meet, but found it difficult. Dad worked on the docks and Mom took in sewing and ironing in the tenement. As much as they worked, they still had financial troubles. They wanted to raise me and my little brother or sister as best they could. David kept in touch as he hired Mom to do his laundry.

"David worked for the New York World. He later published his first novel, *The Great God of Success*. David was a crusader as a journalist. He was known as a Progressive and a muckraker. He exposed the corruption in Congress and caused several New York representatives to resign under public outcry. He also exposed corporate corruption and the abuses of trusts, child labor, and human trafficking. Whenever he wrote and exposed abuses and corruption, somebody's illicit livelihood was brought to light and threatened.

"He found a great deal of evidence regarding the means by which women were offered jobs for passage in the Old County and then sold into prostitution in the United Sates. Most had no education, couldn't speak English and were doomed to an average of five years of torture in enduring the pain and humiliation of prostitution. If they got pregnant, they were forced to get abortions so they could get back to work. If they found a means of escaping the life style, they were discouraged through beatings, torture and other abuses. I said 'five years' because that was David's calculation of their life expectancy. David also began to see a broader link between human trafficking and abortion.

"There was evidence of abortion all over the city. Street workers would find babies in the alleys, wrapped in newspapers. Sanitation workers would find them in dust cans as they emptied them into their wagons. The Foundling Society would accept babies with no questions asked. Mothers would pin a note on the blanket and leave the child at the steps or at the entrance of a police station or fire house. They asked the Society to take care of them. As much as possible, the notes were kept and later given to the child when they would leave.

"David became curious and wanted to discover how widespread the abortion industry was. It was going on all around the city. People were advertising the service as, 'Restoring the menses.' There were advertisements for abortifacients and other chemical or medical 'Relief from the source of your distress.' Although abortion was illegal, it was going on without law abiding, moral people even noticing. You only found the symptoms and evidence of the dark industry if you were looking for it.

"He wanted to determine if the activities were conducted by midwives, doctors, or back alley amateurs. He also wanted to determine to what extent they were self-induced with a coat hanger, a knitting needle or crochet hook. David had quite a reputation, so he was able to get investigation and research money from his editors. He knew Mom and Dad needed some extra cash to get by, so he offered them an undercover job.

"Mom was about seven months along and showing pretty well. David hired them to pose as a couple seeking an abortion. With proper cover, he could expose the places and persons performing the operations to the public. He then planned to write a major exposé of the industry entitled *Human Trafficking and Infanticide*.

"They all felt the story would be a safe assignment, as they had no intentions of actually going through with the procedure. He found midwives and doctors who would not perform the procedure. He found doctors and midwives who would perform the procedure. For the doctors, there was a legal loophole, known as 'therapeutic abortions.'

"The brothels and the places that offered illegal abortion had to find police protection. The police, just like local residents, knew what was going on by the volume of foot traffic to and from the places. That didn't mean the police watched over them for a price. It meant the police, for a price, would simply look the other way and attempt to divert raids when possible.

"One place owned by Madame Fleischer, a midwife who performed abortions, sold abortifacients, or referred the client to another facility. She had a son who was on the police force. Naturally, he offered more protection than the other police who simply attempted to divert raids.

"He watched over his mother's business and kept his ears open to any news, information or rumors traveling through the police network or his informants' grapevine on the street. There were several articles from the series of twenty-one articles already in circulation. People in the business were getting worried they would be shut down or arrested. Both were happening across the city.

"David told me, Officer Fleischer was probably on patrol and met my mom and dad coming out of an interview with Madame Fleischer. Something about them stirred his instincts. He followed them and found out who they were. A few days later, he summoned Dad to a secluded meeting place. That was when Dad went missing. David suspected Officer Fleischer and began to do his own investigation.

"A week later Dad's body was found in the Hudson. He had been shot by a thirty-eight special. Through David's insistence and presenting evidence to police and prosecutors he could trust, they began to consider Officer Fleischer as a person of interest. When the police went to his apartment to question him, they found Officer Fleischer dead, with a single shot to the right temple from his police revolver. They ruled his death suicide.

"According to David, finding Dad's body and determining his killer, gave no comfort to Mom. She went into a depressed state. She stayed in bed until the time of her delivery and died during child birth.

"David was very helpful. He found a place for me in the Foundling Society. He visited frequently and took me to dinner on Sunday afternoons. I kind of always had a childhood fantasy that he would come one day and offer to be my father. I'm sure his work and the fact that he never married kept him from even considering such an arrangement. It's funny how kids think.

"Long after I left the Foundling Society, I began to wonder if I had a special arrangement to be a leader and not have to work so many hours because David was paying some of my support. I want to go back to New York some day and see him. I want him to know

I'm in the journalism business and have been somewhat successful as an adult."

Daryl hung his head, as if he were recovering from an exhaustive inquiry.

Stewart interjected, "Wow! That was a tough childhood!"

Daryl added, "As tough as it was, I can never get over the suffering so many kids experienced. At least there were people like Gladden, Dr. Clark and others in the foundling Society to attempt to alleviate some of the suffering."

Stewart shifted back to the legal concerns and added, "We don't have you out of the woods yet. We still need to find you a job. Would you be willing to do some mining for Victoria back in Discovery for a while?"

Daryl answered, "I think I might. I'm sure the conditions are safer now than they were when...When the mines were run differently. "

Stewart assured, "I'll see what I can do."

They had some small talk with Daryl and assured him they would do all they could to make sure he was gainfully employed by his court date. Daryl said, "Again, I'm thankful you two are working in my best interests. I don't like abdicating my First Amendment rights, but you can't fight city hall."

Stewart answered, "Thank you for your confidence. You are young and this is simply a temporary setback. You are resilient. I know this will all seem comical someday."

After Daryl left, Stewart went to his office to straighten his paper work, make some notes and reflect on the day. He heard Sven out in the hallway. Stewart offered, "Come in and have a seat. Would you like some coffee?"

Sven and Stewart sat and talked for a while. Stewart told Sven the news, "I can get you work, mining. We just have to work out the details and get you up to Discovery. How does Heidi feel about you mining?

"Oh, she alvight vit dat. She glad I verk. Din, maybe ve can get married."

Stewart answered, "That would be great!"

Sven left and Stewart opened his Bible, "'And I will come near to you for judgment; and I will be a swift witness against the sorcerers, and against the adulterers, and against the false swearers, and against those who oppress the hireling in his wages, the widow and the fatherless, and that turn aside the sojourner from his right, and do not fear Me,' says the Jehovah of hosts."

Stewart thought, "What is a sojourner? Let's see…the dictionary says, 'Foreigners or aliens who walk among us.' I need to make a note, Malachi three and five. I love this job! This week I was able to help two orphans, one widow and a sojourner."

"Six o'clock! I'd better get to the hotel for supper!"

Chapter Seven

EDGE OF ETERNITY

As Stewart arrived at the room, everything was in pandemonium. Victoria, it seems, was drifting into and out of consciousness. Whitney had taken charge of the situation. Michael was sent out to retrieve the doctor. Stewart was assigned the task of keeping cold compresses on her forehead. He also took on the responsibility of silently praying. "Lord, please strengthen and comfort Victoria. Heal her and the baby. Give the doctor wisdom and guide his hands. Comfort and strengthen Whitney and Michael."

After some time, Michael returned with Doctor Gilbert. Whitney was becoming perplexed. She said, "I don't know why Victoria had to get herself pregnant. This was probably out of infatuation!"

Michael gave her a serious look and said, "Always ready to voice your opinion. She fell in love. She is pregnant. That is what we have to deal with!"

Whitney realized she had spouted off out of frustration. She regained her composure and asked the doctor "Is it possible to save Victoria by restoring her menses?"

Doctor Gilbert replied, "There is no guarantee either way. We have to be completely legal in whatever is decided."

Whitney continued, "I know it would be extreme, but if the procedure of relieving her distress would save her life, isn't that something we need to consider?"

Michael relieved Stewart of his duties so he could join the conversation between Whitney and Dr. Gilbert. He asked, "What exactly are you talking about?"

Dr. Gilbert answered, "If it can be determined that a procedure is therapeutic, the law allows for the procedure to take place."

Stewart, with a shocked expression, asked, "As determined therapeutic by whom?"

Dr. Gilbert, demonstrating some agitation by the tilt of his head, answered, "Well, by the attending doctor, of course."

Stewart answered, "I'm not an attorney yet, but I will check with James."

Dr. Gilbert said, "In the patient's condition, I am not sure if the procedure would be more risky than carrying the baby to term."

Whitney interjected, "Victoria! Her name is Victoria."

Dr. Gilmore, scowling, said, "Yes, Victoria."

As Michael was sitting and listening, taking care of Victoria, he also engaged in prayer. Stewart was jotting some notes on his legal pad. Doctor Gilbert and Whitney continued their fervent discussion. After a while, Victoria regained consciousness. She motioned for Whitney and Stewart to come closer. With wide eyes and her jaw set in a strained expression of determination, reaching up, grabbing Stewart by the necktie and pulling him closer, she said, "Save my baby!"

Stewart said, "Of course!"

Victoria clarified herself, "If you take my baby, you might as well kill me, too. Write up something legal that says you will not take my baby."

With that Victoria drifted back out. Stewart began drafting a document. When he had something he thought might be legally binding, he set it and his pen on the night table by the bed. They all sat and waited, with Michael and Stewart praying silently. Whitney picked up the nearest book and started reading. She said, "She needs to hear something positive. The baby could respond to voices, too. Isn't that right, Doctor?"

Doctor Gilbert, as though interrupted in a reflective daze, said, "Yes, I suppose it won't hurt."

As they watched, Victoria's movements became agitated, as if she were in a nightmare. Her breathing became slowed and strained. She even stopped breathing for a little while, which seemed to the onlookers like an eternity. Suddenly, Victoria came into consciousness again. In a weak voice, she asked, "Do you have something for me to sign?"

Stewart answered, "Yes, here it is, if only I can find my pen."

Victoria said, "Oh, it rolled under the bed."

Stewart, with wide eyes, looked at Whitney, who said, "Lands, child, how you know that?"

Victoria calmly answered, "I was above, looking down at us. I could see me lying on the bed, unconscious. I could see and hear Michael and Stewart praying. I could hear Aunt Whitney reading. I saw the pen fall off the table and roll under the bed."

Michael asked, "What else did you see?"

Victoria said, "I turned and was walking down a tunnel. I could see Raymond, Father and Mother. I walked toward them in perfect peace. All of a sudden, the light began to grow dim. I heard Raymond say, 'Finish what we started.'

I felt perfect peace. I could go on walking or I could wake up. There was no burden to decide. No guilt or angst. I woke up."

Doctor Gilbert said, "I have heard of these things. Of course, there is no medical or scientific basis for what happened. Not all that happens can be quantified. There is a fine line between the natural and the supernatural, the physical and the metaphysical."

Michael added, "We've been privileged with a glimpse of heaven."

Before Dr. Gilbert left, he gave these instructions, "We've truly seen something amazing here tonight. It appears her will to live is a stronger factor than her grief. She's not out of the woods yet. She'll need to rest as many hours a day as possible. Travel is out of the question for now.

"Find the most nutritious foods you can. She'll discover what she can keep down and what she can't. It might take some experimentation, but she and the baby need as much quality food as she can handle. Try broths with vegetables. Get cheese, small quantities of meats and poultry. Let her eat as much fresh or canned fruit as she wants. Oatmeal and whole wheat toast will also be good. See if she can drink about three glasses of milk a day. You are very fortunate to be at the Straiter. They have one of the best menus in town. You can get room service from around six in the morning until ten in the evening."

Michael thanked the doctor and walked him to the stairway. Stewart stayed a while longer. Whitney looked in on Victoria. "She's sleeping now. Even her sleep seems different. She seems more peaceful. Her color is coming back."

After Stewart received the encouraging report, he said, "Thank God! I thought we were going to lose them."

Whitney reacted, "Them?"

Stewart clarified, "Yes, Victoria and the baby."

Whitney said, "Oh, yes."

After Stewart left, Michael and Whitney sat and talked. Michael asked, "Would you like for me to have some coffee sent up?"

Whitney said, "At this hour? Sure, why not. You know it's amazing. Some of the worst times in our lives are balanced by some of the best memories. Here we are worrying about Victoria. God, I thought we had lost her. Now she hangs in a tedious balance between life and death. I'm assured she is on the life side now and improving. With that worry, here we sit, taking comfort in one another's company, living like kings and queens."

Michael answered, "You know, worry, sorrow and trials reach everybody, regardless of wealth, success, position or power. Life is a delicate flower that soon withers. We have to take the bad with the good and learn to find our repose in the moments of rest between battles. One thing I learned in the war was to not let the gloom of reality and the dread of what was to come overshadow those moments of repose. I guess it goes back to living each day to its fullest and living one day, one moment at a time."

Whitney gazed out the open window at the glow from the city below. "What you're saying sounds great, but is it truly possible to do that and not quickly get caught up in the battle and the dread once you hear the first shot fired?"

Michael answered, "Keep conscious awareness of who you are and how fragile life is."

Whitney pensively said, "I will truly work on that."

Michael's face took on a more serious look. "Whitney, when you were campaigning for women's rights and suffrage, were you also advocating birth control and...?"

Whitney finished the sentence, "Abortion?"

Michael continued, "Yes. Were you an advocate of abortion?"

Whitney answered, "There were two groups. There was Margaret Sanger who advocated abortion. In her opinion abortion and birth control were means of keeping the immigrant population down, whether they were voluntary immigrants or not."

Michael asked, "What do you mean by 'voluntary immigrants'?"

Whitney clarified, "There were the Europeans who came here by choice. Then there were the people of color who were beaten and dragged to come here and work for others. Another group nobody talks about is the women who were tricked into coming here for a better life, but were actually sold into prostitution.

"I feel Margaret Sanger claimed she was advocating for quality of life and destiny of women over their own bodies. As you became an insider in the movement, you got the feeling she really hated children. There was a story of her visiting a tenement where a woman wanted an abortion.

"She already had three children and said she couldn't handle another. Her husband had thrown a baby girl out in the snow and said, 'Leave it.' A neighbor quickly retrieved the child and kept the baby girl until the husband sobered and things settled down. Sanger was heard to say, 'I would gladly throw them all out in the snow and leave them there.'"

Michael sat there and looked shocked. Finally, he asked, "What about the others?"

Whitney explained, "The others were led by Susan B. Anthony. We were in favor of equal pay for equal work, women's suffrage, protection from abusive husbands, health care and assistance for adoption and early child care. We split with the Sanger group over the life of the child, born or unborn."

Michael asked, "When you talked about taking the baby to save Victoria, you were considering the life of the baby as a person, weren't you?"

Whitney answered, "Of course, but if we had to do something that drastic, to save Victoria, we could consider that option. Do you know some women and doctors have considered the baby to not be a person until the quickening – the first moment she could feel the baby move?"

Michael paused, sipped from his coffee and asked, "When do you think God believes the baby is a person with a soul?"

"Oh, Michael, you can't know the mind of God!"

Michael answered, "We can read the scriptures, pray and hear teachings from credible and knowledgeable people. It also seems humans achieve greatness in the sacrifices they make of themselves, not the scenarios in which they sacrifice others."

Whitney responded, "Yes, Michael, but people argue over even what the Bible says. There are so many religions. People have even fought wars over their belief in God."

Michael said, "God can't be proved or disproved. I can't say what happened to Victoria was a real trip to heaven or a dream. I can say she was changed after that happened and even the doctor could not explain it with his science, theory, practice or experience. Faith is not what we see. God wants to have a personal relationship with us. Religion is theory about God and some remote hope that he cares and exists. Faith is living in the realization that He loves us and wants the best for us."

Whitney asked, "Why, Michael, when did you become so religious?"

"Like I just said, I'm not religious. I've found faith. It started when I was a boy. I've always understood there was more to this world than we can see with human eye and understand with the human mind…in the present physical condition we call 'reality.'

I went to Sunday school as a boy. I think a foundation was laid then, although I never made a conscious decision until I was up in the cabin. I studied the Bible, philosophy and history determining to prove or disprove the existence of a loving God. Finally, He became real to me."

Whitney sat with an inquisitive smile and her head tilted, twisting some strands of hair as if she were in deep thought. She said, "By the way, what does God say about the unborn child?"

Michael walked over to the occasional table, picked up his Bible and came back. "This one is specifically about Jeremiah, 'Before I formed thee in the belly I knew thee, and before thou camest forth out of the womb I sanctified you. I have appointed thee as a prophet unto the nations.' That was Jeremiah one and five."

"Jesus rebuked the Pharisees for killing the prophets that He sent to the nation of Israel. Could you imagine killing a prophet, even before he ever had a chance to live outside the womb? King David wrote, 'For Thou didst form my inward parts; Thou didst cover me in my mother's womb.' That was Psalms one hundred and thirty-nine, verse thirteen.

"So, if God knows the kings and the prophets in the womb, does he not know every one of us? Do you want to risk your eternal soul determining the fine line between when God values a living mass of tissue as a person, or a fetus to be discarded like yesterday's garbage?"

Chapter Eight

WANNA BUY SOME SWAMPLAND?

Although Victoria was showing improvement and gaining strength, Whitney, Michael and Stewart made sure she was always attended by at least one of them. On Sunday, Stewart came over so Whitney and Michael could get away for a while. They smelled the aroma of meat cooking from their open window all morning. They decided to attend the buffet at the hotel and maybe take a stroll around town after dinner.

As they arrived in the lobby, they could smell the brisket and other dishes warming in the chafing pans on the side serving table. They were shown their seat and went to the serving line. There were mixed vegetables with corn, peas, and lima beans called succotash, baked white potatoes and sweet potatoes hauled in from the valley. Michael said, "I wonder if Stewarts' family grew these?"

Next they came to the brisket that had been rubbed in spices and slow cooked on a charcoal burner in back of the hotel. There was also chicken that had been barbequed with the beef brisket. Finally, there was a selection of plum pudding, apple pie or crème brûlée. Whitney said, "I won't eat for a week. I hope we can walk this off this afternoon."

Michael responded, "As soon as we take Victoria and Stewart their lunch, we can do that. Victoria is in good hands. For now, let's just relax and enjoy the aromas, the flavors and the company."

Michael had already discussed his plans with Victoria, Whitney and Stewart. On Monday, he was heading back up to Discovery to make sure everything was proceeding in the mines as well as could be expected. Since Victoria and Thomas Mines had become a client of James's law firm, James suggested that Stewart accompany Michael for a couple of days or longer if they discovered he was needed.

For desert, Whitney chose the crème brûlée, and Michael chose apple pie. They sat for a long time, enjoying the dessert and the coffee. They took Stewart and Victoria a tray with an urn of coffee and started out on their walk. Whitney had not been able to see the town all week except in getting to the hotel and catching a glimpse of the city's sky line against the backdrop of the mountains from the windows in the room. She said, "The fresh air and walking are wonderful. This was just what I needed."

Michael nodded in agreement and extended his hand to gently grasp Whitney's. They walked several blocks without many words, but both were beaming with a smile. They finally found themselves back in front of the hotel. When they came to the room, Stewart was taking an afternoon nap on the sofa. Victoria was napping in her room with the door open. They both awoke when the couple came in and sat down. Michael asked, "How was your lunch?"

"Fantastic! It was almost as good as the food we got together in the cabin."

Michael smiled and said, "Yeah, right."

Victoria called for Stewart to assist her in moving out to the living room area. She made a conscious effort to push herself a little harder every day to sit up for longer periods, move around more and rebuild her strength without overdoing it. After she made herself comfortable, she asked, "Aunt Whitney, how was it that you became widowed? I hope you don't mind me asking. We've just been so busy with me and my health problems that we've not had a chance to talk about you yet. You wrote and told us it was a farm accident, but that was all."

Whitney asked, "Are Michael and Stewart packed for tomorrow's trip? This might take some time."

They both smiled and nodded to the affirmative. Whitney began, "Before I tell you how I was widowed, I should tell you how

I became a bride. My friend Nora and I were attending a women's meeting in Indianapolis. She had not seen her brother John in some time. He was ahead on his farming, so he came to the city a few days to see Nora.

"We hit it off very well. In fact, we took a stroll through town like Michael and I just did."

Michael offered a slight frown and turned his head to look out the window. He was wondering if John held Whitney's hand on that walk. He was listening to her account, but also appeared to be day dreaming about his stroll and the possible results. His slight frown turned into a pensive smile.

Whitney continued, "John had been widowed a little over a year prior to our introduction. His teen bride died in child birth. He was fifteen years older than her. We hit it off so well in two days that he invited us to come over to the farm for the weekend before we headed back east. Then, we began writing letters. A year later, he came out east and proposed. We were married and I went back to Indiana to be a farm wife.

"He had three farms, with hired people to run them while he commuted by train among the farms to oversee the operations. The farms were in Missouri and north central and west central Indiana. He also spent a portion of his winters in Punta Gordo Florida. In Missouri and northwest Indiana, he came by the land that had been reclaimed swampland. They were pumping and draining the ground with wind power. His brother, Alex died in Missouri from a ruptured hernia after he attempted to lift some heavy equipment up onto a windmill.

"The area was called the Grand Kankakee Marsh. It was originally five hundred thousand acres of swampland. Before they were rounded up and marched to reservations in the West, the Potawatomie Nation made a huge settlement in the area. They placed spiritual significance upon the area where rivers met. The rivers were the Kankakee and the Yellow Rivers in an area known as English Lake."

Victoria interjected, "Is that biblical or just a superstition, the part about land near the confluence of rivers holding spiritual powers?"

Michael answered, "Well Princess, I don't know. You have to consider the Garden of Eden was estimated to have been located between the Tigress and Euphrates Rivers, which converged into one river. That area, swampy at the time, is considered to be the Cradle of Civilization."

Stewart interjected, "That is also the area where the tower of Babel was built."

Michael added, "That confirms that man can take any good creation and ruin it."

Whitney continued, "Even with the dredging and drainage ditches, the swamp and farm land didn't drain until they broke a natural rock ledge in Momence, Illinois. By the time John came along in the late eighteen nineties, the land was selling for a dollar and fifty cents an acre. He bought five hundred acres near English Lake. The swamp had been a sportsman's paradise with hunting and fishing. It drew people from all over the nation and the world."

Victoria said, "The place sounds like paradise. "Whitney answered, "When John bought his land, Grand Kankakee Marsh was mostly gone. His farm, although the soil was extremely rich, looked like a mud hole. Even with the drainage efforts, John had to pump and drain the land with wind mills. He felt badly that the swamp had been drained and the Potawatomie Nation had been displaced, but that had all been done prior to his purchase.

Victoria asked, "So, what happened to John?"

Whitney turned her eyes down and took a deep breath as she composed herself, "We were married for three years. It was December. He had been to the Missouri farm and came by way of the English Lake farm. We were going to head to Punta Gordy right after Christmas.

"He went to Toto to flag a train. It was less than five miles from the farm. He had done it so many times. Whether it was the driving snow or the dark of night, we will never know. It was probably a combination of two."

Victoria said, "Did you say Toto?"

Whitney answered, "Yes, the town was Toto."

Victoria asked, "Was the town named after Dorothy's dog?"

Whitney smiled and answered, "Funny thing you should ask. L. Frank Baum, who wrote *The Wonderful Wizard of Oz* had a cabin at Bass Lake, a few miles beyond Toto. I'm sure he passed through there traveling between Bass Lake and Chicago. Actually, the town of Toto was named after the Toto Indian Nation. Baum probably named the dog after the town.

"That night I had some kind of premonition. I can't explain it. I was fully awake, sipping some coffee by the stove in the kitchen. I saw John lying face down in the bloody snow. He was leaning on one arm and raising his other hand, saying, 'Whitney.'

"I couldn't sleep. I think I nodded off a few times during the night. The next morning, when I heard a rider in front, I said, 'Something's happened to John.'

"It appears he was too close to the track and the engineer couldn't see the lantern he was using to flag the train until it was too late. John was standing near the track and didn't calculate for the speed of the train. He was sucked into the side of the train due to the speed."

Chapter Nine

BLURRED LINES

Stewart was glad to be going to Discovery. He was meeting Michael, Sven and Daryl at the depot. He and Michael determined he would go for a few days or a week, depending upon what needed to be done. Sven and Daryl were going up for a few days to determine jobs for which they would be best suited to fill and also to arrange their housing.

As Stewart was waiting, Michael was first to arrive. Stewart said, "I can't get it out of my mind. It's amazing that we saw an unexplainable miracle last week."

Michael agreed, "It appeared that Victoria was brought back from the dead."

Stewart continued, "By the changes in her strength, her countenance and her general health, I wonder if we witnessed a miraculous healing. And then, what about Whitney's account of John dying and the premonition?"

Michael responded, "I tell you, what seems like reality is only part of the total spectrum. It's as if we see through a mirror, dimly. There are so many aspects of the spiritual realms that we can't explain in human terms. I pray Victoria was divinely healed. I also pray that God's will be done for Whitney's life."

Sven and Daryl arrived within a few minutes of each other. Stewart introduced all, as none of them had previously met. They settled into their seats with Michael and Stewart in one seat facing Sven and Daryl in the opposing seat. As they proceeded through town they engaged in small talk. After a while Stewart asked Michael, "There's something that we talked about in the cabin. I've mentioned the situation to others and have received several differing opinions.

"You mentioned we went in to war in Cuba because we thought the battleship Maine was sunk by the Cubans. There are also theories that we might have sunk the ship ourselves as justification to start the war."

Daryl added, "There was also the possibility the ship hit a mine that was in place to defend the harbor."

Stewart nodded acknowledgement toward Daryl and proceeded, "It could've even been an accident, caused by overdue maintenance issues. What's your take?"

Michael thought about the question. He smiled as if this were not the first time he had contemplated the different opinions himself. Michael said, "It's good we have a long trip. Even with that, I'm sure I can give you a completely satisfactory answer.

"First, I want to quote you an interesting verse in Isaiah eight and twelve. Loosely translated, the prophet says, 'Do not call conspiracy all that these people call conspiracy. Do not fear what they fear nor dread what they dread.'

"After we got back from Cuba, we were all excited. We received a hero's welcome. The nation was in the state of nationalistic fervor. We had won the war and returned home. Teddy was running on the momentum to test the waters to run as president in nineteen hundred. We were all quarantined for a period of time to determine we didn't bring back any of the plagues. It was a short war and camaraderie was at a peak.

"Then we went home to our private lives. When you are alone after a great campaign, you have time to think. You second guess the reason you went to war. You wonder why you were sent to fight. Then you start reading some of the books and newspaper accounts. You realize you probably shot men who only disagreed with you politically. Sure, we ended Spanish rule in the Western Hemisphere, but that was not the reason we were given when we went in.

"I went back out to mine with Edward. Teddy wrote letters to all the Rough Riders, recruiting anybody he could to assist in his efforts to run for the nomination. I went back to Washington for a week to visit and to sit-in on some organizational meetings.

"It was impressive meeting with somebody I knew personally who was in line to be the next president. He had such an impressive record and history, police commissioner of New York City, governor of New York State, Secretary of the Navy. And now, finally he was a conquering commander of a victorious army.

"The capital was impressive, almost overwhelming. All the extreme architecture, with the huge domes and ornate figures, statues and memorials was a lot to take in in a few days. I was proud to be an American and a veteran. With the upcoming election, and all the political fervor, being right there in the middle of it was a once in a lifetime memory. I learned the Capital had once been used for church services by Jefferson and Madison. They only stipulated that the services be non-discriminatory, not showing any preferences for one religion over any others.

"As I looked closer, I began to notice the small details. One day I was walking up sixteenth Street toward Capitol Hill. I saw the huge structure rising as if it were a manmade mountain. It looked so perfect. As I walked closer, I could see the base of the building. It had external timbers around it to reinforce the walls. People argued whether Washington was built on a swamp or not, but there was the Capitol Building apparently sinking back into the earth, needing to be shorn-up and supported by external timbers. They rebuilt part of it a few years later in nineteen and four.

The thing that amazed me was not the fact that the huge building might need reinforcement and repair, but how magnificent it looked until you saw the foundation. As I looked at other monuments, such as the Washington Monument, I realized it was an obelisk or an Asherah pole.

Sven said, "Vat is dat?"

Michael paused and said, "They were religious fertility symbols used in Baal worship. Baal worship was prevalent in the Old Testaments and Jewish leaders were instructed to tear down the Asherah poles and obelisks. In Baal worship, children were sacrificed. The poles are found all over Europe and the Middle East. Even the Vatican is rife with them.

"I also noticed the gargoyles and other symbols that were in almost every building and in the decorations. The Capitol even had a cellar in the basement called the 'Crypt.' These are symbols of mythology, mysticism and occult practices. I went to a play and saw *Ben-Hur*. It was quite an experience. Now I learn from Whitney that Lew Wallace was from Indiana and was rumored to have written part of the book in English Lake.

"The mix of Christian and secular or even occult influences was quite an experience. I had a dream that night. In the dream, I was standing in a position where I could watch the play. As I was absorbed in the drama, the lighting effects, the plot and the setting, I happened to notice backstage. In front, for everybody to see was a Christian play about the life of Christ. Behind the curtain, I saw stage managers, business men in suits intermingling with the actors. Quickly the play totally faded from the dream. The stage people and actors behind the curtain became bankers, politicians, corporate magnates and members of secret societies. That dream was at least six years ago, yet it is as vivid and haunts me as if it were last night.

Stewart said, " Wow! Do you think you might have been tired from the trip and suffering some latent distress from the war?"

Michael responded, "That's a possibility."

Sven said, "Yah. I haf alvays vondered about so many religions. All claiming to be da only von."

Daryl added, "The members of one church can't agree on what they stand for, let alone find agreement with other churches."

Michael agreed and continued, "There are several popular conspiracy theories. They all involve man reaching for the height of human power through wealth, wars and political upheaval. They involve kings and kingdoms. They are all efforts for the Deceiver to establish his control over the world. There are visible and invisible powers. Colossians one and sixteen says, 'for in Him were all things created, in the heavens and upon earth, things visible and things invisible, whether thrones of dominions or principalities or powers; all things have been created through Him and unto Him.'

"The first conspiracy theory I can think of involves the Rothschild family. They were a European banking family who became so powerful they could almost manipulate the course of wars. They certainly used wars to manipulate the market and amass wealth. They were so wealthy, they helped fund the English army to defeat Napoleon at the Battle of Waterloo.

"The Rothschild family had messengers who carried red leather courier bags. Battles were stopped when the messengers came through. These couriers allowed the family to have news of battles that were won or lost a day ahead of military intelligence and public awareness. This allowed them to use the information to manipulate the market to gain more wealth."

Stewart observed, "When people trust in their wealth instead of God, no amount is ever enough."

Michael continued, "That is so simple, yet so difficult for people to grasp."

Sven added, "Yah, da luf of money is da root ov all efil."

Michael responded, "Exactly. Other conspiracies included the Lincoln and McKinley assassinations. They were completed by lone gunmen. There was knowledge or allegations of accomplices, planners and financial backers in both cases. Some historians trace both assassinations back to banking, secret societies and shadow governments for world domination.

"In Lincoln's assassination, accused accomplices were hung. In McKinney's situation, some prominent people were directly or tacitly accused because of their political affiliations, such as women's rights advocate, Emma Goldman. She was known as an anarchist and a Socialist. Albert Pike, who established the Ku Klux Klan, was also allegedly involved in the Lincoln assassination. He was also very prominent in Freemasonry."

Stewart was looking around the coach to see if he could discern the reactions of other passengers to Michael's accounts. There was a couple with two children who appeared to be too involved in their own conversations to even notice. Stewart saw only one man who was sitting across the aisle and back one seat from Sven and Daryl. He was definitely listening and offering facial expressions and occasionally nodding his head to indicate agreement or disagreement.

Stewart said, "Just because they're labeled as theories doesn't mean they aren't conspiracies. Even though you're paranoid doesn't mean they aren't out to get you."

Michael agreed with a wink and a nod and continued, "The most prevalent theory was the idea that most of our founding fathers were all members of secret societies. Later, there was some evidence to confirm this as Pierre Charles L'Enfant designed all the federal buildings and monuments in Washington to a pattern prescribed by the Masons."

Stewart asked, "What's the significance of that?"

Michael responded, "I found out that Teddy was a Freemason. Most of our presidents have been Freemasons or Deists."

Stewart asked, "So, that would mean we are not a Christian nation, rather a government prescribed by Deists and Masons. Either way, our legal system is based upon biblical principles."

Michael answered, "That's what most people believe. The Masons believe all religions are of equal value. They give equal weight to religions based upon following Buddhism, Hinduism, Islam, Judaism, Mormonism, Humanism, Theosophy or any other cult or secret society that professes to believe in a god. Our legislative branch was modeled after the Roman Empire. Even if the founding fathers were all Christian, some had slaves. There was also a conspiracy theory about Jefferson and Astor. Money and political power are inseparable."

At this point, the man Stewart had been watching got up and stood at the end of Sven and Daryl's seat. Standing next to Sven he was a little taller than Sven was seated. He was almost as wide as the isle. He wore a gray wool frock coat and a dress hat with a slightly rounded dome and small brim all the way around. He had heavy pork chop side burns that blended into a mustache, all gray. His coat was open, exposing a gold watch chain clipped to a button hole and ending in a vest pocket. He stood in the aisle and shouted, "Sirs, you are crazy! I am a conservative and everyone knows America is a Christian nation!"

Michael calmly asked, "What does that mean?"

The man answered, "It means I believe in traditional values and high moral standards. I prescribe to the Constitution."

Michael calmly asked, "Whose values and whose traditions?"

The man answered, "We have modeled our system based upon several Christian-Judeo principles, such as the laws being based upon the Ten Commandments. Morals and traditions based upon religious beliefs."

Michael agreed and added, "We will also succeed or fail as a nation to the extent that we do or do not seek God to bless our nation and follow His principles. But to say 'a god' is not the same as saying, the God of Abraham, Isaac and Jacob, Jehovah and Jesus. That's what the deists were, and a mandated government sanctioned religion was never the intent. We ask God to bless our standard of living, but do we ask God to guide us? To say we are a Christian nation because the Founding Fathers believed in a god is like saying, 'I am saved because my father attended church.'

"When somebody tells me they believe in strong morals, they usually mean, 'Sure I want a moral wife. She is more likely to remain loyal and faithful. I hope my employees or employer are moral people. They are less likely to cheat me. My neighbor should be moral so he doesn't covet my wife or my possessions and kill me for them. My banker and other business associates should be moral so they don't embezzle me and cheat me out of my life savings. My children should be moral so they don't embarrass me or cause me to bail them out of jail. As for me, I'm happy with the way I am. I'm good enough. Don't mess with my liberty.

"Conservatism is not a spiritual belief. It's putting your faith into maintaining a standard of living, nationalism and patriotism, possibly even to include ancestral worship. It can even be a life of acting out a plantation mentality. Sure you believe in Life, Liberty and the Pursuit of Happiness. Does your pursuit of happiness allow you to enslave another individual or family? Does your pursuit allow you to kill or exile the Native Americans so you can have their land? Does your pursuit of happiness include viewing your wife as property to own and manage or as an equal in voting or her right to own property? If you cause your mistress to become pregnant, does your pursuit of happiness allow you to hire a doctor or midwife to kill your baby for the sake of convenience? What about the life of the unborn child?"

The intruder stormed out, shouting, "I am going to the club car where we can agree on matters of spirit!"

Stewart waited until the door slammed behind the gentleman at the end of the coach. "Michael, what were you about to say regarding Jefferson and Astor?"

Michael answered, "Jefferson and Astor became friends through letters. Astor began his fur trading in eighteen hundred and eight by founding the American Fur Trading Company. With the threat of the war, fur trading was suspended. Somehow, Astor came out after the war with a monopoly on American fur trading. Other traders had been around for decades. Some have speculated that he had special favor with President Jefferson for enforcement to turn a blind eye or even provide protection for Astor's continued trade.

"Astor also allegedly wrote promissory notes to trappers for the furs they brought in. Supposedly, he sent his agents out to kill the trappers, recover the notes and make it look like Indian attacks. Astor became so prominent that when he and other bankers suggested the government find a better way to finance itself, his concerns were heard. They began to charter the Second Bank of the United States and Astor was nominated to be one of the five directors.

"He trapped on the Grand Kankakee Marsh and throughout the Northwest Territory and opened Astor House on Mackinac Island. He also invested heavily in real estate ventures in Manhattan. Astoria, Oregon was established by Astor and Jefferson's Corp of

Discovery and became the first permanent settlement west of the Rocky Mountains for, in Jefferson's words, '...planting the germ of an American population on the shores of the Pacific.'

"In other matters, Teddy Roosevelt was a globalist and wanted the Panama Canal and open free trading. I have learned that we probably initiated the Columbian Civil War so Panama would break off from Columbia and allow us to build the canal. Roosevelt's intervention by sending in the navy was labeled 'Gunboat Diplomacy.'"

"Capitalists hate Teddy. It seems if they were true capitalists, they would welcome world trade and the competition to be coupled with the potential increased market. If you actually worship and idolize your own wealth, you want restrictions on the ability of others to profit from the market. That is why capitalists were disdainful of Teddy's trust busting. They call it Socialistic and Progressive. Yet capitalists and globalists agree on moving toward a one-world government and monetary system. So, they are not capitalist, but ruling class socialists. They made sure Teddy was nominated as vice president instead of president so they could control him."

"So you see, there are theories and conspiracies. They all center on war, banking, political upheaval, secret societies and shadow governmental favor or cronyism. The most effective tactic of the Deceiver is to get us to look at the situations and live in fear. He also wants us to blame the symptoms such as man's greed for money and power. He wants us to label each other as conservative, liberal, muckrakers, progressives, nature fakers, whistle blowers, or Socialists. That was why I asked the gentleman what he meant by being a 'Conservative.'"

Stewart interjected, "Conservative is an adjective, not a noun. They might call themselves 'conservative Americans, conservative thinkers, or those who wish to conserve something.' It's interesting these are the same people who say liberals are 'nature fakers' and to conserve nature or reduce pollution is a Communist, Progressive Illuminati plot."

Michael agreed, "There is another whole argument on that issue. The Holy Wars were an effort to commit genocide of Islam. Sure Islam might have threats, but Islam is not the enemy. Dostoevsky mentioned in the *Brothers Karamazov,* a scenario in which a Russian soldier had been captured deep in Asia. He was tortured and threatened with immediate and agonizing death if he didn't renounce Christianity and follow Islam. He refused, so he was flayed alive and died, praising and glorifying Christ."

Daryl asked, "What does flayed mean?"

Stewart interjected, "Being skinned alive."

Michael continued, "In the story, the Islamic torturers were the conservatives. They didn't want their world empire to be threatened by the new and radical principles of Christianity. They adhered and continue to adhere to their beliefs to the point they will gladly kill to maintain them. In their system, even their wives are considered to be property. They have the right to execute their own wives and children for any reason, especially for becoming a Christian.

"In another situation, Jesus rebuked the Pharisees for killing the prophets he sent to them. The Pharisees took simple principles and traditions and made them complex, telling the people they needed the Pharisees to interpret these principles and tell the people how to live. Jesus took complex principles and made them simple, telling people He was the way to heaven.

"They ultimately killed Him. They were the conservatives who did not want this young radical upstart to upset their empires. They were in league with the oppressive and cruel Roman Empire, as long as the practice of their faith did not cause a disturbance or threaten the Empire. That's an example of government sanctioned church and preserving traditional values. Paul, in Colossians two and eight warned, 'Take heed lest there shall be any that maketh spoil of you through his philosophy and vain deceit, after the tradition of men, after the rudiments of the world, and not after Christ.'

Michael continued, "Jesus was not a conservative. He didn't come to fulfill the religions and traditions of man. He came to disturb the world order and establish His kingdom on earth. Some of His followers were zealots. They thought He would recruit troops and call down legions of angels from heaven to bring about an earthly empire. They had to be shocked when he said of his killers, 'Forgive them Father, for they know not what they do.'

"If what you are attempting to conserve of America is some romantic notion and nostalgic image of what America should be, or if you are more concerned about using God to bless America and preserve your lifestyle, you are making an idol of America. Jesus died to save humanity. He lives to upset the world order. Would you die to help establish His kingdom or would you kill to preserve and conserve your notion of empire on earth?"

Daryl asserted, "I wonder if Conner reads the same Bible you read. Are you guys getting hungry yet?"

Sven said, "I could eat."

With that, the men proceeded to the dining car. Over lunch they talked about the scenery, the future, the new jobs and the opportunities. After lunch they returned to their seats in the coach until they switched trains in Junction. After switching trains, Daryl and Sven opted to nap for the two hour ride into Discovery.

Stewart said, "Look, we're almost to Discovery."

As the train chugged and lurched to a stop in Discovery, Stewart, Michael, Daryl and Sven agreed to find rooms at the Inn before meeting for supper. Stewart loved the cool mountain air. It reminded him of the previous year when he found Michael near death on the trail. What were the chances that he would be hiking through at that exact time, on that exact day of the accident unless God had a hand in it? His life was certainly different since meeting Michael.

Chapter Ten

A NEW DISCOVERY

As he sat in the dining room, Stewart imagined that Raymond was probably sitting in this dining room just over a year ago. He might have even caught his first glimpse of Victoria here. Stewart was sure they had eaten here together. He also noticed the alcove separated by the French door. This was where he and Victoria ate with James and Michael, while discussing and preparing for the deposition. The morning of the deposition Edward collapsed. His story ended within days after that.

Daryl and Sven came into the dining room. Stewart watched as Daryl came through the door. His demeanor changed. Stewart was sure Daryl remembered the previous year when he and Raymond both stayed at the Inn and worked in the mines. Sven was a little more cheerful. He was always optimistic. "Dis town looks chust fine. I am sure ve can live well."

They ate a quiet supper. It had been a long day and they were tired from the travel. Stewart and Michael were about talked out for one day. They agreed to meet for breakfast. All four rooms in the Inn were available, so they each had their own room for the night. Daryl said, "I have the same room I had last year. I'm glad I started a fire in the stove before I came down. It could get cold tonight."

The next day, Michael posted a notice on the front bulletin board. He notified the miners to stop work an hour early and report to the office for a meeting. While Michael and Stewart sat in the office, various reactions could be heard out on the plank sidewalk. One miner said, "This is it. They're going to close it down."

Another miner said, "No, we've done so well with less help that we're going to get a bonus before Christmas. Well, I guess we'll see soon enough."

Michael said, "I knew there'd be some anxiety over their futures. I want to allay their fears and let them consider their options as soon as possible."

Sven and Daryl came in and completed their paper work. Michael and Stewart looked through the files to see if there might be any other documents pertinent to the afternoon meeting. After the paperwork, Michael took the three around to show them the town and the mines. Michael and Stewart felt as if the miners greeted them with cordial reluctance.

Michael had already gained their trust, but they wondered why he had a lawyer with him. Most of them realized that Michael would do whatever he could to preserve their jobs and treat them fairly. They also realized that some decisions might have to be made that were beyond Michaels's control.

At lunch, Michael said, "After we eat, would you like to see the shop?"

Sven said, "Dat vould be great!"

Daryl nodded to the affirmative and Stewart said, "Okay. We had a shop back on the farm. Basically, it had a vice, an anvil, a forge and some farrier tools, a monkey wrench, a hammer and some pliers. We had to make do with very little."

Michael smiled and said, "I hope you'll find this one a little more complete."

They finished lunch and walked over to the shop. Michael showed them the saws and woodworking hand tools. He showed them the woodworking and metal lathes, drill press, forge and the vertical mill. Stewart was pleasantly surprised. He exclaimed, "Wow, some of this can be overwhelming. I've never seen multiple machines driven by one pulley system. What's that called?"

Michael said, "That's called a line shaft."

Stewart observed, "Wow! It appears the steam engine drives the main shaft and each machine has a belt connected to the shaft."

Michael agreed, "You've got it. It is not so difficult. Sounds like you're catching on. You learn the basics, one step at a time and then you can do about anything with these machines."

Michael selected some wood that had been stacked to dry. He cut some rough stock, squared it and set it up in the wood lathe. He showed the others the basics and let each have a turn at shaping the piece. Stewart took longer than the other two and finally had to be reminded that the time was drawing near for the meeting. He asked, "Will I be able to finish this before I go back to Wellspring?"

Michael smiled and said, "I thought you might like this."

They were in the office as the whistle blasted, ending the workday. Soon the miners began filtering into the conference room. Michael introduced Stewart, Daryl and Sven again, although almost everybody met earlier in the day. Most of them remembered Daryl from the previous year. One miner asked, "Why do we need a lawyer here?"

Stewart answered, "I'm not a lawyer yet. I'm a legal assistant, working on my license to practice. I'm a friend of the Thomas family and assisting Victoria and Michael in a smooth transition for the future of the mines."

Michael began, "Gentlemen, we have suffered loss. There is no disputing my brother Edward knew how to turn a profit. Victoria has requested that every miner who was with them for more than a year is entitled to a twenty percent bonus. Miners with less than one full year are to receive a ten percent bonus."

The miner who earlier speculated the meeting was to discuss a bonus smiled and said, "I told you so."

Michael said, "There's more. Victoria has decided to sell her holding to Robert Conner."

With that announcement, the entire room let out audible groans. "That crook is going to be our boss?"

Michael said, "Be careful! You never know who might be listening. I wanted you all to know now in case you wanted to make other arrangements before winter. Daryl and Sven will be working with us, at least until Thanksgiving.

"Victoria has a written agreement that no changes will be made affecting your future for three months. We'll be training management to take over. The management will be selected by Mr. Conner. They'll have no say over positions until we turn over operations. If any of you would like to apply for the management positions, we can take your applications."

Someone asked, "Why can't you and Victoria keep the mine? She seemed to be a born leader."

Michael said, "Victoria's situation has changed. She has health issues. I can't share everything yet, but we almost lost her last week. She's recovering in Wellspring with her Aunt Whitney."

One of the miners who had been with the mines from the early days, let out a whistle and shouted, "I remember Whitney!"

Michael smiled and said, "I'm sure you do! Are there any other questions or concerns you might have? We'll continue to operate as normal as possible until the change. Again, I wanted to make sure you would understand your options if you needed time to make other plans."

At supper, Sven and Daryl decided to leave on Thursday and return on Monday with Michael. He would begin work on Tuesday. Stewart told Michael he would wire James to make arrangements.

For the next three days, Stewart followed Michael around to help supervise and learn as much as he could about the trade. He was intent upon determining if there were any legal issues or other loose ends that would need to be addressed with Victoria, James and Mr. Connor upon his return to Wellspring. Michael announced he would return to Wellspring with Stewart and come back to Discovery on Monday. Stewart spent any free time he could find finishing the small table he began on the first day.

At supper on Friday night, Stewart had a proud grin, much like the grin he had when he presented Michael with the crutch he made up in Michael's cabin. He went back outside and brought in the table. Michael said, "That's fine work! You sure you've never run a lathe before?"

Stewart answered, "No, this is the first. I love it! I'm going to check with James to see if I can come up here on weekends. I'm sure I can use the train ride on Fridays and Sunday afternoons to study for the exam. I can probably concentrate better on the train than I could at the office."

Michael said, "I'd enjoy the company. We don't know how long it'll be before Victoria can get back up here. I also don't know how long Whitney will be staying. "

After they discussed the work and travel details over coffee, Stewart stated, "That was some dream you had in Washington."

Michael agreed, "Yes, whether it was just my perceptions or something spiritual, it sure did change my outlook on everything."

Stewart asked, "Aren't most dreams just some subconscious connection you make?"

Michael answered, "Do you remember discussing the Prophet Joel, about restoring the years that had been ravaged?"

Stewart said, "Yes, up in the cabin. You have always explained the Scriptures differently than I ever experienced before. "

Michael continued, "Well the Prophet says a few verses later, toward the end times, "'I will pour out My spirit on all flesh; your sons and your daughters shall prophesy, and your old men shall dream dreams and your young men shall see visions."'"

Stewart asked, "What does he mean by 'prophesy'?"

Michael said, "Most people think a prophecy is a prediction of future events. That might be true to a certain extent, but prophecy is divine inspiration from God through the Holy Spirit. Prophecy is also confirmed by other spiritual leaders who are guided by the Holy Spirit.

"Old Testament prophets usually spoke to a nation and its leaders to repent. Most of chapter two of Joel is about returning to God and repenting. Prophecy might be scriptural like Stephen's historical account before the Sanhedrin. His account in Acts, chapter seven was truly inspired. He was not an educated man, yet he told a Biblical history of faith and of the crimes of the religious leaders who killed the prophets who were sent to warn them. He was so powerful in his delivery; they tore their clothes and dragged him out to stone him.

"When they stoned Stephen, his coat was laid at the feet of Saul of Tarsus. Saul became the Apostle Paul and later said that his ministry was to make plain '... to make all men see what is the dispensation of the mystery which for ages hath been hid in God who created all things; to the intent that now unto principalities and powers in heavenly places might be made known through the church the manifold wisdom of God...' Ephesians three, verses nine and ten."

Stewart clarified, "His mystery, kept hidden in God, was that through the church, God's wisdom would be revealed to rulers and authorities, principalities and powers, of His eternal purpose. In other words, 'Thy Kingdom come, Thy will be done on earth as it is in heaven."

Michael got excited and agreed, "Exactly! Church is projecting a ripple of awareness and consciousness, yet lacking in a wave of action. Church aligns with government to pervert justice, entitle the wealthy and control and suppress the poor. Religion is acceptable to government as long as it is not revolutionary or radical – as long as the people answer to man rather than to God. This is the epitome of conservative thought – keeping religion and the church acceptable to the ruling class and the god of nationalism - true social gospel."

Stewart observed, "The greatness of America is that it allows the churches to function. We should not expect the government, exclusively, to do the function of the churches, such as take care of the needy, defend the defenseless and speak for those with no voice."

Michael agreed and added, "The deception flourishes when we argue over what government should or should not do for people. We should be discovering what the church can do for the people and the influence it is to exert over the leadership of the nation."

Stewart added, "So America could be in trouble. God is pouring out His Holy Spirit. He is sending prophets to this nation and the world. Through his church, He is revealing to world leaders that His kingdom is coming and we should prepare."

Michael said, "That's right!"

Stewart smiled and said, "I find the idea of a prophet to the nation intriguing. I've discovered two things while we were here this week. I love woodworking and making things. I also discovered that God's plan is to reveal his eternal purposes through the church. Count me in."

Chapter Eleven

PARALLEL LINES

Michael and Stewart met for a late leisurely breakfast on Saturday morning. As they ate, they mused over the past year. Stewart asked, "When you were up in the cabin, did you ever think you would be sitting here again in Discovery, eating this fine food or spending time in Wellspring at the best hotel in town?"

Michael answered, "I never knew how it would end with me and Edward. I always hoped and prayed for reconciliation. I had a lot of time to think. Sometimes I would wake up from a dream thinking I was one place or the other, only to be disappointed.

Stewart said, "I remember us talking about that up in the cabin."

Michael smiled and shook his head in acknowledgement, He continued, "When I was awake, I spent most of my time surviving. I had to keep from wondering about things that might or might not happen. The main concern I faced was to not squander the present worrying and fretting about the future or regretting the past, or thinking of the good old days."

Stewart concluded, "Our talks have left such an impression on me."

They finished breakfast and proceeded to the station. Stewart looked around town and was glad he would be coming back often, if James agreed to the proposed arrangements. The air was fresher up here, even with the heavy smell of coal and charcoal burning. The leaves had just begun to turn. The air felt cool and crisp, like mid-autumn down below. He did not want to miss the short time the leaves would be in full color before dropping off for the winter. Seasonal changes transpired more quickly up here.

They caught the train and settled in for the ride. As the train moved beyond the imaginary line separating Discovery from wilderness, Stewart asked, "You told us about the verse in Isaiah warning us not to call everything a conspiracy. What if there are conspiracies involving the government?"

Michael answered, "Oh, there are conspiracies involving all governments. The enemy of God has had an agenda from the beginning. We're not to dwell on whether the symptoms are conspiracies or not, or allow them to be our motivation. Do you remember the rest of the verse? It said, 'Do not fear what they fear, nor be in dread.'"

Stewart continued his questions, "If we're not to be in dread or fear, what about the teachings of the prophets and Jesus, warning us that those dreadful days are on the way. Some persecution is already happening to others around the world, due to their faith. Whether we experience them in our lives or not, there will come a day…"

He paused for a second to finish his thought, "…even in this great country, people will be rewarded for turning in family members for believing. They will be persecuted by neighbors, employers and authorities for expressing and acting upon their beliefs. These things don't happen overnight. They take years of planning, desensitizing and buildup. How do we get from those warnings, skip conspiracies and get to the outworking of the prophecies? The prophecies say we will be handed over to judges, magistrates and governors. These are government officials."

Michael thought for a second and said, "That's an interesting question. Paul warned the church in Thessalonica the same thing. 'Let no one deceive you in any way. For that day will not come, unless the rebellion comes first, and the man of lawlessness is revealed, the son of destruction, who opposes and exalts himself against every so called god or object of worship so that he takes his seat in the temple of God, proclaiming himself to be God.'

"Daniel, twelve and four says, 'But thou, oh Daniel, shut up the words, and seal the book, even to the time of the end: when many shall run to and fro, and knowledge shall be increased.'

"Here we are rushing here and there. The prophecy was kept secret for about twenty-four hundred years. Now, we see how Daniel's vision of a knowledge explosion is being fulfilled."

Michael said, "The story follows two sets of parallel lines. There is the original motivation for world conquest, raising oneself up to be god and persecuting the true church. It is the plot that leads to a one world government, a one world monetary system and the mark of the beast. It began when the serpent told Eve in the Garden of Eden to eat from the Tree of Knowledge of Good and Evil. He told her if she did, her eyes would be opened and she would be like God and she would not die. He convinced her that God had been withholding information to which she was entitled. She could only obtain the information by disobeying the direct voice of God and taking the matter into her own hands. It was such a subtle, reassuring whisper but held grave consequences.

"That's been the same pattern man has followed ever since. The Tower of Babel was the next example. Man attempted to reach the height of heaven without the blessing, inspiration or empowerment of God. Most religions are exemplified by the Tower – humans attempting to reach God by their means rather than taking the hand which God extends from heaven. Look at the edifices that are built to reach God and to channel God down to earth.

"Evidence indicates Nimrod was using the occult sciences to build a portal to heaven. The people said 'Let us build a city and make a name for ourselves, otherwise, we will be scattered abroad over the face of the earth.'"

"So the people, with Nimrod as their leader, built a tower of bricks. They also wanted to memorialize themselves. God said, 'Behold, they are one people, and they have one language, and nothing they propose to do will be impossible for them.' Like the world religions, the builders of the Tower were scattered and God confused and diversified their language. Since God scattered the people, pagan religions have been preserved by disappearing into the shadows. Esoteric languages, occult sciences, astrology, mysticism and mythical legends, secret societies, governments and symbols continued in efforts to reach God. They also perpetuate the practices and knowledge through elaborate structures and ancestral worship and through architecture and memorials. Most modern religions have embraced and perpetuated some of the symbols of sun worship, from elaborate steeples, architecture and ornate buildings.

Stewart clarified, "So, at that time, Nimrod openly set himself in defiance of God and the Deceiver will do it again through the Antichrist in the temple claiming to be God?"

Michael continued, "By contrast, the Judeo Christian heritage has been handed down through the verbal Torah, and written scrolls, and later when the printing press was invented to print the Bible. Jewish rabbis are converting to Christianity and revitalizing the connection and relevance of the Old and New Testaments. When

Jacob was traveling from Beersheba to Bethel, he stopped for the night and laid his head on a stone. He had a dream in which he saw a ladder reaching to heaven and the angels of God were ascending and descending on it. He heard the Lord say, 'I am the God of your father Abraham and the God of Isaac.'

"Jacob built a stone memorial to God, not to himself. Later Jesus told Nathanael He had seen him lying under a tree in a vision. Jesus said, 'Because I said to you that I saw you under a tree, do you believe? You will see greater things than these. Truly, I say unto you, you will see the heavens opened and the angels of God ascending and descending on the Son of Man.'"

Stewart asked, "The God of Abraham, Isaac and Jacob had a glimpse of a portal to reach heaven? That portal is through Jesus?"

Michael answered, "Yes these things will happen after the temple is rebuilt in Jerusalem. To confirm that He is working now and we are not to dread what they dread or fear what they fear, Paul assures us in Second Thessalonians two and seven, 'For the mystery of lawlessness is already at work. Only He who now restrains it will do so until he is out of the way.'

"If you look at Matthew twenty-three, Jesus spent the whole chapter publicly rebuking the Pharisees. He ended by lamenting over Jerusalem killing the prophets that were sent to them. While He and the disciples were leaving the temple, some of them pointed out the buildings. These were the same buildings that were originally built by Solomon, destroyed by the Assyrians and Babylonians and rebuilt by Nehemiah.

"He used the buildings as a metaphor of his pending death. He told the disciples not one stone of these buildings would be left upon another. He also told them that in three days He could rebuild them. Of course, He was referring to His resurrection and not to rely on temporal structures or physical objects to reach God. When asked by a disciple when the kingdom of God would come, Jesus replied, "The kingdom of God is not coming in ways that can be observed; nor will they say, 'Look, here it is!' or 'There it is! For behold, the kingdom of God is in your midst.'

"Then in Chapter twenty-four, he warned the disciples about the end times of the earth. You were right in saying government will not be friendly toward Christians, even in America. There will be wars and rumors of wars. Nations will rise against nation. There will also be natural disasters such as famines and earthquakes. Jesus warned, 'You will be hated by ALL nations.'

"The other set of parallel lines is between Israel and America. When Samuel the prophet was getting old, his sons were acting judges and acted wickedly. You see, God grants special grace for three categories of people on earth. He appoints, anoints, promotes and empowers people chosen as spiritual leaders, rulers and judges. In Second Chronicles, chapter nineteen, verses five through seven, Jehoshaphat told the judges of the Lord, 'Consider what you do, for you judge not for man but for Jehovah; and He is with you in the judgment. Now therefore, let the fear of Jehovah be upon you; and take head to do it, for there is no iniquity with Jehovah our God, not respect of persons, nor taking of bribes.'

"That means those appointed by God to act in His behalf on earth. He not only gives them special grace to act in that responsibility, He assigns great responsibility and repercussions for those who take the task lightly or irreverently. He says, 'How long will you defend the unjust and show partiality to the wicked?' He goes on to instruct the judges what they should be doing in administering justice: 'Defend the cause of the weak and fatherless; maintain the rights of the poor and oppressed. Rescue the weak and needy; deliver them from the hand of the wicked.'

"As I said, Samuel's sons were acting wickedly. They turned aside to dishonest gain, took bribes and perverted justice. The leaders of Israel came to Samuel and asked for a king. He told them God would be their king. Samuel warned them of the potential for the abuses of the government of man. He said their sons would be drafted and made foot soldiers to run ahead of the chariots. They would be assigned to build weapons and war equipment for the chariots.

"Daughters would become servants, perfumers and cooks and bakers. The king would take the best fields, vineyards and olive groves. He would also take ten percent of their seed and flocks. With God as the king, ten percent was voluntarily given to the temple and the temple priests were entrusted with the proceeds. The people of Israel were also instructed to take care of the poor and needy, share from their produce, forgive debt, charge no interest and extend hospitality to the foreigners among them.

"They wanted Samuel to appoint a king anyway. In those days, in Israel, the government came to the prophets for direction. That is one way America departs from the Judeo heritage. It was as if a king who had the luxury of creating a draft, enforcing servitude and confiscating land and resources; thereby concentrating on war and luxuries like perfume and baked goods. He had time to think about preemptive wars so he could confiscate land, people and resources from other countries.

"Without the king being able to concentrate on resources, more was spent on the work of the church and survival. Through the lineage, Saul became king. David replaced him, and Solomon eventually was appointed the king of Israel. David wanted to build the temple for the Lord and to permanently house the Arc of the Covenant. God denied David the privilege due to the many wars he fought and resulting deaths.

"Even though God appoints and approves a nation's leaders for service, the leaders are still accountable to God. They are fallible and human with flaws. Human leaders can be a blessing or a curse. That's why our system has checks and balances built in.

"When Solomon completed the temple, he threw a huge celebration and held a solemn dedication. He revealed to the people that if they followed God, He would bless them in this place and in their land. He warned them that if they turned from God and His ways to serving other gods, they would lose the blessing.

"In America, whether the founding fathers were Christian or not, they wanted a nation sanctified by God. They wanted religious freedom so the people could follow the gods of their choice and seek direction and blessing in self-governing to the fullest extent achievable by human beings. They deified the god of 'Reason.' They said, 'We hold these truths to be self-evident.' Coupled with the freedoms of self-governance came the responsibilities.

"Washington held a similar dedication at the Federal Building. The Federal building was not in Washington. It was in New York City, the nation's temporary capital. From there, they proceeded up Wall Street to a little church on the hill for a prayer service. Washington gave a similar warning. The Federal Building later became the center of the banking industry.

"Solomon was considered to be the wisest man in the world, both during his lifetime and since. When asked by God what he desired, he said, 'Now, oh Jehovah my God, thou hast made thy servant king instead of David my father; and I am but a little child. I do not know how to go out or come in…Give your servant an understanding heart to judge thy people, that I may discern between good and evil.'

"Solomon began in humility saying he was only a child. He asked for wisdom and God granted it. In fact, God visited him personally twice in his life. Solomon later became proud. He was told not to take on the daughters of the neighboring nations as wives. He did so regardless of the warnings. With all his wisdom, he still stumbled. He used slaves from his own people to build the temple. He also built a temple to Moloch in which children were sacrificed. Before he died he saw his nation divided in half by a civil war."

Stewart interjected, "Wow, America was almost divided into two nations over slavery!"

Michael agreed, "In the example of Israel, the nation was breached exactly where the dedication had taken place. The temple wall was destroyed and the Assyrians tore down the temple, defeated Israel, and led the captured survivors off in chains after stealing their gold and plundering their resources.

"Assyria and Babylonia fought for dominance over each other and over the entire world. All the empires in history began a quest for world domination as soon as they felt they had an economic and political system that was working. From the Assyrians and Babylonians, through Alexander the Great, Rome, and Napoleon, they sought world conquest. As they found their economic and political systems were flawed, they used force to bring their own subjects into submission. As they expanded into world conquest, their weakened political and economic systems could not sustain their expanded efforts. They all ultimately failed, but consistently revealed that tyrants began to consider how to conquer additional nations and the world.

Stewart asked, "If we are, in fact a nation seeking to follow God, do you think we should learn from the example of Solomon?"

Michael continued, "A breach in America would exist where the dedication occurred. The dedication at the Federal Building would be the site of the breech. The Federal Building is now where a major portion of the gold is stored that backs up our paper currency - the banking center of the United States. Could a similar breach occur in America's wall of protection? It could if Americans make money an idol. That street is called Wall Street."

Stewart observed, "Doesn't America face other dangers besides placing their trust in money to save them?"

Michael added, "In America, the founding fathers were considered to be the wisest men in the world. Like Solomon and Daniel, they were educated in literature, history, mythology, and science. Jefferson even spoke several languages. With no formal education and as young as he was you would almost have to consider that Jefferson and the others had a special and anointed gift of wisdom and knowledge from God.

"By contrast, with all their learning and training, Daniel, Shadrach, Meshach and Abednego never turned from God, even when they were ordered to do so. That was why they were thrown into the fiery furnace or the lions' den. It seems that Solomon confused the lines between myth and faith. Jefferson even wrote his own Bible. He adhered to strong moral values, but denied the miracles of Jesus. His belief system was a type of moral and rational humanism, a type of pride where man thinks he can be good through learning and education. He denied the virgin birth, the resurrection and, therefore the empowerment of the Holy Spirit.

Stewart observed, "So Jefferson believed in morals to save the nation, without the personal relationship with the Savior. Don't we face the same hazards?"

Michael looked pensive and said, "Sure there are other perils. Although they may seem like separate issues, they are all related at the core. We learn from history so we don't repeat it. Look at the all the great nations in the past. When they became obsessed with nationalism, moral decency without godly empowerment, sacrificing their children, obsession of the supernatural, entertainment and nostalgia, they began to crumble at the foundation.

"We have our political tensions which are constructive and useful in the arena of government and legislation. In fact our republic was fashioned after the Roman model of citizenship. Democracy lasts as long as people are responsible to keep it.

"We have those supporting big business and big bankers. We have the Progressives who believe salvation comes through government. We depend on patriotism or nationalism. These are good things, but are secondary to depending and believing in a loving God. We have the nostalgia of thinking of the good old days. People who say, 'The good old days' just have a poor memory.

"Washington prayed for and dedicated the nation to God, although he often referred to God as the Great Architect of the Universe. He said he was motivated to go to battle and risk his life so people could worship the God of their choosing. The Quakers and Pilgrims were Christian. They believed in being citizens of another nation, the kingdom of God. Even though we have turned from our roots and heritage, there is hope."

Chapter Twelve

CUTTING EDGE

Before leaving Discovery, Michael asked Daryl and Sven to come to dinner at the Straiter, on Sunday. Back in Wellspring on Sunday evening, Michael made an announcement. "After Victoria has her baby and we get this mining situation behind us, I am going back to Indiana to farm with Whitney."

Victoria asked, "Is that all you plan to do?"

Michael answered, "One step at a time.

Victoria jokingly asked, "Are you afraid of change or commitment?"

Michael, who was feeling philosophical said, "Although people resist life's changes, life is linear and dynamic. It goes on with or without us. Change occurs voluntarily and transformation occurs as events that are beyond our control. The events we think we can manipulate, we try. The events that are beyond our control are like unseen forces that arrange and change our situation. Sometimes, it's like a huge knife in the hand of God that cuts and separates relationships and conditions. He rarely lets us settle into comfort and complacency."

Turning toward Whitney and smiling, he added, "Or fuses people together. May we all be together!"

Daryl and Sven offered their congratulations. The entire scene was one of warm and congenial celebration. Stewart looked a little more serious. Victoria continued to glance in his direction. Michael continued, "Whitney still has two of her three farms since she sold the Missouri farm last fall. She will need competent workers to help, if anybody is interested."

Stewart answered first, "Daryl and Sven might want to consider making arrangements other than mining by then. When Connor discovers they're working for him, he will probably fire them. I hope to be a licensed and practicing attorney in Colorado soon. I don't think I could leave James in the lurch, especially after investing so heavily in me to obtain my license."

With Stewart's announcement, Daryl and Sven looked pensive as if they would seriously consider the opportunity. Whitney and Michael stared into each other's eyes with a joyful expression. Victoria looked away as if she was in deep thought. Michael stated,

"Well, everybody will have time to think. Whitney has decided to stay until the baby is born."

Victoria continued to improve. She was not bed ridden, but did not venture far from their suite. Stewart arranged for her and Whitney to move to Ma Peterson's boarding house, as it would be far less expensive than the Straiter. Ma Peterson had two rooms available, and she could use the business. She assured Stewart that she would also love to care for Victoria and the baby, however long she was needed.

As time went on Michael, Sven and Daryl spent their time in Discovery. They had a few months to make sure the mines were running efficiently for Connor's possession. Michael came back every other weekend to visit with Whitney and Victoria.

Stewart found himself looking forward to Fridays, when he would have six hours on the train to rest, see sights and study. The return trip to Wellspring on Sundays was spent in the same manner. He found he could get more work done on the train than in the office. James's law business continued to grow, so there were constant interruptions. Stewart loved the weekends in Discovery.

He spent time at meals with Michael in the Inn. Then, after he and Michael discussed business and legal matters, he spent time in the shop. As he worked, he found himself obsessed with the shop work. He worked each weekend until he had a pair of occasional tables for Sven and Heidi, a pair for Michael, and a pair for Victoria. He figured Daryl had no use for the tables, so he bought him a new Kodak.

For the time being Michael stayed in the Thomas house. Daryl and Sven, since they were not as experienced as the other miners, filled in as needed. They were considered helpers. Daryl was well liked for his easy going demeanor and his sense of humor. Sven was appreciated for his ability to accomplish huge tasks that might have taken two other men to accomplish without him. They also spent several hours each week packing and crating the items in the Thomas household.

Michael talked with Victoria each time he returned to Wellspring to determine which items she wished to keep and which she wanted to leave at the house. She instructed Michael to keep any of Edward's clothes that he could wear. She also wanted him to have any personal items he would like to keep, such as guns, knives, and other articles of monetary or sentimental value.

About half way through the transition period, Victoria realized she would probably never see the house again. Dr. Gilbert determined she would probably deliver around Christmas. Any travel prior to delivery would simply be too risky. After Thanksgiving, Connor would own Discovery and the mines. There would be nothing there for her to see.

Daryl returned to Wellspring about once a month. He had no reason to spend time in Wellspring other than finding himself bored in Discovery. Sven also returned about once a month. Daryl and Sven liked to spend the time together on the train talking. On each alternate weekend, halfway through the month, Heidi came to visit Sven. They decided to get married the weekend after Thanksgiving. They also told Michael they would go to Indiana to farm.

Stewart was in the office about a week before Thanksgiving. He read "For the word of God is living and active, piercing to the division of soul and spirit, of joints and marrow, and discerning the thoughts and intentions of the heart."

Stewart was in deep thought as James came in with an envelope. On the outside was printed, "Colorado Bar Association. Official Documents. Handle with Care." He excitedly tossed the envelope onto Stewart's desk. "I haven't opened it. I wanted you to be the first to see it."

Stewart said, "I hope I passed." Opening it quickly, he paused and gave a huge sigh of relief!

James said, "They don't send rejection letters as 'Official Documents.' I am buying you dinner tonight!"

Stewart and James decided where they would go to celebrate. After James left the office, Stewart started to think about his obsession with working in the shop. The equipment was now packed and crated, ready to go to the farm. He thought of Victoria. Would she and her baby stay in Indiana or would they visit and return to

Wellspring? What did she have in Wellspring to keep her? What would he have in Wellspring other than his work?

Ma Peterson grew close to Stewart and his new family. She realized some of the group would only be around until Christmas and some would go to Indiana. Others had not announced their plans as of yet. She decided to have the entire group over for a Thanksgiving feast.

At dinner, Michael made another announcement. He said, "I am going to Indiana in a week. I'll be staying about ten days to two weeks. I want to be back before the baby is born.

"Sven, you and Heidi can go at that time if you're ready. There is maintenance to do. You could also set up the shop, since you're familiar with the machinery."

Sven said, "Ve vill be ready."

Michael turned to Daryl, "Have you decided whether you want to go or not?"

Daryl answered, "I'll go when you go to determine if I think I'd like it there."

Michael said, "Fair enough."

Ma Peterson asked Michael to give the blessing. He agreed, "I'll give thanks, but first I want to hear why each person is most thankful."

Sven volunteered, "I am most tankful for Heidi. We vill be married dis veekend. I am also happy for new life vit her."

Heidi agreed, "I have Sven for husband and ve hear back from Immigration. Ve learn ve are United States citizens."

At these two announcements, everybody clapped. Stewart volunteered to go next. "I'm thankful for my new family. I'm not happy that we will all be separated soon. Oh, by the way, I am a licensed attorney."

Daryl said, "I agree with that. I'm happy to not be in jail and to have options available to me. Maybe I can thank my attorney for that. I guess the future is as bright as we make it."

James said, "I'm thankful the law business is growing. God gave me and the rest of us a huge blessing in bringing Stewart to us last spring. I'm thankful for a wonderful mother. I feel she's not only my mother, but would be mother to the whole world if she could."

Everyone said, "Amen."

Ma Peterson added, "I'm just happy we're all family."

Michael stated, "I'm happy to be alive. If Stewart hadn't found me on the trail a little over a year ago, I'd be buzzard bait."

Whitney added, "Oh Michael, you are so eloquent in the way you phrase things. I'm happy to be reunited with Michael, wherever that leads. I'm sure it'll be an adventure."

Victoria looked pensive. As she spoke, her eyes became tearful with deep emotion, "I'm happy to soon be a mother, God willing! I'm also thankful for those who have become my family. Even though I lost Raymond and Father this year, I've become close to so many who've made huge sacrifices for my health and the health of my baby. Aunt Whitney, you have always been like a mother to me. Uncle Michael, you have actually been closer to me than Fath..."

She paused while she attempted to regain her composure, "Sven and Daryl, I want to thank you for filling in at the mine and moving my household. As you well know, I couldn't have accomplished that task."

She turned to face Stewart, taking his hands into hers while tears were flowing down her cheeks. After composing herself, she said. "Dear Stewart, I can't even put into words how I feel. You gave of yourself so freely for Uncle Michael. You sacrificed six months of your life. For me, you took care of the entire legal work and played nurse maid. I am grateful! Sometimes, I almost feel as if we were..."

Catching herself and realizing the true emotions she almost betrayed, Victoria stopped and reiterated, "I'm so grateful. I just hope, by my going to Indiana, we are not separate..."

Again, she stopped speaking for fear she might have said too much. She wanted Stewart to know how she felt. She did not know when or if she would actually have the chance to tell him. She was not sure if she could describe or admit her feelings to him or even to herself, especially since she was still in mourning.

Sensing her predicament, Michael said, "Let's live in such a way as to restore the years."

Stewart sat very quietly during the meal and the warm talks around the hearth after dinner. As he thought, he constantly glanced at Victoria, attempting not to stare and hoping not to be noticed.

Chapter Thirteen

EDITOR-IN-CHIEF

The Denver and Rio Grande began chugging into Union Station about four in the morning. Daryl was disappointed. He wanted to see Chicago, even if it was from the tracks at pre-dawn. He consoled himself thinking that after they caught the Monon Line they would still see some of the city. They had a two hour layover. The sun might be up by then. It would certainly be up later as they arrived at the farm in English Lake. Their goal was to visit the farm and catch a train at the Rye Depot in Toto and continue to Warren County.

After visiting the first farm and another three hour train trip, Daryl was already tired of farming. Michael and Sven were observant and astute in asking the current tenants the right questions. They enjoyed the conversation about the farm as they continued their lengthy train ride. After a day on the farm in Warren County, Michael and

Sven busied themselves with farm related issues, such as introducing themselves at the grain elevator, visiting the equipment and feed dealers and other everyday details. They decided Sven would go back to the English Lake farm after the first week.

Daryl determined that if he was going to leave Colorado behind, he needed to know more about the area than the farming. He had a feeling farming might only be part of his reason to uproot and come to Indiana. He asked about the closest town and made arrangements to go to Williamsport the next day. As he arrived in Williamsport, he secured two nights at the Warren Hotel and ate a late afternoon lunch. Before lunch, he toured the town. He saw a brick courthouse with a one hundred and fifty-five foot tower, Citizen's Bank, jewelry store, woolen mill, some attorneys' offices, grain store, black smith shop, general store and a building with an "IOOF" sign.

As he stepped into the café, he thought to himself, "This is an awfully small town."

As the waitress brought his lunch, he asked, "What's there to do around here?"

She replied, "Oh, just about everybody farms, or does something that supports farming."

Daryl asked, "Is there a newspaper?"

The waitress smiled with a type of half smile half smirk expression. "Yes, the office of the *Wabash Watchman* is down in Old Town. The editor is brilliant, but eccentric."

Daryl asked, "What do you mean?"

She reflected upon her answer and said, "He's won several awards for journalism. He's exposed politicians and other crooks. He just has some different quirks - his ramblings and ravings when he's not writing. He drinks some. I guess he was gifted for writing."

Daryl asked, "Is Old Town within walking distance?"

She replied, "Sure, just go down Monroe until you get to Fall Street. North Monroe becomes Fall Street. East Monroe Street turns to the left. Stay on East Monroe. Make sure you stop by Williamsport Falls, down under the bridge. They are the highest in the state, about ninety feet."

Daryl replied, "Wow!

"Yeah, right here in town! After the Falls, go on down East Monroe until you get to Market Street. If you run into the Wabash River, you've missed Market Street. The office is way at the other on end on the corner of Market and Washington Streets."

Daryl thanked the waitress and paid for his lunch. As he walked, he thought how the houses looked well-constructed. The yards were bigger than in the mining and other mountain towns. There was more space here. The Falls were not running much at this time of year. He observed how the running water had cut through the relatively soft sand stone, cutting the deep groove into the shelf and depositing large sections of debris below.

As he progressed down Monroe Street, He noticed how the houses in Old Town were more Victorian and had widow watches, towers, spires or high cupolas, much like most river towns had. "Finally, Market Street!"

He was disappointed as he reached the newspaper office. As he stood starring at the front, he observed, "*Wabash Watchman*, only twice-weekly newspaper in Warren County. Richard Douglas, Editor-in-Chief."

Daryl wondered why a horse and buggy was tethered in front of the office. A small paper sign was posted below that on the door, "Out."

From this point, Daryl could see the Wabash down beyond a beach that was at the end of Washington Street. He walked down to the beach. As he was taking a few pictures with his Kodak and skipping stones on the river, he had a funny feeling he was being watched. He also smelled cigar smoke. Shortly, a voice called out, "Can you take pictures with that Kodak or do you just point and shoot it?"

Daryl looked for the direction of the voice. There behind a sycamore tree in the late afternoon twilight, he could see the source of the voice and the cigar smoke. He answered, "I do alright."

As Daryl walked toward the man, he could see a tall man of medium frame that might have been athletic in his younger days. He still had broad shoulders and long legs, but what appeared to have once been a well maintained waste line was approaching the same girth of his chest. He had gray hair, almost white, down over his ears and a full gray beard, cropped evenly all around. He had a large mustache that flowed out over the beard on his cheeks. He wore gray pants, a black vest and a gray smock coat, all wool. He wore a black felt hat with a crease in the top and uniform brim around it that did not dip up or down toward the front or the back.

"I'm Daryl Daily. I'm not from around here."

The man replied, "I can see that."

Daryl said, "It gets melancholy down here about this time of the day."

The man added, "Especially, this time of the year. I've had my fondest childhood memories here and seen my worst nightmares realized."

As Daryl stared back at the man, wondering what to say next, he said, "I like your hat. It reminds me of the hats the reporters in New York wore. What type is it?"

The man said, "I guess you would call it a fedora. Been to New York, have you?"

Daryl smiled and said, "Yes."

The man said, "Excuse my manners. I guess it just took me a minute to recover from someone encroaching upon my space. I am Richard Douglas, Chief of the Wabash. My moderation is my only extreme. My humility is my only source of pride. My adherence to flexibility is my only source of rigidity. Fairness is my only bias. Toward balance is the only direction in which I lean. I don't have many enemies, but my friends don't like me much either."

Richard took on a more serious appearance and asked, "Would you like to see the newspaper office?"

Daryl exclaimed, "Of course!"

They walked back up the embankment to Washington Street. Daryl observed, "You are literally on the edge of town here."

Richard answered, "Well I figured nobody would be able to build closer to the river. That is public land behind. I have the benefits of town at my front door and the country behind, as long as the Wabash doesn't flood."

The office was small. There was a counter and a desk in the front room. Inside the counter was a glass covered display case with old newspaper articles mounted on photo mounting board around the sides. On the base and glass shelf were several artifacts that appeared to be arrowheads, spear heads, tomahawk stones and war hatchets. In the center of the room was a door to the press room filled with printing type and equipment. Daryl noticed a door to a closet-sized room in the back corner. "What's that room?"

Richard answered, "That's the dark room."

Daryl said, "So you have a darkroom. Do you have a photographer?"

Richard said, "None at the present time. We are a twice weekly, so I can't afford to hire a photographer. I would like to have one I could pay on an assignment basis."

Daryl said, "I might be interested in doing some assignments."

Richard looked at Daryl as if he could discern his ability by his physical appearance. "That is interesting. I'm taking a trip to Lafayette for a couple of days and thought I'd like to have a photographer go along. I could pay your travel, room and food, and maybe fifty cents a day on top of that. Let's go talk over supper. I'll give you a ride uptown."

They rode up Washington Street to Fall Street. At Fall Street they rode back north toward uptown. As they crossed the tracks, they came to a restaurant and inn called the Wabash. Richard asked, "You don't mind eating in a former saloon do you? Governor Hanly closed down our saloon."

Daryl said, "Not at all."

The waitress greeted Richard as if she was very familiar with him. Over supper Richard and Daryl continued their conversation. Daryl asked, "What's this assignment you are talking about?"

Richard began, "I'm going to Battleground just north of Lafayette near the Wabash and Tippecanoe Rivers. There is talk about erecting a monument at the Battleground to commemorate the Battle of the Tippecanoe. I think it will make a good feature story. If the public is asked to pay for it, they should know about the effort and potential cost."

Daryl answered, "I'll go. I just have to get word to some people that I will be a few days longer than I originally thought."

Richard answered, "We'll go the day after tomorrow. If they have a phone, you can call. If not, the telegraph office is just down the street. Bring some warm clothes. We'll be outside most of the time."

Daryl said, "And my Kodak, of course."

Richard agreed, "Of course." He took a silver flask out of his pocket. After looking around to make sure he was unnoticed, he poured some in his glass. He offered Daryl some but Daryl preferred to stick to his coffee.

Daryl asked another question, "You said your fondest memories and your worst nightmares were on the River. What about those?"

Richard replied, "Oh and I see you're a journalist too? Are you sure you want to hear an old mans' ramblings? I usually write my stories, not knowing if anybody reads them or not."

Daryl said, "People are probably reading your accounts or you wouldn't keep publishing them. I'm sure you can spin a yarn."

Richard observed, "Outspoken and direct. I like that. Well here goes. I grew up on Washington Street, just up from the office. That's where I earned the self-acclaimed title of Chief Richard of the Wabash. When we were small, we roamed the river from the landing to Pine Creek, a couple of miles up the river. If we were able to get away, we were on that river.

"Every spring, we could expect a jon boat to float down from somewhere up the river. The river didn't always close completely shut, but formed deep crusts of ice along both sides. As the ice melted in the spring, it would tear somebody's boat loose that had been left too close to the shore. Sometimes they would not float well enough to support a small gang of renegades. When we got them, we collected pitch, boiled it down and patched the boat as well as possible. That was how they used to build the barges that traveled the Wabash in earlier times."

Daryl asked, "Were you ever afraid of drowning?"

Richard said, "You know kids. We were indestructible. We had no fears. After the spring flood waters receded, the bank would dry and crack. The mixture of clay in the silt made the bank appear to be clay tiles with huge cracks between them, drying in the sun. We gathered the tiles and built forts and cabins. Then we took willow branches and made a roof. One time, when we came down in the morning, we found somebody sleeping off a drunk from the night before. We poured his bottle out on the landing. I can't imagine doing that now. Then, we refilled it partially with water from the Wabash. We were a stealthy bunch.

"After we got the bottle replaced and tied his shoestrings together, we stood off in the woods and pelted the cabin with dirt clods. When he awoke, he grabbed the bottle and took a swig. That was when we saw the real look of shock. As he began to regain his senses and remembered where he was, he shouted, 'I'll get you kids.'

"Then he stood up and attempt to walk, only to fall flat on his face. He was so embarrassed by the time he got the shoe strings untied or busted off, he never showed his face around our camp again.

"We also made bows and arrows, and spears out of the willow branches. They weren't very sharp or powerful, but they weren't accurate, either. To put somebody's eye out, we would have had to aim completely away from the person."

Daryl observed, "That's where the Indian relics came from in the display case?"

Richard smiled and nodded to the affirmative. "Yes, we found a bunch."

Daryl asked, "Those have to be some of your best memories. What were you referring to when you said, some of your worst nightmares?"

Richard looked pensive and took another drink. As he filled his glass, he continued, "When I was about eight years old, we heard about the Pottawatomi 'Relocation.' We learned they would camp here one night on their way west. My family and several families of Christian folk arranged to have blankets, clean water and some food provisions to distribute to the natives.

"The army commanders balked, and at first refused us to allow the assistance. There were so many women and families pleading to help, they finally gave in. Afterward, we went home. That was the only time I ever saw my father break down and cry. He kept sobbing about the despair and the unfairness of forcibly uprooting a group of people. He was changed after that.

"We later learned that four native children died before making it the twenty or so miles to Illinois and on west. It was difficult for me to enjoy the river the following summer. Whenever I went down there, I felt like I was returning to the scene of the crime."

Daryl just sat. He didn't know what to say when he saw the tears in Richard's eyes.

Richard continued, "I learned that the early settlers had burned out the natives that were living on the bank between Pine Creek and the Washington Street Landing. Allegedly, they placed a curse on the settlers. The courthouse and other parts of Old Town have burned since then. Who is to say curses are not allowed to alight and are just superstition?

"My perspective of the Native American changed after looking into their faces. I realized they were as human as any of us. They had a right to life, liberty and the pursuit of happiness. Although we continued to terrorize the banks of the Wabash, it was different after the night of the encampment of the Pottawatomie's. The event was later called the 'Trail of Death.'

"While my dad was still alive, we went west to visit the reservations. We were told the natives were well taken care of. We wanted to discover, firsthand, how they were treated. The reservations were stark and bleak. The vegetation that grew best was tumbleweeds. Alcoholism and despair were common. As we sat down to eat with a family, the father said, 'Stir the puppy up from the bottom.'

"After returning, my father took heavily to the bottle until his death. Hey, it's getting late. You probably better get to the Warren. We have a lot to get ready tomorrow for our trip on Thursday."

Chapter Fourteen

PROPHET'S REWARD

Richard met Daryl for breakfast on Thursday at the restaurant in the lobby of the Warren Hotel. A half block walk after breakfast and they were at the depot waiting for the train. Daryl asked, "Why is there an Old Town and a New Town up here? Was it because of the flood plane?"

Richard answered, looking over at the tracks, "You see those tracks? They dictated the layout of the town. As the railroad gained importance, river traffic just died out."

Daryl asked, "What do you think about the motor car? I've noticed a couple around town. Do you think they'll ever threaten the railroad?"

Richard laughed and stated, "They're too impractical. The motor car might be a costly and fascinating hobby, but they'll never haul the passengers or the freight the Iron Horse can move."

As Richard finished his statement, a whistle was heard in the distance followed by the chug of the locomotive and the hiss of steam. Richard looked at his watch and said, "Here she comes, right on time."

As they left Williamsport on the Illinois Central and Western, heading east, Daryl watched out the window. Within a few minutes they reached the Pine Creek trestle over the narrow canyon, exposing eighty foot cliffs on both sides. Daryl said, "I thought this was supposed to be flat land."

Richard said, "It is except the creek and river valleys and canyons. When the glaciers came through, they eroded the land as they melted."

Daryl observed, "Out at the farm, you can see flat land for miles. I think it's less than twenty miles from here."

Richard added, "The Pine Creek Canyon, connecting to the Wabash River Valley is the fine line separating the forested river valley from the Great Planes."

As they settled in for the two hour trip, Richard began telling the history of the battleground. "The battleground we are visiting is of great historical significance, yet few outside the area know about it. Prophetstown was established near the confluence of the Tippecanoe and Wabash Rivers."

Daryl acknowledged, "I've heard the Indians placed spiritual significance upon the confluence of rivers. The people I am here with also farm at English Lake."

Richard brightened and said, "English Lake, I could go on about that! Are you here with Miss Whitney's friends, out on the Goodwine Farm in Jordan County?"

Darryl smiled a surprised expression and said, "How did you know?"

Richard said, "It's a close knit community, even if it is spread out over so many acres and miles of farm land. Besides, that Miss Whitney is some looker!"

Daryl said, "I never know exactly how to take her."

Richard said, "That is no accident. Her feminine wiles allow her to be in control when necessary or disarming if appropriate. She is the type of woman who makes a boy feel like a man and a man feel like a boy."

Daryl agreed, "I've never been around a woman like her. It doesn't matter if she is old enough to be my mother, I find her extremely charming and attractive."

Richard said, "Do you think she would have been able to keep those farms if she weren't a shrewd business woman?"

Daryl said, "Well, I know she has been a strong advocate of women's rights."

Richard smiled and said, "Her own included!"

Back to my story, "Presidential campaigns have been launched at Battleground, in more ways than one. That's where Harrison won on 'Tippecanoe and Tyler, too.' Long before that, William Henry Harrison had been appointed governor of the Indiana Territory, the area that consisted most of the six states surrounding Lake Michigan and Ohio. The area later became known as the Northwest Territory. Two brothers of the Shawnee Nation began to form a confederation of the remaining tribes throughout the area. Tecumseh was the leader. His younger brother was Tenskwatawa, which meant 'Open Door.' He was a medicine man also known as 'The Prophet.'

"White settlers had been engaging in confrontations with the Indians. Composed of recruits and full time soldiers, they marched into Indian lands and ravaged crops and towns. The Indians returned acts of reprisal and harassed many towns and settlers. In early days, the Indians formed a loose confederation of several tribes. The Indians were not accustomed to prolonged military engagements. They used what we would call 'guerilla tactics,' ambushing an area or settlement and then moving on.

"Tecumseh was a brilliant student, fluent in several languages, and a gifted warrior. The Prophet was the runt of a set of triplets and never acquired the status of 'warrior.' He lost an eye in a hunting accident as a child. He was known more for being a trouble maker and a drunk. Legend has it that he awoke from a drunken stupor and claimed to have been visited by the Great Spirit. He began preaching abstinence from white man's alcohol and other customs such as clothing, foods, tools and methods of survival."

Daryl interjected, "You might say he was a cultural and political conservative."

Richard smiled, "I have never thought of it that way. I guess so."

Daryl said, "You don't know them yet, but I have been engaging in lengthy conversations with Michal and Stewart. Sven and I have taken several train rides together and talked of politics, philosophy and religion. Sven will probably be farming the English Lake farm."

Richard said, "I think I would like to meet them, except for the religion part."

Richard rummaged through his briefcase, found some notes and continued with the narrative, "Tecumseh was quite an orator and diplomat. He spent his time travelling around building the confederacy of the Indian nation. He realized the Indians could not withstand the wave of white immigrants, pouring into the wilderness. He reasoned, however, that if the Indian Nation exhibited enough unity, the settlers might honor their multiple treaties and push only to the Mississippi, leaving them alone to live in peace.

"Harrison was getting worried by the sheer number of Indian tribes combining forces. He attempted to discredit the Prophet and wrote a letter to all the tribes gathered at Tippecanoe. He challenged them to provoke Prophet to demonstrate some super natural event of Biblical proportion. He stated, 'If he is really a prophet, ask him to cause the sun to stand still or the moon to alter its course, the rivers to cease to flow or the dead to rise from their graves.'"

"Prophet and Tecumseh received the letter while visiting a friend along the White River. The brothers met in private for about an hour. Afterwards, Prophet requested that all in the village assemble to hear his response. He stated, 'Fifty days from this day there will be no clouds in the sky. Yet, when the Sun has reached its highest point, at that moment will the Great Spirit take into her hand and hide it from us. The darkness of night will thereupon cover us and the stars will shine round about us. The birds will roost and the night creatures will awaken and stir.'

"Fifty days later, at about noon on June sixteenth, eighteen and six, a total solar eclipse covered the region. About a thousand Indians were gathered for the event. Needless to say, Prophet gained great credibility and influence."

Looking amazed with eyes and mouth wide open, Daryl asked, "How did he know?"

Richard smiled and said, "I don't know."

Richard continued, "Harrison was visited by Tecumseh in Vincennes. Harrison asked him why he was fighting and attempting to build a coalition. Tecumseh told Harrison to sit on a bench. He moved toward Harrison, who kept sliding to the end of the bench. As Tecumseh pushed, Harrison stood up. He said, 'This is what you are doing to us.'

"Harrison decided to strike while the iron was hot. He marched from Vincennes on September twenty-eighth with the Fourth Regiment of the U.S. Infantry. Harrison's force consisted of about one thousand men. They marched along Indian trails and chopped their way through the wilderness along the banks of the Wabash. They stopped to build a supply depot and named it Fort Harrison, near present day Terre Haute. Altogether, they traveled about one hundred and twenty-five miles. They brought supplies by wagon, walking live cattle along for fresh meat."

Daryl clarified, "So, even back then Harrison knew that preparation for war included training troops and obtaining provisions. He coupled this with creating propaganda to build your case against the enemy, gaining support from his side and discrediting the enemy from the enemy's side."

Richard stopped and looked out the window. "Yes, I guess that's true. Look, those buildings are the southern edge of Purdue University."

They rode a few more minutes and crossed a trestle over the Wabash. A few more blocks and they screeched to a halt at the Fifth Street Depot, a Romanesque building combining style and function. Richard said, "We have two hours before the Monon comes through to take us the last ten miles to Battleground. Let's walk a couple of blocks to Loeb's and Hene Department Store. Have you ever had lunch at a soda fountain?"

Daryl answered, "Yes we had one in Wellspring. I've been here. We came south on the Monon and switched here to travel on to Pence."

Richard clarified, "So you have been through Battleground?"

Daryl answered, "I guess so, but it had no significance to me last week."

After lunch, they headed back to the depot and caught the Monon. The train rumbled through town, and merged with Ninth Street. Within a few minutes the conductor came through and said, "Battleground, next stop."

As the train slowed for Battleground, Richard pointed to an iron fence on the ridge. "That iron fence runs the circumference of the actual battleground. You'll be familiar with the area in the next couple of days."

They checked into the Harrison Inn and met in the lobby until supper. Richard spent the time interviewing local residents to get any more information he could about the Battle of the Tippecanoe Battleground or the proposed monument to be placed at the site. Daryl looked through the *Lafayette Journal* and *Courier*, dated June sixth, nineteen hundred and six. He found an article written by one of the battle survivors, Isaac Naylor, who had been a circuit judge.

The next morning, Daryl and Richard met for breakfast. They walked back south through town, past the Methodist Church Camp cabins and sanctuary. Richard began his narrative of the fight. "The night of November fourth, Harrison and company camped at the landing in Williamsport, near Pine Creek. They marched to within fourteen miles of Prophetstown on the fifth. The afternoon of November six they arrived here within sight of Prophetstown."

Richard pointed due east and said, "You could see the tops of the smoke columns from their fires here. A delegation was sent by Prophet to meet with Harrison. They advised Harrison to camp in the wet prairie of Brunette Creek, reasoning they could have water and a flat place to camp. Harrison also realized the creek valley was surrounded by small brush and steep ridges all around. If the Prophet decided to attack, the troops would be in a vulnerable spot.

"Harrison knew Tecumseh had ordered Prophet not to engage in battle until he returned. Although the delegation assured the troops they would meet the next morning to discuss peace, Harrison decided to camp on this rhomboid shaped plateau. It was cold and rainy that night. Harrison ordered the soldiers to camp in formation, fully clothed and ready, sleeping on their weapons. The soldiers started with camp fires to dry out and warm up, but realized they were more visible sitting near the camp fires surrounded by darkness.

"About four in the morning the first Indians crawled into camp through the cold and wet grass. They entered right there, where the gradual slope ascends up from the plateau from the Brunette Creek wet prairie. Prophet told the Indians they were protected from illness, bullets and bayonets. He watched the battle from Prophet's Rock just west on a ridge extending up from Brunette Creek."

Richard and Daryl walked the perimeter of the battleground and looked out over the valley where the Indians told Harrison to camp. They visited graves of the American commanders who had been killed in the battle. Daryl asked to walk up to Prophet's Rock. When he climbed the forty foot ridge behind the rock, he looked out over the battlefield. As he was taking pictures, he dropped the Kodak. The camera bounced once as he quickly reached out and grabbed it in midair. Richard, watching from below yelled, "Good save!"

Daryl examined the camera and climbed back down. He said, "This might sound weird, but I forgot all about it. I had a dream last night that I dropped my camera. I had never been to Prophet's Rock, so I didn't recognize it in my dream. Now I know it was this scene."

Richard laughed, "Oh you've just been immersed in this stuff for the past couple of days. It's all explainable by Dr. Fraud. Let's go get some lunch."

Daryl said, "Don't you mean Freud?"

Richard smiled and said, "No."

As they walked back to the Harrison to eat, Daryl could not so easily shake the camera incident from his thoughts. That afternoon, they walked east about a mile, over to the prairie where Richard attempted to determine the approximate location of where Prophetstown sat.

The next morning, they caught the Monon back to Fifth Street Depot. As they were waiting to catch their train back to Williamsport, a man approached them. He was trim, clean shaven and wore a modest wool plaid suit. He wore a fedora with a slight brim. Richard smiled, gave the man a hug and said, "Daryl, this is Richard Douglas Junior, although he doesn't like the 'Junior' part. Richard, this is Daryl Dailey. Richard will be accompanying us to Williamsport."

As they rode back across the Wabash Trestle and past the campus, Richard Senior began explaining why Richard had joined them. "Young Richard is a campus minister here at Purdue. He also travels out into the wilderness of Warren County to minister on alternate weekends. He happens to be going back to Williamsport this weekend."

Daryl sat across from and facing the two Richards. Daryl asked young Richard how Prophet could have known about the eclipse. Young Richard answered, "I've been studying the Indian ways and comparative religion for some time. They certainly were spiritual. How the Great Spirit relates to God, Yahweh and Jehovah is difficult to determine. Only God and Prophet know if he faked the prophecy of the eclipse with prior knowledge."

At this Richard, the Editor-in-Chief got up and crossed the isle to a vacant seat. He leaned back, brought his legs up on the seat and pulled his hat over his eyes. Young Richard continued, "I guess we have lost him for a while. Jesus said, 'He that receives a prophet in the name of a prophet shall receive a prophet's reward.'"

Daryl asked, "What's a prophet's reward?"

Richard answered, "Rewards can be both positive and negative. Ezekiel was given an assignment by God. He was told that he would be a watchman for Israel. He said that if Ezekiel was told to warn the wicked and they did not heed the warning, the unrighteous people would die. God added that if the wicked died without the warning, their blood would be on Ezekiel's hands. If he warned them and they refused to turn from their sins, Ezekiel would not be held accountable. The Good Book says the wicked would die. It is not specific how Ezekiel would be held accountable for not warning them.

"Most of the prophets, except Isaiah became depressed when God gave them an assignment. Eliajah wanted to go into the wilderness and die. Moses argued with God and was able to include his brother, Aaron in the assignment. He said Aaron was more fluent and skilled in his speech. That sounds kind of like Tecumseh and the Prophet.

Moses was adopted into the Pharaoh's family as a son. He became second in command in the greatest nation on the earth, at the time. When he defended one of his own people by killing an Egyptian, he was forced into forty years of exile in the dessert prior to setting his people free and leading them out of Egypt.

"The Hebrews were in Egypt because some four hundred years earlier, Joseph had dreams and was able to interpret them. Joseph also became the second in command of Egypt. In his position, he was able to save his family and establish the Israelite population in Egypt. To do so, he went through being sold into slavery by his brothers and imprisonment. He said, 'They meant it for evil, but God meant it for good.'

"Daniel had dreams and visions. He was appointed to be the second in command of Babylonia, again, the most powerful nation in the world. Daniel and Joseph were appointed by God to speak to the existing governments. They also anticipated times of shortages and warned their leaders. The leaders were able to set aside reserves and yes, tax the people so the nations could get through the lean times. Daniel came to power by way of a death sentence in the den of the lions.

"Jonah was given a prophetic assignment, but ran in the other direction. He was told to warn the city of Nineveh of God's judgment. He feared man rather than God, because prophets could be killed, exiled or imprisoned by the nation's political or religious leaders. This happened more frequently when the religious leaders formed an unholy alliance with the ruling political powers. The best example was Rome and the Jewish religious leaders. We'll get into more on that later. Jonah was worried the Ninevites would heed God's warning and repent. He would be embarrassed if God relented from destroying them.

"Like I said, Jonah tried to run from God. He boarded a ship. The ship ran into a storm. The crew members discerned that somebody on board was running from God. We are not told the crew members' spiritual condition or status, yet they could discern the conditions. Jonah confessed and asked to be thrown overboard.

"Realistically, in the middle of the sea, in a storm, he probably did not expect to survive. He was swallowed and spent three days in the belly of a huge fish. Those three days were a harbinger of Jesus going to the grave, and his resurrection, conquering hell and death. So the fish ejected him and he ended up on the beach. He warned Nineveh. They heeded his warning and just as Jonah predicted, they turned from their wickedness. Jonah was mad and still wanted God to destroy the city. So, a prophet's reward can be a blessing and a curse. The greatest part is the reward of turning from wickedness to righteous.

Daryl said, "I had a dream on the first night at the Inn. I told your dad about part of it, but he downplayed it. Is he a spiritual person?"

Richard smiled and said, "He won't admit it, but he is a spiritual person. He is just not religious."

Daryl continued, "In the dream, I dropped my camera off a large boulder or ridge. I caught it in midair, undamaged. The next day that actually happened on Prophet's Rock. The thing I didn't tell your dad was that after I caught the camera, in my dream, I was soaring behind it. I was actually flying with the camera extended in my hands, taking pictures.

"The next night, I dreamed I was traveling along a dirt road. I came up over a wooded ridge, as the road descended into a peaceful valley. As I approached a large clearing in the valley floor, I discovered the ruins of a great mansion. All that remained were corners of the mansion that were a story to a story and one half high of brick and chimneys, partially crumbling. There were some large pieces of burnt wood on the ground, still smoldering. The dream then turned to a strange village. I was flying over several buildings. Most were two and three story brick houses. There was brick rubble with windows blown out and holes the size of a man in the walls in random places. Do you think my dreams have significance?"

Richard said, "I do not claim to be a prophet, but I know dreams and prophecies have three sources. In some, God is telling us something significant. In others, we are only projecting our own hopes and desire or fears. I'm not sure, but others can possibly be from the Deceiver."

At this point, the Editor in Chief stirred, took his hat down and rejoined the two. He said, "You didn't tell Daryl the best part about Prophet's curse."

Young Richard said, "I figured you had already told him. Besides, you were sleeping. How do you know what we were talking about?"

The Editor-in-Chief just gave a mischievous smile. Young Richard, glancing skeptically at his father, continued, "The Prophet predicted that Harrison would become the father of the great land. He also predicted that Harrison would die in office and every great father elected on the even score of years would die in office. Harrison was defeated by Van Buren in eighteen thirty-six. He was elected in eighteen forty. He gave a lengthy inaugural speech in the rain, in January, without a raincoat, caught pneumonia and died thirty days later. He was the shortest term president."

Daryl gazed in disbelief. Richard continued, "Every president since Harrison, elected on the even twenty year interval has been assassinated or otherwise died in office. The prophets in the Bible could be killed for a wrong prediction, or for just offending the political or religious leaders. Harrison, who did not receive Prophet as a true prophet died at the height of his power, and demonstrated how human he actually was. An expedition sent up Wildcat Creek to capture or kill Prophet shortly after the battle at Tippecanoe was bogged down in a blizzard and had to retreat. Prophet died of old age in Kansas."

Prophet's Rock

Chapter Fifteen

MUST BE LOVE

Richard wrote his article. It was a call for a memorial to be erected at Battleground whether state money would be used or collected from private sources. His article was different than most being published at the time. The others were about honoring the heroes from the American military. Richard also called to commemorate the memory of the lost life style and the once great people who were forcibly uprooted and exiled or killed. Daryl published some photos of the days at Battleground. Daryl told Richard he would be back in a month or two.

He caught the train back to the farm to meet Michael. They rode to Lafayette and caught the Monon Line north. They met Sven at the Rye Depot in Toto and continued to Chicago. On the trip, Michael talked about farming and getting back to Wellspring. Sven was excited about the English Lake farm and Daryl handed both a copy of the article and his photographs.

Once in Chicago, they had lunch at Union Station. Michael excused himself and looked around in a few stores near the station. Sven and Daryl knew Michael missed more than the town of Wellspring. As their train left the station, Daryl asked, "Did you know Williamsport had a jewelry store?"

Michael answered, "I did not."

Daryl asked, "Did you find anything interesting in the jewelry store close to Union Station?"

Michael smiled and said, "Maybe."

After reading the article, Michael said, "I'd like to meet Richard. He sounds like an interesting character."

Daryl agreed, "Oh, he's a character alright. I told him I'd attempt to work part time for the newspaper and part time for you, if that'd be alright."

Michael said, "That sounds great! You have a gift. You need to use it. There will be times when farming takes most of our time and effort and times when we are not busy at all."

The three had various conversations in the lengthy return trip to Wellspring. Daryl spoke of both Richards and Williamsport. He was very optimistic of the challenge of making the *Watchman*

a daily instead of a twice weekly paper. Sven discussed Heidi and
their future at English Lake. Michael attempted to talk about
farming and Indiana. He subconsciously and unintentionally
mentioned Whitney in about every conversation. Almost every
time Michael got a dreamy look and mentioned Whitney, Daryl
and Sven gave a knowing smile to each other. Michael was oblivious
to the inside joke.

They reached Wellspring on Monday afternoon and went their
separate ways after agreeing to meet on Sunday at Ma Peterson's for
dinner. Michael made an arrangement to move into the boarding
house next to Ma Peterson's, as she had no rooms left. He also made
arrangements for equitable payment for meals which he or Whitney
requested and were for guests who were their employees, as opposed
to the regulars who stayed there.

He first saw Whitney Monday evening. He relayed his
perceptions of Indiana and the farms. He also told Whitney
that he would like for her to accompany him for dinner, alone
on Wednesday night. Whitney agreed. Michael was busy all day
on Wednesday. He arranged for a carriage and told Whitney
they would need the blanket and should stay close under it to
keep warm in the cold December air. During supper, Whitney
kept watching Michael as he was acting very unusual. She said,
"Michael, you seem different since you've returned from Indiana.
You seem jumpy and somewhat nervous."

Michael responded, "For some reason, I feel guilty. I feel like a kid who is contemplating snatching the cookies from the cookie jar."

Whitney smiled and said, "Whatever are you talking about?"

Michael said, "I missed you. While we were gone, I thought of little except you. I thought of the years we could have been together - years that we will not be able to get back. I thought of how I need you. I can't waste one more day letting the past rob me of a future, a future with you. Whitney, will you marry me?"

As he said this, he pulled a small box from his coat pocket and handed it to Whitney. Whitney thought she knew what was coming, yet she was overwhelmed with emotion. "Michael, I was beginning to think you would never ask me. I thought you were getting to know me and thinking you didn't want to get married. Yes, Michael!"

Michael said, "If Princess has her baby soon, we can set a date. How is she doing?"

Whitney answered, "She is doing very well. After the one episode at the Strater, she has been improving almost daily. Of course, I made sure she ate right and rested most of the day, every day. She would have nothing to do with complete bed rest. I think she'll deliver in the next week or so, maybe around Christmas."

Michael said, "Christmas is on a Tuesday. "How would you like to be married on Christmas Eve?"

When the newly engaged couple arrived back at Ma Peterson's, they found Stewart and Victoria sitting in the living room, watching the fire and talking. When Michael and Whitney told them of the plans, both were excited, but not surprised. Victoria jokingly asked, "Does this mean I should call you Uncle Michael?"

Michael said, "You have never been required to, that's totally up to you. I won't be any more of an uncle to you than I've always been, just because I'm marrying your aunt."

Victoria anticipated the news. She found herself excited for the couple, yet surprised that she had mixed feelings. Mixed feelings should have come as no surprise, however. Her hormones had influenced or controlled her emotions for the last eight and a half months. She was grieving the loss of her father, her husband and she was carrying her first baby. Thoughts of the mine and the house in Discovery crossed her mind every so often. Yet, she was surprised how little she missed those trappings.

With all these emotions, she found that something else occupied her conscious and subconscious thoughts. She caught herself worrying about the future. Even though Victoria had a strong support structure, she worried about raising a child by herself. Being a proper woman, she also contemplated how people would accept an unmarried mother in Indiana.

She thought of Stewart often. It did not help that he lived in the same house, even though his room was upstairs. She experienced guilt that, as a grieving widow, she should feel the way she did. She attempted to rationalize her feelings with the idea that Stewart had been so helpful and self-sacrificing. Of course she would think about him when they shared every meal together, when he read to her and they talked in evenings and on weekends.

Being a person who had to believe she could control her emotions, Victoria found any justification, even denial for the feeling she could not control. Maybe once the baby was born, she would get back into her old rational state. While Stewart was at work, when she wasn't sleeping, she read everything she could. Victoria found herself drawn to books that included or were likely to include a love story. She studied them, not as an atheist would study the Bible to find loopholes, but as a philosopher would search for truth; or as a pastor would attempt to drive home the final point to convict the sinner.

Victoria wanted to know love in her mind as a teacher would understand and explain a theory and illuminate the concept for the learner; or a lawyer finding the right evidence to conclusively defend the innocent or convict the guilty. Her obsession was not for the disengaged or impassionate understanding of the philosopher, student, defender, prosecutor, the jurist or the judge. It was for the emotional acceptance and belief of the true believer - all in with no reservations.

Whitney noticed Victoria's dilemma. While Stewart was at work and the other men were away, she sat down to discuss the situation with Victoria. She said, "Princess, these are emotional times."

Victoria answered, "Once I have the baby, things can get back to normal."

Whitney countered, "Honey, things will never be what we call 'normal' again. Things will always change. I can see that you and Stewart have a strong bond, one that is rare in a couple that's not married."

Victoria answered, "Oh, I am so appreciative of all that Stewart has done."

Whitney said, "It's obviously more than that. Actually, you are not even dating. What is your relationship?"

Victoria responded, "I really don't know. The uncertainty is making me a wreck."

Whitney continued, "What Michael and I had so many years ago was as close to anything I could imagine as your situation. We were so busy with life, though. You and Stewart have had a chance to grow together almost as a couple with responsibilities, yet denied the emotional and physical satisfaction. I would hate to see the two of you let that get away. I lived every day of my life thinking about Michael, wondering if he was safe; if he was lonely; if he was thinking about me."

Victoria responded, "Aunt Whitney. I can't allow myself to need somebody. I have to prove I can take care of my baby by myself."

Whitney asked, "Why? Princess, your father is dead. You don't have to live up to his expectations any more. You have to live your life."

With this statement and realization of its truth, Victoria sat and cried. Whitney moved over closer and held her. Suddenly, Victoria jerked and felt a deep contraction. Stewart came in the door from work and Whitney asked him to see if Dr. Gilbert was available. He left immediately. After about two hours, Stewart returned with Dr. Gilbert. Whitney informed the doctor the water had broken, He said, "Hopefully, it won't be long now."

Shortly after midnight, Doctor Gilbert came out and said, "It's a healthy boy. He might be a week or so premature, but healthy."

Stewart jumped up and said, "And Victoria?"

Doctor Gilbert said, "She is fine, weakened and tired. With some rest, she will be fine."

Michael and Whitney had their wedding the following Friday, December twenty-eighth. The pastor from Ma Peterson's church performed the ceremony. Michael said he did not mind the wait as he had never been a great uncle before. The pastor was gracious enough to wait until baby Raymond was put down for his nap to perform the ceremony. Stewart stood and Victoria sat next to Whitney as witnesses for the couple. With a new baby in the house, they did not ask the others to attend.

Chapter Sixteen

BACK HOME IN INDIANA

Early in nineteen O' seven the Williamsport court house burned down. There was speculation around town about the curse the Native Americans had placed upon Williamsport when the early settlers had burned them out. The records were saved but the structure was a complete loss. Plans were made to begin the overwhelming and cumbersome process of building a new one on the existing site.

Michael and Whitney, Sven and Heidi, and Daryl decided to leave for Indiana at the end of January. Victoria had to decide whether Raymond would be able to travel that far being only five weeks old. Stewart dreaded the idea of being alone. He also knew that he dreaded more than just being alone, although he would not allow himself to admit his feelings.

Stewart was sitting in his office on an early midwinter morning. As he picked up his Bible, he was thankful to be in Wellspring. Although survival in Michael's cabin was an adventure the previous January, he thought how nice it was to be living in a boarding house, with heat and water and meals provided. He read a couple of verses from Proverbs twenty-eight and verse one, "The wicked flee when no one pursueth; But the righteous are bold as a lion. For the transgression of a land many are the princes thereof; But by men of understanding and knowledge, the state thereof shall be prolonged."

Stewart contemplated the verses. "When you are guilty, you lose confidence. When you are right with God, you have the confidence of God's approval and empowerment. When the country is under submission to God, it has wise rulers who maintain order. When the country is in rebellion, there are several claiming to be in charge and chaos results."

He contemplated the Civil War and Lincoln's assassination. The country had been in rebellion since its founding. Although God blessed the nation, the guilt of slavery had its results. It took the blood of over six hundred thousand Americans to eradicate the evil roots of slavery.

Stewart read the next three verses, "A needy man that oppresseth the poor is like a sweeping rain that leaveth no food. Those who forsake the law praise the wicked; but such as keep the law contend with them. Evil men do not understand justice; but those who seek Jehovah understand all things."

Stewart thought of the irony that the writer of these verses ultimately oppressed the poor and caused a civil war in his own nation. Solomon had built a temple for Moloch in which children were sacrificed. He thought about how much he loved Victoria's baby, Raymond. He also pondered how Vitoria would have given her own life to save him. He remembered the shocking revelation that mothers sacrificed their babies right here in the United States and if the practice was allowed to continue, how the nation would be judged.

Stewart was reminded of how thankful he was to be in a profession in which he could seek justice and resist the wicked. He wondered about Robert Connor and, how he used the law, his position and his wealth to oppress the poor and praise the wicked. He wondered how the men in Discovery were doing under the new ownership of the mines. He heard that Connor had rejected the recommendations to promote management from within and appointed an acting manager named Winston Barlow.

As he was sitting in the office meditating upon the verses, he heard a familiar voice coming from the reception area. Soon, Michael's head appeared in the doorway to Stewart's' office. "Got time for an old friend, and I do mean old."

"Michael, what a surprise! What brings you down here?"

Michael said, "I thought you might have time for breakfast with a client."

Stewart said, "Sure, let me grab my coat. Didn't Ma Peterson or Whitney fix breakfast for you?"

Michael smiled and said, "Ma Peterson is a great cook. Sometimes, it is a little crowded there. Whitney has many strengths and admirable qualities. Cooking is not one of them."

Stewart left a note on James' desk as nobody else was in the office this early. They walked a few blocks in the blustery morning wind to the café where they ate the previous time, the one in which Stewart ate his first morning in Wellspring. As they sat down and ordered coffee, Stewart asked, "What's on your mind?"

Michael said, "You know I'm not one to pry into your personal life."

Stewart said, "Yes, and I respect that."

Michael began as if broaching the subject was very difficult, "You know we're leaving in a couple of weeks. I've noticed that you seem to be distancing yourself from Victoria."

Stewart answered, "I'm giving her space. Out of respect for the memory of Raymond, I'm honoring her time of mourning."

Michael said, "She thinks you are not interested in her because she's a single mother."

Stewart with wide-eyed amazement, answered, "That's impossible! I love Raymond as if he were my own son. I lo…really respect and like Victoria. She is a strong woman, and is a valued client."

Michael said, "I think of Whitney and myself. We wasted so much time that we could've been together."

Michael could perceive from Stewart's silence, he was contemplating their discussion. They finished breakfast and Michael told Stewart, "I'll go on back to the boarding house from here. Think about our talk. There may be only a few weeks left to act upon it."

Stewart assured him, "Oh, I will! This has been on my mind daily."

Michael assured him, "No worries, no regrets."

As the next two weeks passed, Stewart found himself at the boarding house less and less of the time. He buried himself into his work and gave James a good sixty hours of production a week. He found a club near the office where he could exercise daily, with a rowing machine, punching bag and dumbbells. He also found an industrial school that had an evening class. He rationalized that he could continue to learn more about the machines with instruction. Maybe he was distancing himself from the others so he would not be so lonely after they left. The more he determined to take control of his life, the more he found it already spiraling out of control.

The day he dreaded finally came. No amount of activity or self-denial could remove the pain, only delay it a little. They had already delayed the departure one week to make sure Raymond was strong enough to travel. They also did all they could to determine if the weather would be suitable for a two day trip with a newborn infant.

Stewart took Friday morning off to assist the group in getting to the station. As the train boarded, he shook Michael's hand and gave him a hug. He hugged Whitney. She said, "Please come and visit as soon as possible. You might find you want to stay."

As Stewart smiled, in his mind, he agreed without voicing his comment, "That's exactly what I'm afraid of."

As he embraced Victoria, she could say nothing. She held him tight and cried. He returned the embrace as his eyes welled with tears. Finally, he was able to whisper into her ear, "I will miss Raymond and …"

Just then, the train whistle blew and the conductor shouted, "All aboard."

Whitney tugged Victoria's coat and Michael carried Raymond onto the coach. Stewart ran along the landing beside the train, watching as Michael and Whitney waved from inside. He could only see Victoria's profile with her face buried in her handkerchief. He thought back on Michael's words, "No worries, no regrets."

As the travelers settled in for the ride, Whitney attempted to comfort Victoria. "This will all work out somehow."

Victoria said, "I could not hear if he finished his sentence. He said he will miss 'Raymond and...' just as the whistle blew. He was whispering and I couldn't tell if he said more. I'll never see him again."

Michael asked, "Did you ever tell him how you felt?"

Sobbing, Victoria said, "I hinted. It wouldn't have been proper for a widow to throw herself at a handsome young bachelor."

Whitney asked, "When have you worried about what others thought, except for Edward?"

Victoria said, "Besides, I didn't want to be desperate. If I was desperate, he would know and be driven further away."

The remainder of the trip included several conversations of reassurance coupled with thoughts of thanksgiving for the new family. Victoria was comforted by the fact that her closest relatives were now married. She could not replace her mother and father, but Whitney and Michael were as close to her parents as possible. She was thankful they loved Raymond so much. She never had to worry about somebody holding him, feeding or changing him. Michael always offered to carry Raymond's basket when they switched trains at the stations. They finally arrived at the station in Pence. Daryl was there to meet them with the carriage.

Over the next two months, Victoria received a letter from Stewart every two weeks. Although he attempted to be professional and impersonal at first, his letters over time began to betray the feelings and emotions he attempted to hide from Victoria, but mostly from himself. He continued to bury himself in his work and other activities. Keeping no record of the letters, he could not remember what he had actually written and what he had thought he had attempted to suppress.

He remembered all the times he and James discussed honesty. They determined that honest people didn't need good memories. They only needed to tell the truth. It was those who were attempting to deceive who always needed to remember the details of what they told people, so as not to be caught in a lie. Due to loneliness, he continued writing, not realizing that his feelings were portrayed more accurately than he could admit to himself. Victoria kept the letters and read them over again and again, looking for evidence of love and cherishing them in her heart. She also continued to read every book that spoke of love.

They began to attend a church in Pence. Pastor Richard Douglas came to preach every other Friday night. He ministered on campus at Purdue every other Sunday. He came to Williamsport on alternate weekends and ministered to the small congregation in Pence on Friday evening. After the first service, as Michael greeted him, Richard said, "I am sorry for the inconvenience of meeting on Friday night."

Michael smiled and said, "Oh, that's alright. Friday after sundown is actually in keeping with the Sabbath."

Chapter Seventeen

TIME IN A BOTTLE

It finally came! Victoria read a letter from Stewart stating that he had been with James' law firm for one year and had earned a vacation. He was coming to visit in a month! Victoria's joy and excitement soon turned to apprehension. Would he think she was still fat from the pregnancy? Would he still have any feelings for her? Would this visit cause him to walk away and feel he had completed all he was obliged to do toward her and his respect for the memory of Raymond?

The months leading to the arrival of the letter had been times of great anticipation and apprehension. Sure, this was the first letter resulting in the promise of definitive action. Stewart would be coming to visit. In those months, Victoria began to doubt the letter would ever arrive. Maybe the letters in those months that tended to lean toward Stewart's true feelings of love for her were just his coping with the loneliness of the winter in Wellspring. He had attempted to use work, the athletic club and the industrial school to allay his fears of loneliness. After all, she, Michael, Whitney, Sven and Daryl were gone now and he had his own life to live. In his position and in constantly making new contacts and experiencing new connections, he would find somebody.

Whitney was first to notice. Victoria was becoming animated. The emotions and hopes she attempted to suppress over the months could no longer be denied. In sharp contrast, she also exhibited self-doubt and uncertainty. These were rare qualities for Victoria, especially as she had been a successful business woman, an heiress and now settling into her role as mother.

She could not wait to see Stewart, yet she dreaded his visit. Her days fluctuated from flying by to standing still. She looked at Raymond sleeping and anticipated how he would be in a few years waiting for Christmas. She remembered her childhood, how she anticipated Christmas, thinking, minutes were hours, hours were days, days were weeks, weeks were months and then, it was all over until another year. Sitting on the porch, rocking him gently and watching him sleep, Raymond caused her to remember so many thoughts of her childhood.

As she watched Raymond and continued to think, her thoughts were again mixed. She wanted to drink in the precious moments she and only Raymond shared. The moments when Raymond was nursing, totally dependent upon her for survival, not worrying about the future or the present. Holding him in the middle of the night when nobody else was around as if time stood still. The next moment she thought about Raymond growing up without a father, going to school, encountering bullies, falling and skinning his knee or worse. Just then, Michael came in from the field. Victoria announced, "Stewart is coming in a month! I just got his letter in the mail."

Whitney came out to the porch and sat next to Michael. She said, "I heard the news. That's fantastic!

Michael responded, "Great! I can't wait to see him. Is he well?"

Victoria said, "From his letters, he seems to be doing well."

Whitney asked, "Do his letters reveal anything else?"

Victoria smiled and said, "I can't say for sure. I keep looking and reading between the lines, hoping that my desires and emotions aren't clouding my perceptions, causing me to read something into the situation that's not there."

Michael said, "If it is meant to be, it will work out."

Victoria asked, "But don't you and Whitney feel as if it was supposed to work out for you, and yet, it took so long?"

Michael thoughtfully replied, "We might have let life get in our way. Maybe it was supposed to take this long. Either way, I couldn't be happier than I am now."

Victoria said, "I'm finding it difficult to live by that philosophy. Maybe I'm still emotional from having Raymond. Maybe I'm adjusting to the move. I want Raymond to stay little forever, yet I want to see him grow up without ever scraping his knee. I'm happy now, but I don't want to delay further happiness. I don't want to have high expectations, only to find they weren't all I hoped for. "

Michael comforted Victoria with, "One day at a time, Princess."

Victoria agreed, "I know, Uncle Michael. It's just so difficult. Things go by so slowly out here."

Whitney said, "I've read about these emotions. They're completely normal for a new mother. Your body is adjusting to the change in hormones. Your emotions are adjusting to the new love and responsibility. Of course, I can't say from personal experience."

Victoria asked, "Do you ever regret not having children?"

Whitney looked pensive and replied, "I feel I was blessed to be able to take care of you. Those were wonderful years. I love you like a daughter. I didn't have to go through the pregnancy, change diapers or stay up nights nursing."

With this statement, Victoria moved over and sat between Michael and Whitney. Michael placed his arm around both of them. Victoria said, "My life has not gone according to the normal plan, but I have been blessed to be part of your lives."

Michael said, "What we consider normal could be just average. God wants us to live in the exceptional. You'll see."

Whitney agreed, "It seems uncertain now, but you'll look back on these times as some of the best."

Michael said, "We need to start looking around to see if anything exists out here that would be a good place to celebrate."

Whitney said, "Daryl told me about a place that Richard, the Editor-in-Chief, has taken him for supper. It's only about fifteen miles from here. It's a resort with a European restaurant. You can even hob-knob with celebrities there."

Victoria, with a surprised expression asked, "Out here in the middle of nowhere?"

The next afternoon, Michael brought up the carriage. They went two miles south to Pence Road, turned east and proceeded for a few miles. They passed the new grain elevator and crossed the tracks at Stewart, the intersection of the rails and the county road. Victoria said, "I like the name of this town."

Whitney looked at her and said, "Princess, Stewart isn't the only one who is not forthcoming with his feelings. I think you've got it bad. "

They rode further to an intersection with a few houses and a depot called Sycamore Corner. Shortly, they came to Judyville. It was a thriving community with a hotel, a granary, a general store, a black smith shop and a huge farm mansion. Victoria said, "Something about this town reminds me of Discovery. Of course, there are no mountains and they have farming instead of mining."

Michael said, "That's ironic, as Judy uses a script system much like your father used. His employees buy almost everything from his general store, using Judy money."

As they proceeded east, they noticed the land beginning to have small rolling hills instead of flat prairie as far as the eye could see. They rode through Carbondale and turned right onto a county road for a few miles south to Hunter Hill Road and wound through huge green trees and around to Lovers Leap and the Hunter House. Suddenly, the hill overlooked a deep valley that was about a mile wide and flat, surrounded by gently sloping canyon walls. Toward the side of the valley furthest from them, they could see a building that was grander than anything they had ever visited or seen in pictures. It was nestled in a wide hollow at the bottom of the Pine Creek Canyon.

As they drew closer, they could see people strolling around on the grounds. There were men pulling mowers behind mules. There was a nine hole golf course, tennis courts and a baseball diamond, a solarium and a brick colonnade and a koi pond in front of the resort. The building was a sprawling Victorian design with large spires and balconies. People were lounging in the shade in white wooden chairs and chaises on the massive veranda across the front of the building. The hot August afternoon was held at bay by the sycamore and pine trees and the cool deep walls of Pine Creek canyon. Further to the east, up a slight incline and toward the back canyon wall, there were some other buildings, including a gazebo and a chapel.

A bellman approached the carriage and asked, "Is there any luggage?"

Michael said, "Yes, we each have a valise."

A porter asked, "Will we be stabling the horses?"

Michael said, "Yes, just water and oats. Maybe a good currying. We shouldn't be the only ones enjoying this luxury."

As Michael watched, the bellman took the luggage. A stable hand took the carriage and tied the horses to the hitching post. He unhooked the horses from the carriage and led them to the stable. As Michael turned and proceeded toward check-in, he offered to carry Raymond and said, "I could sure get used to this."

They entered a majestic foyer with parquet tiled floors and a fountain in front of a huge stairway. To one side was the desk of solid walnut, with walls of solid walnut paneling. The other direction led to the dining hall. The high ceilings had hardwood trimmed beams with flat plastered panels between. Huge crystal chandeliers hung from the beams and green marble columns with German silver trim supported the beams at their intersections. There were German silver curtain rods, Tiffany windows, and hardwood floors with colorful wool runners.

Michael requested a suite with two bedrooms. Victoria read while Raymond took a nap and Michael and Whitney took a stroll around the property. They all liked the idea of "dressing" for supper as they were not expected to do so since staying at the Straiter in Wellspring. After the walk, Whitney told Victoria, "I'll watch Raymond while you go downstairs for a mud bath."

Victoria said, "Seriously, I couldn't do that."

Whitney said, "Oh, it's quite normal. That's what most people are here to do. Go ahead, you'll enjoy it."

Victoria reluctantly agreed. She went to the women's bath area in the basement. There were mosaic floors, onyx partitions and low sturdy beds with an air mattress on canvas stretched over strong wooden frames. Victoria watched as the attendant placed a four inch layer of hot mud on the table. She then assisted Victoria to lie down on the table. Another layer of warm mud was placed over Victoria, leaving her face open.

She lay in the mud, resting and relaxing as the therapeutic effects worked wonders on her. After the prescribed time, she was assisted from the mud, hosed herself off in the shower room and was given an alcohol massage. People usually experienced such a deep level of relaxation that their legs felt rubbery after the bath. She went back upstairs and took a long nap.

As they entered the dining hall, they could see Daryl at a table toward the other end. He noticed them and motioned for them to sit with him and two other gentlemen. The host quickly arranged the tables to accommodate for six adults and a high chair. Daryl beamed and said, "This is Chief Richard of the Wabash. You've met Richard Douglas, circuit preacher. I'd like you to meet Michael and Whitney Thomas and Victoria Warren."

Richard smiled, stood up and kissed both ladies' hands, shook Michael's and said, "I've heard a lot about you all. Daryl is a better photographer than story teller. His descriptions of the two ladies were inadequate compared to the live specimens."

Victoria blushed. Whitney smiled. Michael said, "We've certainly heard a lot about you. When Daryl is with us, he talks about nothing but you and the paper. Pastor Douglas, it seems strange meeting you outside of church."

Richard responded, "Well, preachers have to eat, too. You know Chief Richard is my father, don't you?"

Whitney said, "Lands, I never made that connection!"

Victoria looked around. She was still in awe of the grandeur of the resort. The tables each had a white linen table cloth and napkins, silverware and serving dishes and fresh cut flowers. The vinegar and oil bottles resembled medical flasks with frosted glass stoppers, neatly arranged in a silver caddy. Up close the trimmings on the chandeliers were brass and glass resembling emerging buds on a willow branch. Huge silver samovars filled with coffee and serving dishes sat on walnut side tables around the room. Porters and waitresses served the tables. The porters wore maroon jackets and white gloves. The waitresses wore dark dresses with white aprons.

After eating dinner, ordering dessert and coffee refills, Michael asked Richard, "What's the story behind this place?"

Richard settled back and said, "Since I'm already finished eating, I will entertain you while you eat. The story begins with a Story."

Daryl and Pastor Douglas looked at each other as if they had heard the story before and rolled their eyes in respectful admiration. Daryl sighed, "Might as well settle in."

Richard began, "In eighteen hundred and eighty-four, a Civil War veteran named Samuel Story returned to his home here in Warren County. His body was racked with pain from age, rheumatism and fighting the war. He lived on a modest farm in Pine Creek Valley. The place was called Cameron Springs. The property he leased was swampy and boggy with no drainage. He decided to dig a drainage ditch across the farm. While he was digging, knee deep in mud every day, he found the symptoms of rheumatism, kidney troubles and other physical ailments began to diminish. He attributed it to the water and the mud, as he was drinking large quantities of well water to rehydrate.

"Cameron Springs, the village right up the hill behind us, was named for Postmaster, 'Uncle Billy Cameron.' In eighteen eighty-nine, the town became known as Indiana Mineral Springs. Henry Kramer, a twenty–four year old entrepreneur and adventurer arrived on the scene. He bought the rights, and began selling the water in bottles all over the world. Kramer earned enough capital to begin the process of building this resort. He completed the project and opened on December twenty-fifth of eighteen and ninety. The town name was changed once again in nineteen and one to Kramer."

Michael observed, "This is an amazing place with an astounding history. I could spend more time here."

Chapter Eighteen

WOVEN THREADS

The day arrived. Victoria could stand the anxiety no longer. She waited at the station with Michael, Whitney, and Raymond. Finally, they could hear the distant chugging of the locomotive. The train lurched to a stop. In a moment that seemed like an eternity to Victoria, Stewart was standing on platform. He ran to Victoria and embraced her. He held on tight, unable to conceal his true feelings. Victoria could not conceal her elation, either.

Finally, they separated as Michael and Whitney moved closer. He hugged Whitney and gave Michael a gentleman's hug-handshake combination in which the right hand remained clasped in a handshake while the left arm reached over the other's right shoulder. Stewart took Raymond from Whitney and held him at arm's length in front of him, studying his face, stating, "He sure resembles his father. I missed all of you!"

Whitney in her typical forthright fashion, said, "Oh, for heaven's sake! Who did you miss the most?"

Stewart, a little embarrassed by Whitney's directness and happy for the mandate, took Victoria's hands, looked her in the eyes and said, "I honestly missed everybody, but I obsessed over you. I…I… love you!"

Victoria looked shocked and over-joyed at the revelation. Although she had imagined and hoped for this moment, she appeared to be attempting to determine that it was reality and not just another of several imagined scenarios. As she regained her composure, she said, "I love you, Stewart Taylor."

Stewart became even more emboldened and admitted, "I've loved you since the first time I saw you. Can you imagine how difficult it's been for me to honor the memory of my dead friend, your baby's father and your time of mourning?"

Victoria said, "Yes. I can imagine. I miss Raymond immensely, but my life and little Raymond's life must move on. I felt the same way, but had to maintain the appearance of propriety, and be a 'proper' grieving widow."

Whitney said, "Alright, that's settled! We need to get Stewart's luggage and go home. We have church tonight, and I'm sure Stewart would like to have little time to relax and get ready."

Michael said, "Thank God!"

Stewart loved the service. Although he attended church regularly in Wellspring, visiting this church for the first time reminded him of the time he first visited the church in Wellspring. That was such an uncertain time, yet one of extreme elation. He and James had won the trial in which he was falsely accused and could have become a wrongfully convicted felon. Instead, in assisting in his own defense, he found his calling in the profession of law. Several conflicting and complementary thoughts raced through his mind.

Life was just as certain now, yet just as uncertain. He had a good job in Wellspring, yet he suffered the uncertainty of whether he could go forward with his relationship with Victoria. He thought how the only way one could be satisfied with life was to become complacent and never hope for more. He thought back to the cabin and remembered that he was content there, yet not complacent. He rationalized that contentment was the assurance that he was in the right place at the right time, doing what he was supposed to be doing. He was there because he was on a mission to get to Wellspring. Wellspring had become lonely. Maybe it was time to move on.

As Stewart was thinking, he was also listening to the sermon. He had the ability to juggle several things in his mind at one time. Sometimes it was a blessing. Other times it was a curse. It was a blessing when he could sort and arrange thoughts, prioritizing as needed, dropping some as necessary. It became a curse when he felt the compulsion to simultaneously follow all the thoughts through. Mostly, he could focus excessively on some to the exclusion of others.

He remembered back to Wellspring from the time Victoria and the others left. As he attempted to control his life and fight the pain and loneliness by filling the void with activity, he could no longer discontinue any activity. He buried himself into every constructive impulse which came to him at the time. He not only had to be successful and conquer his career, he had to be successful at recreation and his new hobbies. He had to conquer them. He realized how relaxing it was to be visiting with no agenda, pretty much at the others' discretion and direction. Maybe it was time for a clean start.

Pastor Douglas was wrapping up the sermon. He said, "The disciples clung to the person of Jesus. In spite of repeated warnings and admonitions to not cling to Him, they hoped he was going to use His leadership ability to overthrow the oppressive alliance between the Roman government and the religious leaders."

In Acts, chapter one, "He told them He must go so the Comforter could come and empower them from on high. They asked, 'Lord, dost thou at this time restore the kingdom of Israel?'

"He answered, 'It is not for you to know times and seasons, which the Father hath set within His own authority. But you shall receive power, when the Holy Spirit is come upon you; and you shall be my witnesses both in Jerusalem, and in all Judea and Samaria, and, even to the uttermost part of the earth.'"

Stewart had seen nothing but the town of Pence and the farm and thought, "This has to be the remotest parts of the earth. How will we be His witnesses both in Jerusalem and Samaria?"

Pastor Douglas continued, "After Jesus was crucified by the religious leaders and the Roman government, the disciples were waiting and hiding. You can imagine how they felt. The leader in whom they trusted was brutally tortured and murdered. Witnesses had seen them all with Jesus daily. They were waiting and praying, knowing in their hearts and minds, the authorities were only delaying in rounding them up while formulating their final plans how to dispose of so many revolutionaries.

"God had different plans. After fifty days came the day of Pentecost, the first recorded events of manifestations of the outpouring of the Holy Spirit. Peter addressed the issue by quoting the Prophet Joel. In Acts, chapter two Peter said, 'And in the last days it shall be,' declares God, 'that I will pour out my Spirit on all flesh, and your sons and daughters shall prophesy, and your young men shall see visions; and your old men shall dream dreams.'"

As they were leaving the church, Victoria introduced Stewart to Pastor Douglas, who said, "I've heard so much about you. I half expected you to walk on water."

Stewart looked a little embarrassed and replied, "Oh, Michael is an honest man, but tends to exaggerate a little about his friends."

Pastor Douglas smiled in Victoria's direction and said, "It was not all Michael talking about you."

Victoria blushed and said, "We better let Richard greet the others."

The next day they proceeded to Mudlavia. Michael, Whitney and Victoria took a two bedroom suite and Stewart rented his own room. At supper, they met Daryl, the Editor-in-Chief, and Pastor Richard.

After they ordered supper, Michael said to Pastor Douglas, "The verses in Joel you quoted last night are my favorite of the prophets. The verses preceding the passage you quoted about the Holy Spirit speak of the restoration of the years that were ravaged. I felt like my restoration began as I forgave my brother. That was after Stewart found me up on that trail.

"After that, I was able to tell Edward I forgave him before he died. I was also restored to my relationship with my niece, Victoria. Most of all, I've been restored to more than my previous relationship with Whitney. Although it might appear we wasted those years, I feel they have been restored. If I have only one year of happiness, or if by the grace of God I am allowed more, it will be the happiest time of my life."

As Michael finished his statement, with tears in his eyes and obviously deep emotions, Whitney gently grasped his hand and smiled. She added, "I have to second that."

Stewart attempted to glance in Victoria's direction without being too obvious. She was already glancing at him. They smiled as they held the gaze. He reached for her hand. Finally, they realized the others were contentedly staring in their direction.

Michael asked, "Does it seem the Holy Spirit has been on hold since the day of Pentecost and since the rest of the Book of Acts was written?"

Richard paused in deep thought and answered, "There have been reports of miraculous events such as those recorded in the Book of Acts in mission fields around the world."

Stewart said, "Maybe America needs to be more primitive. It seems that our faith in science, industry, politics and reason has negated our need for the Holy Spirit."

Pastor Richard said, "That is why Jesus taught about not putting new wine into old skins or sewing new fibers onto old cloth. The new wine and the new cloth are symbolic of the Holy Spirit. Old religion based upon the traditions of man will not hold. I hear reports of a spiritual revival taking place right now in the United States. It is occurring out on the west coast, in Los Angeles at a place called Azusa Street. The pastor is William Seymour."

Michael asked, "How have you heard about the revival?"

Richard answered, "It has been documented in the press, although my father chooses not to publish anything about it."

Richard the Editor defended himself, "I report on facts that I can see, or from credible witnesses, not fanatical accounts of alleged mystical occurrences."

Pastor Richard smiled and continued, "Besides, I met William Seymour. He sends out ten thousand newsletters recording the activities at Azusa Street."

At this time the meal was served and talk was replaced with the clinking of silver utensils upon fine china. The guests ate leisurely and deliberately so as not to allow the meal and the moment to pass by too quickly. Occasional sighs and groans of satisfaction could also be heard.

Michael asked, "How did you meet him?"

Richard said, "He was in Indiana. His father was a freed slave and decided to remain in the service of the Union Army. His service led him through the southern states of Louisiana, Mississippi and Texas. He became disabled and was unable to provide for the family. One time, they claimed as their meager assets one old bedstead, one mattress and an old chair, totaling in value of fifty-five cents.

"Due to the Reconstruction Era Klan threats, Jim Crow laws and other prejudice of the South, William decided to head north to Indianapolis. He was working at three luxury hotels downtown while studying at the seminary. I met him in class. He found me a job in one of the hotels.

"He was a large black man, blind in one eye from childhood malaria. Some of his detractors claim he was illiterate. He was very bright, especially for having no prior formal education. He was a hard worker, waiting tables and studying at the seminary. He was also very passionate about living the life he was preaching. He believed in one man marrying one woman, refraining from excessive entertainment and studying to show oneself approved."

"In one of his newsletters, A.W. Orwig offered an account of his visits to Azusa Street. He wrote of an incident which was relayed to him by a young reporter. He said the reporter had been assigned to visit a meeting and write an unfavorable article about the mission. The reporter was foreign born and spoke his native language and English very fluently. During the service, a lady sitting next to him turned and spoke in his native language. She spoke of his rebellious heart and directly about his sinful life.

"Afterward, he asked her if she knew the language she spoke. She said she did not. He asked if she knew what she said. She said she did not. He went forward, repented and became a Christian. When he told his editor he could not write a derogatory story about

Seymour and the Mission, he was told his services would no longer be needed."

Michael said, "That's how the outpouring of the Holy Spirit is supposed to work, to convict sinners and strengthen believers through God's miraculous language and prophecy!"

Sometime, during the coffee and conversation Stewart and Victoria snuck off for a stroll around the grounds. As they were walking past the chapel, Stewart tried the door. It was unlocked, so they went in and sat down. Stewart began, "You know you've ruined it for me."

Victoria looked somewhat surprised and asked, "What?"

Stewart continued, "You've ruined my ability and desire to remain alone."

Victoria looked intently. As she sat in the pew, Stewart got up, reached into his pocket and pulled out a little box. He got down on one knee. "Victoria, will you marry me?"

Victoria had actually not seen this coming. She stammered. "I don't want you to think I'm desperate. I am not needy. I...I... Of course, I'll marry you!"

Stewart kissed Victoria with a very passionate kiss. As they were walking back toward the dining hall, Stewart held Victoria's hand. Suddenly reality came back to him. "Where will we live?"

Victoria answered, "We can live on the moon. I don't care as long as we're together."

When they were in sight of their party in the dining hall, all conversation stopped. All present could see that something significant had occurred. Stewart announced, "We're getting married right here at the chapel. Pastor Douglas, will you do the honor?"

Whitney asked, "Have you set a date?"

Victoria answered, "That is to be announced. We have so many details to work out."

Whitney assured her, "Don't worry! You'll have time. This is your time. We're the supporting cast."

As the others returned to the farm on Sunday afternoon, Stewart stayed another night. He was going into town the next day to look around. He checked some apartments and inquired in a couple of law offices. He wanted to determine how difficult it would be to get his license to practice law in Indiana. He entered the office of McCabe and McCabe. James McCabe was practicing law, with his son Edward after serving as a justice in the Indiana Supreme Court. McCabe told Stewart he could license him after a short apprenticeship, and coincidentally, would need help in the near future. McCabe said, "The new governor came from here and is stirring up a lot of work with his prohibition and newly signed law allowing involuntary sterilization."

Chapter Nineteen

THE LAST RESORT

Stewart was shocked. He asked, "Upon what criteria can they impose sterilization?"

McCabe answered, "Insanity, criminal history or pauperism."

Stewart was amazed, "Back in Wellspring, James and I never heard of anything like this."

McCabe told Stewart, "I am easing myself out a bit and reducing my case load. I expect Edward to take over. Before I hire you, I want to test your aptitude. Here, go in the next office and read this, then come back in here for an oral argument."

Stewart took the brief. It was entitled, "Horse Meets Motorcar." He read it over and went back to McCabe's Office. Both McCabes were in the office. James motioned for him to come in and sit down.

McCabe said, "That didn't take long. Are you ready to answer some questions?"

Stewart said, "Do I get to use the brief?"

"Sure. Who was the defendant?"

Stewart answered, "Indiana Mineral Springs, doing business as Mudlavia Resort?"

"Who was the plaintiff?"

Stewart said, "Elmer Baker was named as the plaintiff."

"What is the nature of this case?"

Stewart said, "Baker filed a complaint against Kramer, or Mudlavia for damages. The case was heard and the claims were denied. Baker filed this action in Indiana Supreme Court. The Supreme Court upheld the lower court decision."

McCabe said, "Finally, what was the nature of the damages?

Stewart smiled and said, "Baker claims the carriage used by Mudlavia to transport guests from the Attica Depot back and forth from the resort to the train scared Baker's horse and he lost control. The horse was so frightened by the whirring and chugging noises and lunging action that he bolted, resulting in damage to his carriage and injury to himself. Baker further claimed that the unnatural presence of the motorcar and the speeding should not be allowed on the same roads as horses."

McCabe smiled and said, "Good job! I think you get it."

Stewart smiled and said, "Do you think these motorized carriages will catch on?"

McCabe said, "Time will tell. I know Kramer can carry more people more quickly each day with his motor carriage, than he could with several horse-drawn conveyances. What do you think were the motives of Baker?"

"Oh, I think he thought Kramer has plenty of money and probably has made people envious or offended them in some other way. Baker thought he could possibly cash in on some of Kramer's fortune."

McCabe smiled again and said, "There is one other area where legal action could transpire. Hunter House up on Lover's Leap, behind Mudlavia, also has a horse drawn carriage. They go to the depots in Attica and Williamsport and park in front of the Mudlavia sign. When Kramer's motor coach isn't there, the driver shouts, 'Mudlavia.' People ride to Hunter House, thinking they're going to Mudlavia. We've heard some complaints and some have demanded a refund, but nobody has filed suit yet."

Stewart summarized, "So everybody wants to make money from Kramer's success?"

"I believe so."

Stewart finalized his plans and left the office. He spent the rest of the week on the farm and reluctantly left on Saturday morning. The only way he was able to tear himself away from Victoria and return to the loneliness of Wellspring was with the assurance it would be for a short time. He studied most of the trip back to Wellspring from a book of Indiana laws and a packet of miscellaneous briefs, newspaper clippings and articles that McCabe gave him. One article was a year old, from the *New York Times,* dated July six, nineteen and six, under the location of "Winona Lake, Indiana," the headline stated "Taggart Gave Gamblers Full Sway, Says Hanly; Indiana Casinos Opened or Closed at Chairman's Nod. Winnings Put into Safe. Attorney General Charges That Taggart's Suits to Cancel Casino Concessions Are Bogus."

Stewart was busy in the office on Tuesday morning. James stuck his head in and asked how the trip went. Stewart sighed deeply and asked James to come in and sit down. "Do you want the good news or the bad news first?"

James, smiling and looking not at all surprised, grinned and said, "Give me the good news."

Stewart returned the smile, suspecting that James already knew where the conversation was headed, "Victoria and I are engaged!"

James, deciding not to make this any easier on Stewart, said, "Great! When is the ceremony and when is she moving out?"

Stewart composed himself and said, "That's the other side of the coin. I will be returning to Indiana in two weeks, unless you need me longer."

James smiled again and said, "I could see this coming. I am excited for you. Besides, since Connor is busy with the mines, business has returned to the level where I can handle it. I'll look for a practicing attorney or another apprentice to train."

Stewart said, "One other concern. Will you and Ma Peterson be able to come to Indiana for the wedding?"

James assured him as he stood up to shake Stewart's hand, "We'd love to."

Two days later, James brought in Frank Steady to introduce to Stewart. Steady had recently been fired by Robert Connor. It turned out Connor had accused Frank of disloyalty for disagreeing with him over legal matters. James figured the guy had some scruples and courage if, as an employee, he was able to disagree with Connor.

Stewart spent the remainder of the two weeks preparing for the move. At work he brought Frank up to speed on his pending and current cases. He didn't have many possessions, so packing was easy. He reduced the time at the athletic club and the industrial school to short sessions and mostly bidding "good byes" to the people he had recently met.

He remembered back to just over a year and half ago when he strode into town so triumphantly. Was it the realization of the naiveté of youth; or the gaining life's experiences that changed his perspective since then? When he arrived in town he felt he could conquer any obstacle. He would be triumphant through any tragedy.

Then, the uncertainty of the trial provided a dose of reality. At least he now had empathy for his clients who were in a legal scrape with few others believing their innocence. Maybe it was the loneliness and his compulsive compensation that made him realize he had conquered neither himself, nor the city. He thought back upon Proverbs sixteen, "He who rules his spirit is mightier than he who conquers a city."

On the last day in Wellspring, he stopped by the gun shop and picked up his Winchester. He also bought a leather case so the gun would not be too threatening to other passengers during the long train ride. At least, in Indiana he and Michael could shoot the gun. What comfort he took in the realization that in a few days he would be back with his newfound family, in a new setting with new challenges. He kept busy so the two weeks would go quickly.

They met him at the station on Sunday evening. He stayed at the farm that night. After everybody else had retired into the house, Stewart and Victoria sat on the porch discussing their dreams and hopes. Victoria said, "I talked to Pastor Douglas Friday after church. He said there might be difficulty in using the chapel at Mudlavia for our wedding. It appears the Chaplain is Presbyterian and doesn't allow pastors of other denominations to perform ceremonies there. I guess so many weddings are performed for people from out of town, that it's hardly an issue that couples request their own pastor."

Stewart said, "It could also be that he wants to control the little bit of authority he's been given."

Victoria answered, "I'd like to believe the best in people. We have to be careful not to judge other's motives, when we don't know for sure."

Stewart agreed, "Yes, I know. I think I've become more skeptical of people's intentions and motives since I've been practicing law. If we are believers, it doesn't matter to which, if any, denomination we belong."

Victoria said, "That's true. We'll see about it and find out if we need to make other plans. It's just that you proposed there. The place is special to me."

Stewart said, "As long as we're together, it doesn't matter where we get married. I'd even be happy if a justice of the peace performed the ceremony."

Tears formed in Victoria's eyes as she answered, "My first marriage was performed by a justice of the peace. I'm not superstitious, but looking back on it, we were so rushed. I fell in love with Raymond very soon after I met him. Maybe we were rushing to get out from under Father's rule."

Stewart replied, "Raymond was charming. I can see how he captured your heart. We will have a church wedding."

Victoria moved closer to Stewart and said, "Thank you. I knew you'd understand."

Stewart said, "I need to go into town tomorrow and begin work. I also need to settle into my apartment. I don't know how many hours I'll have to work this week, so I can't promise I'll be back home until Friday evening."

Stewart went to Williamsport on Monday morning. He unpacked his clothes and got settled into his apartment. It had one room with a bed on one side and a small sofa separating the bed from the small kitchen area. The toilet was a common bathroom downstairs shared by the tenants of the four apartments in the building. He was glad there was a café next door. On Monday afternoon, he was able to meet with McCabe to begin his first briefing. After McCabe assigned him a case, Stewart said, "I read the New York Times article. What's the current status?"

McCabe looked at the clock, sat back down and began. "French Lick is a resort in southern Indiana. It's owned by Thomas Taggart. He was a United States senator and Mayor of Indianapolis. He's now the head of the Democratic National Committee. Nobody goes to the White House from the Democrats without first going through French Lick. They've kick off national campaigns there.

"Hanly, as you know, is from Williamsport. He was born in a log cabin, across the line in St. Joseph, Illinois. He came to Warren County and dug ditches on a farm in Jordan Township for two years while studying for a teaching certificate. Then at Williamsport he began teaching. While teaching, he became a lawyer. He beat local politician, George Cronk and served in the United States House of Representatives from eighteen ninety-five through eighteen ninety-seven. He became governor in nineteen and five.

Stewart said, "That's amazing! Hanly's a Republican. How did he move up so fast in politics? He came from such humble beginnings to the United States Congress and then to governor of the state. That seems like it would take some financial backing."

As Stewart was sitting there thinking, his eyes opened in an expression of amazement. "The richest person in this area has a resort. Of course, this is a dry county and there is no gambling at Mudlavia."

When Stewart looked in McCabe's direction, he noticed a wry smile. McCabe said, "There is no known activity which could be considered illegal at Mudlavia."

Stewart smiled and said, "I find it hard to believe that people don't engage in a friendly game of chance for monetary gain, or certain entertainment might be provided for the visiting wealthy and well-known. I can't imagine that almost any type of service might not be provided for a price."

McCabe asked, "Have you seen the Wabash Watchman and Richard's latest editorial?"

Stewart said, "No, I haven't."

McCabe said, "Take a look at it when you get a chance. I couldn't tell you this before, but since you work here now, I'm not violating client confidentiality. Kramer came in one day and handed me a check for five hundred dollars. I asked what it was for. He answered, 'I might need you to represent me if I ever get sued.'"

On Wednesday, Victoria took the carriage to Mudlavia. She asked to see Mr. Kramer. Kramer asked the porter, "Who is Victoria Warren? Is she charming or particularly pretty?"

The porter said. "Yes, I would say both."

In annoyance Kramer asked, "What the Dickens does she want?"

The porter answered, "I believe it's a matter concerning the chapel."

Kramer said, "Show her in."

As Victoria entered the room Kramer appeared to be preoccupied and finally glanced up. During the hesitation, Victoria studied the office. Kramer had a solid oak desk. The room was lined with richly stained oak paneling and trim. There were oak book cases along some walls. In one corner, a top hat sat atop one of the book cases. Leaning in the corner was a cane like gentlemen carried in the big cities. Kramer was a massive man with a huge mustache connected to his sideburns. He wore a dark wool suit coat and a gray vest with a gold watch chain.

As he looked up, he did a double-take and began to smile a seemingly genuine smile. As he stood to greet her, Victoria found it curious that he wore dark gray wool trousers with a black satin stripe down the outside hem and had spats on his shoes, a mode of dress one normally saw in New York or Chicago when people were stepping out in style. He said, "Please sit down. What may I do for you?"

Victoria began, "My fiancé and I are new to the area. He is just starting his job today at the McCabe Law Firm. I live with Whitney and Michael Thomas on the old Goodwine Farm in Jordon Township."

Kramer, appearing to become a little disinterested said, "Yes?"

Victoria continued, "We would like to be married in the Chapel on the grounds."

Kramer said, "I see no problem in that. I usually don't handle these matters."

Victoria continued, "It appears there's some little snag in the fact that we would like to use our own pastor, who is not an ordained Presbyterian minister."

Kramer said, "Policy is policy."

Victoria began her final plea, "Mr. Kramer, you are a powerful man. I am sure details of any policy that happens to be in place are subject to your final say and discretion as you see fit."

Kramer sat a little more erect and said, "I will look into the matter."

Victoria said, "We'll be staying here this weekend. May I have your answer by then?"

Kramer said, "I'll leave it at the hotel desk."

Victoria thanked him and excused herself. Before she left the grounds of the resort, she walked back to the chapel and found the pew where Stewart proposed to her. She sat there dreamily pondering her future with Stewart. As she sat there, she offered a prayer for the expectations she envisioned and asked for a little consideration on the request to use the chapel.

After leaving Mudlavia, Victoria proceeded two miles south through Pine Creek Canyon. She drove up the hill and for another mile into Williamsport. In town she located the McCabe and McCabe Law Office. She went inside and introduced herself. Stewart heard her and came out to see her. He introduced her to McCabe. "We can grab some lunch across the street if you like."

They ate lunch and he showed her the apartment. She said, "I guess this will be alright as long as you are coming out to the farm on weekends."

Stewart could discern her disappointment with the apartment. "I know you're used to better surroundings than this. It is only temporary, and I just sleep here. We have to decide where we'd like to live once we're married."

Victoria said, "While I'm in town, I'll check into the housing situation. Oh, by the way, would you like to go to Mudlavia for the weekend? The Pence Aces play the Mudlavia Cascarets on Saturday. We know some of the players on the Pence Aces."

Stewart said, "I'd love to. I'll meet you there on Friday after work. Where did they get the name, Cascarets?"

Victoria answered, "It's one of the most famous and most advertised products of Sterling Remedy's Company. It's an alternative to smoking to help smokers quit."

That afternoon, Stewart went to the library after work. While looking for Richard's editorial, he came across an interesting document. It was a book by James Geikie, entitled *The Great*

Ice Age. There was a book mark on pages seven hundred and twenty-four through seven hundred and seventy-five. Stewart casually opened the book to the marked section, *Glacial Phenomenon of North America.* He read a passage that explained the formation and the study of Lovers Leap and large dune-like wall of the Pine Creek Canyon, directly behind Mudlavia to the north and west.

From the passage, he gleaned that Lovers Leap had formed from three converging glaciers. The glaciers were located west across the plains from Judyville. Another came through Lafayette and formed the Wabash River Basin. The third came from the north and formed Pine Creek Canyon. Stewart thought back to the discussion with Michael in which the Indians assigned spiritual significance to the confluences of rivers. How much more significance could be attributed to the convergence of geological formations that caused the rivers? Of course, he reasoned, "The God who created glaciers and rivers could determine the spiritual significance or insignificance of any land or water formations He chose."

He located and read Richard's editorial. He was surprised how direct and honest the questions were. Richard was also careful to ask questions without drawing any conclusions of his own. He had a knack for motivating the reader to a state of curiosity, to draw one's own conclusions and seek further explanations of the facts.

FOLLOW THE MONEY

It has been over a year now. I waited for my competition, the Review Republican to ask questions and investigate the actions and motives of our elected officials. Nothing has been forthcoming yet. This editorial is not to question the actions or the inactions of other newspapers. Remember the words of Thomas Jefferson, "If given the choice of a government with no newspaper and a newspaper without government, I would choose the latter."

Have you ever wondered how our governor came from a humble origin in a log cabin in Illinois? How did he work as a ditch digger and then a school teacher, while studying to be a lawyer, and then find the connections and resources to win a seat in the United States House of Representatives? Who did he know to reach the elevated position from an obscure town like Williamsport?

In his crusading to legislate morality and eliminate gambling, alcohol and other sin, is he enforcing suppression of those evils more judiciously by those of opposite political persuasion and in direct competition with his own political backers? Is he using his good office to police opponents in other parts of the state more judiciously than in his own back yard?

When morality is legislated, does the legislation change the moral fiber of the people? When alcohol and gambling are outlawed do people desire them less? Are people's consciences molded by the law? Or, on the contrary, does not history illustrate that limiting the legal attainment of commodities tends to make them worth a greater price to those inclined to risk the free market to provide such commodities. Is it not ironic that those most inclined to tout the benefits of the free market are also those most likely to impose their morality on the market?

Stewart finished work a little early on Friday afternoon. McCabe stuck his head into Stewart's office and asked, "How'd it go for your first week?

Stewart replied, "Oh, it was fine. The pace is a little less hectic than it was in Wellspring, although I know it'll pick up as I work into a full case load."

McCabe said, "Why don't you go ahead and take off. Since you're going to be at the resort, you should try a mud bath. They're very relaxing. Be ready to hit it head-on on Monday."

Chapter Twenty

BOTTOM LINE

Stewart took McCabe's advice. He didn't want to spend any more time than he had to in his lonely, hot apartment. Indiana could be very sultry in a small upper story apartment in a mid-September Indian summer. He caught the carriage at the depot and headed out to the resort. After checking-in, he went downstairs and took his first mud bath. After he showered and went back up to his room to get dressed, he took a stroll around the grounds.

He noticed his perceptions were different than they were three weeks ago, when he proposed to Victoria. That weekend the resort had a magical air about it. It seemed like a fantasy land or a different world, nestled in the cool shade of the Pine Creek Canyon. It was like stepping onto a southern plantation in which everything was provided. The only efforts expected of individuals were to dress and feed themselves. Both feeding and dressing took on a more significant air here as they were both done to accomplish ceremonial and ostentatious results.

The genteel atmosphere of the Gilded Age had even reached this seemingly remote area. Stewart heard of famous visitors, such as James Whitcomb Riley and John L. Sullivan, World Heavy Weight Champion.

Stewart wondered if the guests could obtain everything they wanted and if what happened at Mudlavia stayed at Mudlavia. He knew enough about human nature to realize that people tended to act differently in a strange and exotic environment than they would at home and around familiar faces of friends and family. Whether seeking outright hedonistic pleasure or entertainment, entertainment was surely a premium here, "Forget reality; Relax; Enjoy!"

After the walk, he returned to the veranda to wait for Victoria, Raymond, Michael and Whitney to arrive. A piano player was serenading the guests from a baby grand. Stewart learned that Paul Dresser, writer of *On the Banks of the Wabash* used to serenade the guests on occasion. Of course, local residents claimed he wrote the song at Mudlavia. Stewart wondered, as he listened, if Kramer had a passion to bring culture to this remote area, or if he figured he could make more money by hiring quality entertainment. Maybe giving back in some way was his subconscious justification for amassing huge amounts of wealth or just another way to promote his wealth.

As he sat in the cool breeze, the relaxing setting and the effects of the mud bath caused him to drift off into a very deep sleep. He dreamed he saw a man looking into the hallway, pausing at the doorway to place some money on the table. He then took his hat, looking in both directions before proceeding down the hallway, glancing down as he passed Stewart.

He dreamed he saw large back rooms filled with cigar smoke and men sitting at poker tables, or at a dealer's table playing Blackjack or feeding slot machines around the edges of the room. The men were consuming large amounts of whiskey, either from the bar in the room or from hip flasks they flashed at intervals after ordering a soft drink into which they would pour the contents. He dreamed about the room that existed near the mud bath and shower area in the basement that was touted as "Indiana's first therapeutic massage parlor." If someone requested, were they provided, for a price, more than just therapeutic massages?

He dreamed he saw a woman checking into the doctor's office and receiving a prescription for something to relieve her distress or to restore her menses. Were doctors performing procedures that were more certain to obtain the same results, and then telling the client to remain at the resort for a week until he was sure she was alright? He awoke with a jolt as Victoria gently shook his arm. She laughed and exclaimed, "McCabe must be working you extremely hard!"

A little shocked at his dreams and a little embarrassed, Stewart said, "The mud bath and the setting were so relaxing, I must have drifted off. I had some disturbing nightmares."

Victoria acknowledged, "You were totally out."

At supper, conversation was light and lively. Michael asked, "So, how was your first week in Indiana?"

Stewart answered, "It was great! My room is a little small and stuffy, but it seems like a different world here. I know McCabe is taking it easy on me until I get settled in."

Victoria smiled and throwing her head back and raising an arm, with an enthusiastic flair of the dramatic, announced, "We will be able to have our wedding in the Chapel."

With a surprised expression, Stewart asked, "How did you find out?"

Victoria said, "Oh, I just received a letter from Mr. Kramer as we checked-in."

She showed it to Stewart:

Miss Warren,

Plan to proceed with your wedding and the complementary use of our Chapel. With your charm and ability to deal with people, I am sure it will go well for you.

Sincerely,

Henry Kramer.

Stewart focused his gaze more directly in Victoria's direction, "All right, what have you done?"

Victoria smiled a little guiltily, a trifle self-satisfied and said, "I paid a short visit to Mr. Kramer before I came to see you at work. I simply treated him as I would have treated my father and appealed to his sense of power and control, seasoned with a subtle flavor of logic."

Stewart asked, "Were any feminine wiles included?"

Victoria batted her eyes at Stewart flirtatiously and said, in her best southern accent, "Why, Mr. Taylor, if those wiles exist, they cannot be suppressed."

Whitney laughed and said, "Well, maybe we have more than one lawyer in the family!"

Stewart agreed, "I pity the poor defendant who falls under Miss Victoria's prosecutorial vigilance. I envy the defendant who receives the grace of her defense. Justice balanced by mercy."

Michael said, "Amen!"

As they ate and conversed, Stewart participated in the conversation while playing the detective. He watched the other diners in the large dining hall to see if he could catch a glimpse of a flask pulled from a coat pocket or purse and poured them into a soft drink sitting on the table. He watched to see if individuals entering or exiting the dining room to other parts of the hotel appeared to be nervous or guilty in their demeanor.

With mixed emotions, as he watched he could detect no illicit activities. He was happy that his optimistic outlook on human nature had remained intact. He was a little disappointed that his hunches had provided no direct evidence of malfeasance, misdeeds, misdemeanors or felonies. Maybe Mudlavia was the real deal and could make enough money without resorting to cronyism, arcane services and illegal commodities. Perhaps the elimination of the competition or the providing of products and services that increased in monetary value when outlawed or scorned by society, were not necessary."

The night's sleep was exceptional. Stewart was still relaxed from the serene setting, good food and the mud bath. They met for breakfast the next morning and enjoyed more good food, coffee, pie and conversation. Each weekend here seemed like an entire vacation. Unless one played tennis, swam in the pool or golfed, the desire existed to stroll around the grounds just to walk off the ill effects of eating rich meals without any physical exercise.

Daryl had been working for the Wabash Watchman all morning. He joined the group for lunch and could justify attending the ball game as part of his work since he was a member of the "Press." As Daryl entered the dining room, walking toward the table, Stewart noticed a waiter talking to the desk clerk. They were definitely looking at Daryl and talking about him. Apparently the waiter had summoned the clerk to come in and verify Daryl's appearance. They did not realize Stewart had perceived their observations. Maybe they were just saying, "Yes, he's the sports writer, covering the game." Maybe, they were saying, "There goes that kid who works for that dreadful editor, who sticks his nose into everybody's business."

Maybe it was the slow pace of the game on the warm afternoon. Maybe it was the lack of physical and mental exercise Stewart was experiencing. He found himself more engaged in Daryl's conversation with Pastor Douglas, than in keeping track of the game. About the middle of the second inning, Daryl launched into a series of questions that seemed to be somewhat premeditated.

Daryl, in working with Richard and attending Pastor Douglas's church was attempting to reconcile conflicting thoughts. Richard inundated him with the constant preaching of the need to be able to verify all facts with solid evidence, coupled with Editor Richard's keen logic and understanding of human nature. This was countered by the spiritual, other-worldly message that Pastor Douglas seemed to focus upon—an attempt to reconcile the incompatibility of political rhetoric with the theory and practice of radical Christianity. Pastor Douglas' message was definitely a message that the Kingdom of God is in this world, but not of this world.

Daryl asked, "Is capitalism mentioned in the Bible?"

Richard looked somewhat surprised and answered, "The Bible says that one who is able to and chooses not to work should not be fed by others."

Daryl stated, "That's more a matter of personal responsibility than an economic or political system."

Richard agreed and said, "The parable of the ten talents talks of investing yours or somebody else's resources to gain something back. It is not just the talent as a monetary unit. It is more of a matter of investing yourself as well as the capital provided by yourself or by others and gaining a return for them. It is risking your ingenuity and initiative."

Daryl asked, "What about Communism or communal living?"

After this question Richard said, "Hey, these questions are awfully organized. Are you sure you are not writing an editorial or exposé on me?"

Daryl said, "I hadn't thought of that. Good idea. I'm not going to write an exposé or editorial, but maybe I'll do an article."

Richard said, "Do you remember our talk about prophets at Battleground? Joseph had a dream and was able to predict seven abundant years followed by seven years of shortage. He advised Pharaoh to take twenty percent from everybody's crops and herds each year to be set aside and used during the lean years. Joseph's family even ventured to Egypt and was saved. That was what led to the eventual enslavement of the Israeli people in Egypt.

"This isn't from the Bible, but the Pilgrims and Puritans had to live in a communal manner for the first couple of years in America. They arrived during various seasons, did not understand hunting and farming or the cold harsh winters. Several died. Some say they would not have survived at all unless the Indians taught them how to farm, hunt and fish. After learning the art of survival, they moved out on their own and no longer shared everything in common. Some speculated they did not prosper until they experienced the initiative of self-reliance. They were not afforded the luxury of land ownership and self-reliance until they learned to survive. They needed each other and the Indians to get through those first years.

"In Acts, after the Pentecost, the disciples and new converts were sharing everything. New converts were added daily. If anybody had needs others would sell their possessions to provide. The power of God was working through the church, not a building, but the body.

The main point was that the people gave freely and voluntarily. If the government had mandated redistribution, that would have been communism or socialism.

"The bottom line is that God does not depend upon any political or economic system. He is not bound or threatened by world philosophies or tyrants. When the nation listens to the voice of the true prophets, the people prosper. When the people pray for and submit to the leadership of their country, they are blessed. When people resolve to build His kingdom rather than worship a dictator, country, economic or political system, or ancestors, they are blessed. It's a fine line of distinction to pray for your country and the ruling authorities and speaking out against injustice, if called to do so, without worshipping your country and making it to be an idol.

"Don't be tempted to limit your perspective to arguments of conservative, progressive, Republican or Democrat. These are illusions placed before us to make us think we actually have a choice. The government will eventually oppose the true church. Elaborate temples that worship ancestors and tradition rooted in forms of pagan worship will be allowed to remain. The true church will be forced to go underground and meet in homes just like in the books of Acts.

"There are those who are working to establish a one world government of wickedness, a one world monetary system and the mark of the beast. Conversely, there are those who seek to establish the kingdom of God—bottom line."

Chapter Twenty-One

NEW WINE

Stewart arrived at the office early, as he liked to do each day. He read: "The idols of the nations are silver and gold, the work of men's hands. They have mouths, but speak not; eyes have they, but they see not; They have ears, but hear not; Neither is there any breath in their mouths. They that make them shall be like unto them; Yea, every one that trusteth in them."

He made a note, Psalms one hundred and thirty-five, fifteen through eighteen. He noticed that most of the Old Testament, especially the prophets, warned about making idols out of material resources, and mixing their faith with the religions of the other nations. Another problem was the people needed a god they could see, even if they created it. People, through the ages, have also wanted to build a shrine or temple to house God. The God of Abraham,

Isaac and Jacob could not be seen, reached, verified or contained in even the fanciest shrines.

Stewart loved working early in the office. The cramped, stagnant apartment offered no inspiration nor did it alleviate any feelings of loneliness. He was technically not on the clock yet, so he could work writing legal briefs, researching case law, studying for his license, reading whatever he wanted to read or praying.

About seven-thirty, McCabe stuck his head into the doorway of Stewart's office. "At it early, I see?"

"Yeah, I like to get an early start. Once we're open for business, we never know how many interruptions we might face. I can get a lot done before eight."

McCabe asked, "Have you and Miss Warren set your date yet?"

"No, I was going to discuss that with you. I assume we don't get vacation time until we have worked a year."

McCabe confirmed, "Yes, that is our policy."

"Do we have any down time at Christmas?"

McCabe said, "This year, Christmas is on a Wednesday. We'll probably close between Christmas and New Year's Day."

"Thank you; I'll discuss this with Victoria."

Victoria liked the idea. She wanted to have enough time to date and be romanced as a single woman, prepare for the ceremony and arrange housing that did not include living in Stewart's apartment. She wanted a place of their own, so Stewart could still be close to work. Raymond could have his own room. He would also have neighbor children for play time. Her only drawback was the idea that their wedding would be on Whitney and Michael's anniversary.

She discussed the idea with Whitney, "Do you think it would be strange for us to marry on your anniversary?"

Whitney responded, "Not at all. A new bride wants everything to be unique and original. Whatever time Michael and I have left on this planet, we could celebrate our anniversaries together. Years from now when we are dead and gone, you and Stewart will have the uniqueness of the day, yet I think you will remember that Michael and I shared the same anniversary date."

Victoria said, "Yes, I guess you're right. I don't want to beat every detail to death. It's just that with Raymond and me, we were so rushed. We were more worried about getting away with it and not answering to Father. Stewart and I can plan and do this however soon or late we like; hopefully, sooner than later."

Once the date was set, Victoria and Whitney launched into activity. Michael and Stewart learned early in the process to stay out of the way unless their help was requested. They found that their opinions mattered little once the date and location were decided. Victoria looked at a house on Fall Street. It was the largest brick home on the entire one mile section that began at the falls on the junctions of Fall Street and Monroe Street and ended west where Fall Street came to a tee at Washington Street.

Stewart objected, "We don't have to start with such a big house."

Victoria said, "No, we don't have to, but if we can afford it, we might as well start with the one we like. We wouldn't have to move every few years like so many families do. This is ideal! We will have a big yard and enough room to grow as a family. We'll be so close to everything and the farm is less than an hour away. We can go there on weekends as often as we like. We will have room for Michael and Whitney or other visitors."

Stewart had been Victoria's and Michael's attorney in Wellspring. He knew that Victoria inherited a good amount of money from her father and did well in the sale of the mines. Until this moment, he never thought of her money again. Now, the money became an obstacle. Would anybody think he was marrying for the money? How was he to make a reputation for himself, if he married a rich widow? Why should it matter?

Stewart saw an example of an exercise machine in a Sears Catalog. Over a couple of weekends in the farm shop, he built himself a crude, but simple replica. He incorporated the use of fly wheels for resistance in rowing and pedaling; hoisting of free weights on pulleys to work his major muscle groups and cause his heart rate to surge. He wanted to continue the benefits of the exercise routine he had started in Wellspring. He realized how much better he felt each day and how exercise made the emotional and mental work related stress melt away.

He hated the time he lived in the apartment until he could find a way to exercise. Before he was able to build and move the exercise machine into town, he took long walks. He remembered back in the cabin how walking, hunting, chopping wood and drawing water were his major sources of exercise and how fit he felt at that time. Now, the hills and valleys in and around town afforded ample challenge to work up a good sweat.

Stewart also determined to read two hours a day. He found a book by an English author named Sir John Lubbock, *THE USE OF LIFE*, dated eighteen and ninety-eight, who said:

> Rise early, give to muscles and brain their fair share of exercise and rest, be temperate of food, allow yourself a reasonable allowance of sleep, take things easily, and depend upon it, your work will not hurt you. Worry and excitement, impatience and anxiety, will not get on in your work, and may kill you in the end, or at any rate hand you over a victim to some attack of illness; but if you take life cheerfully and peacefully, intellectual exertion and free thought will be to the mind what exercise and fresh air are to the body, they will prolong, not shorten your life.

Stewart found himself filling the void; anticipating the day of the wedding by laboring to give McCabe a full week's worth of work. He also exercised five days a week; read two hours a day and wrote an hour a day. He spent hours studying for his license, balancing this with calculated relaxation as time was available. Weekends were spent in the farm shop. He soon returned to the pace he experienced while living alone in Wellspring. Due to his youth, he did not realize he was neglecting the necessity of rest, recuperation and reflection. Recreation was more like exhaustive, planned and excessive "wreck-creation." At least he was too tired by the end of the day and week to feel the loneliness. Then, on the weekends, he saw Victoria, Raymond, Michael and Whitney.

Thanksgiving came and went. Sven and Heidi came down from the English Lake farm for the four day weekend and celebration. They also attended church on Friday night with Pastor Douglas. Their first year on the farm had an exceptional yield. Victoria had also received a letter from James and Ma Peterson that they would be attending the wedding.

Victoria announced the plans for the wedding ceremony. She said, "We're planning to invite people to Mudlavia for the week, celebrating Christmas at the resort. We're encouraging people to join us as early as they choose. We'll hold the ceremony on Saturday, the twenty-eighth and move into our own honeymoon suite. Guests are welcome to stay at the lodge and celebrate New Year's Eve with us as they wish."

Whitney said, "That is different, yet not surprising. Victoria, you've always liked to do things a little differently than most."

Victoria smiled and said, "We feel there is enough room at the resort for everybody to spend as much time as we like together and enough for privacy for a newlywed couple."

She looked at Stewart, with the realization she had not mentioned the privacy and honeymoon aspects of the marriage in front of other people before. He gazed back at her dreamily. She blushed and returned to the conversation. "We are not interested in waiting until spring or summer. The resort offers a rare setting not found in most places. I understand Kramer really puts on a feast and celebration during the whole week between Christmas and New Year. He is even giving us and members of our party a group rate since things are slow at the lodge during the winter."

Times of loneliness passed more quickly for Stewart with his self-imposed work and "relaxation" schedule. Following three months of work and preparation, McCabe leaned into his office one morning and said, "I've been studying your written briefs and the oral arguments you've presented, and I've determined your time of apprenticeship is over. Apparently, the Indiana Bar Association feels the same way."

He placed a framed copy of Stewart's license on the wall and said he applied for it three weeks earlier. "Congratulations, you've earned this. We'll have to discuss your pay today, too."

The time came and guests arrived. Christmas dinner at the resort was one to remember. The main entrées included roast turkey with cranberry sauce, small filet of veal a la financiere, and roast prime rib of beef with au jus. Side items included peach fritter with vanilla sauce, mashed or glazed sweet potatoes, Brussel sprouts, asparagus, lettuce and tomatoes with mayonnaise. Desert included plum pudding with brandy sauce, mince pie, pumpkin pie, assorted cakes, and tutti-frutti ice cream. There were also mixed nuts, figs, raisins, camembert and Roquefort cheeses. Drinks included coffee, Postum, milk, green or black tea, cocoa to order and Mudlavia Spring Water. There were no written warnings, only rumors that drinking too much of Kramer's water could give a person the "green apple quick steps."

James informed Michael and Victoria that he had heard reports that Discovery had become a ghost town. "Connor attempted to keep the mines open, but could not keep good workers. Unless he stayed in Discovery to oversee things, the workers stole him blind. I guess they justified to themselves if they worked for such low wages and were treated as mules, they would get what they could and get out."

The wedding was held in the chapel on Saturday. Guests included James and Irene Peterson, both generations of the McCabe family, Sven and Heidi, Editor Richard Douglas, with Pastor Douglas officiating. Victoria finally met Stewart's parents. Whitney and Michael stood as witnesses for the couple. Heidi and Sven were holding Raymond as he watched and played intently.

As the music, Pachelbel's Canon in D played on the organ, Michael walked Victoria down the aisle. At first glance of Victoria, in her white formal dress, Stewart gasped and sniffled. As he attempted to control his emotions, he heard his dad sniffle. They each kept attempting to control their emotions causing the other to sniffle. Before Victoria stopped to join Stewart, she handed Whitney her bouquet and gave her a hug. She turned to Stewart and grasped both their hands in front of them. Stewart bit his bottom lip and cried like a baby without the use of his hands to wipe his eyes.

Pastor Douglas said, "Who gives this bride?"

Michael said, "Her aunt and I."

Pastor Douglas said, "The first recorded miracle performed by Jesus was at a wedding in Canaan. The teachings of Jesus and the apostles include several references to weddings. The church is the bride of Christ. When asked why John's disciples fasted and the disciples of Jesus seemed to be celebrating most of the time, Jesus responded, 'The groomsmen do not mourn while the groom is with them.'

"There are a lot of symbols present here. Victoria and Stewart have decided to have a weeklong festival similar to a Jewish festival. They want to share their special time with friends and family. They also acknowledge that the public ceremony of marriage is like the water baptism. They die to the individual and become united as one. Although they become as one, they do not lose their individuality. They grow and encourage, motivate and help each other. They each learn to live for the other, thereby completing them. Victoria, in her young life has already experienced the loss of a husband. God preserved a remnant of that marriage through the birth of young Raymond. Stewart is accepting responsibility to be a husband and a father.

"Jesus said that unless a grain of wheat falls on the ground and dies, it remains alone, but if it dies, it bears much fruit. Jesus spoke of Himself as the bridegroom. He acknowledged that He must go so the purpose of His ministry could be fulfilled on earth. The disciples wanted to keep him in his bodily form, not realizing the extent of His ministry.

"The water was symbolic of the water of baptism. Jesus changed it to wine, which was symbolic of the Holy Spirit. The water of baptism was a symbolic death and cleansing of the body. The water that became wine was the symbolic introduction of the Holy Spirit for the purpose of empowerment.

"After the water was changed to wine, some was taken to the chief steward of the wedding. He commented that people usually served the good wine and when people had enough to lose their powers of perception and discriminating taste, the cheap stuff was brought out. He was amazed in this situation because the good wine was saved for last, symbolizing the Holy Spirit is greater and deeper than the initial rebirth and baptism. The couple will share in communion to symbolize the end of their individual lives and to commit to each other and God to go forward, growing in relationship, first with Him and then with each other."

When Pastor Douglas read the vows Stewart had prepared, Stewart was gazing into Victoria's eyes. He just stood there. Victoria squeezed his hands. He realized he was supposed to repeat the words Pastor Douglas had spoken. He was able to regain his composure and repeat them. Victoria instructed Pastor Douglas that she would say her vows from memory not repeating them after him. She looked into Stewart's teary eyes and said, "Stewart, I, I love you."

At least she had the original vows she had written to refer to later. They rationalized the vows were between them anyway, so whenever she read them, it was more personal than reading them before the crowd.

As they turned to face the crowd and Pastor Douglas introduced them as Mr. and Mrs. Stewart Taylor, Raymond broke loose from

Heidi and toddled over to them. Stewart scooped him up and embraced him. Pastor Douglas said, "And Raymond."

During the reception, McCabe told James, "Well, your loss is my gain. I have never had anybody with the work ethic Stewart has brought to the office."

James agreed, "I hated to lose him, but realized early, he would eventually move on. We weren't big enough to offer him a partnership. Then, I saw the way he looked at Victoria. He thought he was hiding his feelings when he first met her. He didn't succeed very well, even for an untrained eye. I was surprised he let her move back to Indiana without telling her how he felt in the first place."

McCabe agreed, "Knowing Stewart as I do, I'm sure he was honoring Victoria's mourning time. Whether self-imposed or by societies standards and boundaries, we have come up with one year as the time to mourn."

After the reception, Stewart and Victoria moved into the honeymoon suite. Most of the wedding guests stayed around the resort through the New Year's celebration. On January first, Stewart and Victoria moved into their house on Fall Street. Their brick house was a Queen Anne, structure with a round tower and spire on one corner and picture windows overlooking the porch. The windows in the front were leaded glass. The lower story had stained oak trim over the doors and around the base. The interior doors were pocket doors that hid into the walls. There was a fireplace in the parlor, living room and master bedroom.

A large porch wrapped around one corner with a limestone block foundation and columns. The back porch was a glass enclosed solarium. The second story had a balcony off of the alcove next to the inside of the round spire. An oak stairway ascended from the living room and extended up to the third floor spire, which Stewart used for his study. From there he had windows that overlooked the front yard and Fall Street. The remainder of the third floor was unfinished. Stewart vowed that he would, someday, finish it out for occupation. For now, there was plenty of room for a family of three or four.

After the move, Stewart began to reduce his self-imposed schedule. He only worked at the office five regular days. If he was up early studying, he was in his home, comforted to know he was near his wife and son. He cut his exercise time from one hour to one-half hour a day, and walked to and from the office, about a mile in each direction. Visiting the farm became optional leisurely visits.

Stewart also made it a priority to read more novels, as they were educational and entertaining. One particularly interesting novel was one he found on one of McCabe's bookshelves. He borrowed it and began reading it right away. The title was *Futility, or the Wreck of the Titan*. The book was not widely read. It was written by Morgan Robertson and published in eighteen ninety-eight.

Stewart was drawn to the title because of the word "futility," as he had been studying the book of Ecclesiastes. He was also becoming increasingly interested in the ever expanding field of transportation.

The book was a fictional account of the imagined greatest ocean going vessel of the day. The ship was fabled as "unsinkable" and struck an ice berg on an April night in the north Atlantic, just four hundred miles from Newfoundland. The ship lost about half of the two thousand five hundred passengers aboard because they only had life boats for a small number of passengers, as required by law.

Victoria asked, "How do you like the book?"

Stewart answered, "It is very interesting, but I still prefer novels to be more credible."

Chapter Twenty-Two

ARE YOU CRAZY?

During the second week of January, Whitney and Michael announced they would take the train to Florida and stay for about two months. It had been a busy year with a lot of changes. They wanted to finally take the honeymoon they had deferred for the previous thirteen months. Whitney had family in Punta Gorda, which was Spanish for "Fat Point." Punta Gorda was below Sarasota and on the Peace River. Phosphate was mined there and shipped around the world for agricultural purposes. The mineral was first shipped exclusively by barge until the railroad was extended there in the previous two years.

They loved the tropical climate. It was difficult to believe the weather was so warm in the winter months. Michael found some other men who had a boat large enough to fish in the Gulf. Michael spent most afternoons, fishing for sheep heads, flounders, sharks or tarpons. Both wondered how everybody was doing on the farms. From letters, they kept track as much as possible to concerns and developments. Everybody was healthy and surviving the winter. Sven and Heidi were able to keep the cattle, hogs and chickens fed and watered at English Lake. Sometimes, snow could blow unabated across the flat prairie, making winter a challenge.

It was now late February. Stewart was working in his office when McCabe came in and sat down. "Do you want to go to Indianapolis for a few days?"

Stewart said, "Sure, what's going on?"

McCabe explained, "We have a strange case to consider. A local family claims their daughter was placed in the insane asylum against her will and with no material evidence. She was a student at Purdue. They claim she was dating the son of a prominent Lafayette politician and made assertions that differed from the son's version."

Stewart asked, "Does the record show who had her committed?

McCabe answered, "That is confidential until we do some investigation."

Stewart asked, "Couldn't he have just been honorable and direct if he didn't want to see her anymore? Did he have to use family influence to have her committed?"

McCabe retorted, "Be careful! Don't jump to conclusions. I suspect this case will be an onion that reveals more as each layer is peeled back. Her name is Cynthia David. She is at the Central Indiana Hospital for the Insane. You'll need to take her statement and collect any other pertinent evidence you can."

Stewart went home for the evening and told Victoria about his trip. He began packing his travel bag and determined if he had adequate travel supplies. On Wednesday morning, he caught a train east to Indianapolis. The location of the asylum was on the outskirts of town on East Washington Street. Since Stewart did not know how long he would be, he arranged to secure a hotel room downtown at the Canterbury and took an interurban to the asylum.

He arrived at the asylum in the early afternoon. The structure was actually eight large buildings resembling medieval castles. The front revealed four stories. Each story had two double hung windows with awnings over the tops. At each end was a square tower that was almost twice as tall as the adjacent section of wall. Each tower had a round vent on each of the four sides.

He checked in at the front desk of the administration building. An attendant showed Stewart how to get to Ward Three of the Women's Building. The large gray oak trees, lacking any foliage gave Stewart an eerie feeling as if they were huge twisted sentinels guarding over the grounds. As he came up the stairway from the outside entrance and into the foyer area, there were some patients in wheel chairs. One stared into a corner of the ceiling twisting her hair and offering a pained expression. Another sat, writhing her hands in a compulsive nervous gesture and looked up at Stewart, almost as if she expected something.

Some were partially covered with blankets. All were wearing an off-white type of hospital gown that looked as if it had been worn and laundered for several years. As Stewart passed one patient, she screamed a loud shriek that made him jump and caused the hair on the back of his neck stand up and his heart race.

The ward had an overwhelming acrid odor that resembled a combination of cooked cauliflower and cabbage, only stronger and more poignant. Stewart wondered if Cynthia David would be able to comprehend their conversation or if she would exhibit some of the same physical and mental symptoms of the women sitting in the foyer and hallway.

They finally came to a conference room. A young lady was sitting in a chair, with her elbows gently resting on the table. Before he noticed she was wearing the same hospital type gown as the other women, Stewart momentarily thought she might be a hospital employee. As Stewart took a closer look, he noticed that her long brown hair was not as neat and clean as it would have probably been if she were allowed to care for herself in a non-institutional setting. He was a bit taken aback at her modest beauty and countenance.

She stood, extending her hand and said, "You must be Stewart Taylor. I was told you would be seeing me today. My name is Cynthia David."

Stewart said, "I'm glad to meet you."

As he stood staring at her, with a surprised look, Cynthia became a little uneasy. "What is it? What's wrong?"

Stewart feeling a little embarrassed said, "I'm sorry. I don't know what I expected. I saw so many of the residents on the way in. You simply don't look like you belong here. Please, sit down. Take your time and tell me your story."

Cynthia began, "They've been giving me drugs that make me feel sluggish and very slow, mentally."

Stewart reassured her, "I understand. We'll get you through this."

Cynthia continued, "I was in my second year at Purdue. I fell in love. I thought I was in love. He seemed like such a nice young man. His family was so successful. His name was Fredrick Schulz. His father is Congressman William Schultz from the Tenth Congressional District. Frederick was a Political Science major. He was also an intern for his father during summers and whenever he could find some time to work in Washington.

With his family and their connections, he thought he might be able to continue the family name if his father moved up the ladder, vacating the Tenth District. I don't know if they were realistic or not, but he also spoke of the senate, the governor's office and...even higher.

"Of course, he was so charming and positive, I believed in him. I believed that with the right woman supporting him, he could reach any goal he set for himself. He told me that after college we would get married. As I said, I thought I was in love. I thought he loved me, too. Things went faster than I liked. I didn't want to disappoint him. I allowed him to do more than I should have prior to getting married."

Cynthia had been very cool and collected in giving her account until this moment. Stewart attempted to reassure her. "Take your time. I can wait until you can talk."

Cynthia regained her composure and continued, "He took me to meet his family in July. They attempted to be cordial, but could not hide the fact they believed I was beneath the station Fredrick should occupy in life. During dinner, his father asked, 'What nationality is the name David?'"

"I told him my father was of Jewish descent and my mother was Romanian. Her maiden name was Dumitru."

He said, almost looking disappointed, "I see. What does your father do?"

"I said, 'He owns the wagon wheel factory. They don't make as many wagons as they used to. Now, they make very nice hard wood furniture. He and mother have sacrificed so much to send me to Purdue.'

"I found myself defending my parents and I didn't like myself for that. He had been very nice to me up to that point. He then seemed cold and distant. Mrs. Shultz asked me about our relationship. I called her son Freddie. She corrected me and said, 'You mean Frederick?'

"By the start of school I was sure that I might be with child. I found myself daydreaming about my baby. I pictured a son who would have great leadership capability and determination. He would have so much from both families. If his father and grandfathers could be great leaders, or successful businessmen, with the trail they blazed for him, who knows. I began thinking of myself as Jeremiah's Sanctuary. He would be a prophet to the nation. I knew things would be difficult to explain to my parents, but I knew they would forgive me and love my son – their grandson.

"I told Freddie about my condition. He told me he would take care of everything. He said he knew of a doctor who could 'relieve' my 'distress.' I said, that sounds like killing my baby. I would have nothing to do with it. I never saw him again. I tried to find him in some of the places on campus we used to meet between classes for a cup of coffee, or to sit on a bench. I left messages at his dorm, but he never got ahold of me.

"Two weeks later, I was arrested and taken to jail. The next day, they took me to court. Some lawyer, I didn't even know, read charges against me. He claimed I was unstable, mentally ill and promiscuous. They presented a list of professors who they claimed could corroborate their accusations, although none showed up to testify. I was not allowed to see the list.

"They said it was in my best interest to be hospitalized. After they brought me here, two doctors came to question me. They said it was to evaluate my condition. A few days later, they took me in for a procedure. When I awoke, it felt as if my insides had been torn out. I was sore for a week. My menses returned. Maybe, I was never with child."

Stewart asked, "What court were you in?"

"I think it was Tippecanoe County Superior Court, in Lafayette."

"Who was your judge?"

"These details are so difficult. I was in such a state of shock. I think he was Judge Halstead or something like that."

"I'll check the court dockets for that period and see if I can determine the details. These should have been available to you or your family."

Cynthia continued, "I think you'll find a lot about this situation that was not normal, logical or legal. I'm just glad my mother and father finally found somebody who would look into it. They didn't even know where I was for two weeks until they came to Purdue and talked to my roommate."

Stewart assured Cynthia he would do his best. She sat almost exhausted and stunned. Stewart left the hospital knowing he would have an uphill battle to determine the facts and events in this case. He knew beyond logic that the whole situation was not right. He asked to see records pertinent to Cynthia's hospitalization. The clerk at the desk kindly refused, "You'll need a court order to see the documents. You know, for the patient's right to privacy."

Stewart knew the attendant was right, but looked shocked. They claimed to protect Cynthia's privacy, but had already violated so much more. He knew the privacy of others was being protected. Stewart returned to the Canterbury for the night. It reminded him of the Straiter in Wellspring, but was more luxurious and larger. He ate dinner and went to his room for the night. Sleep was sporadic. He read awhile to take his mind off of the day's experiences. When he finally fell asleep, he was visited by nightmares of the images of the asylum and Cynthia's story.

The next morning he determined where the Marion County Courthouse was located. He filed the petition with the clerk. She told him to check back after lunch. After lunch, Stewart obtained the order to see the files. He headed back out to the asylum. He presented the order to the clerk, who showed him to a conference room. Stewart waited until she brought the necessary documentation to him. As he read the papers, he was shocked. The document from the Tippecanoe County Court, signed by Judge Halstead, ordered confinement due to "mental instability, and promiscuity."

As he read the hospital papers, he found a reference to Cynthia's diagnosis, "Paranoid and delusional, with symptoms of neurasthenia." The prescribed treatment was, "Lithia carbonate treatment, coupled with confinement and observation." He found another document, signed by two resident physicians that ordered, "Sterilization, due to mental instability, promiscuity and questionable genetic makeup."

As Stewart returned to the Canterbury, he remembered what James Peterson and McCabe had instructed him, "Do not get emotionally involved with cases and clients."

For the first time since he had been in the profession, Stewart had second thoughts about the grandiose ideals of justice and mercy associated with the practice of law. He knew he would recover from this case over time, but how extensive was the damage to Cynthia and her family? How could she be the only one who was declared promiscuous in a two person relationship?

Stewart was at the office bright and early the next morning. He discovered the order was based upon an Indiana law that had only been signed the previous year, by Governor Hanly, the order of which McCabe warned him. With this early abuse and lack of due process, what devious purposes could this law allow? As he researched the law further, he discovered that individuals could also be involuntarily sterilized for "criminal behavior and pauperism."

McCabe wanted to be briefed first thing. He said, "I doubt that we can do anything about the wrong suffered by the Davids. We'll have to be careful how we proceed in obtaining her freedom. Laws like these involving the mental health industry don't have the same due process as the criminal court system. All the evidence is subjective - subject to the opinions of the practicing professionals in the industry. If we're too aggressive in our approach, Cynthia could be locked away indefinitely. She fell in with the wrong family."

Chapter Twenty-Three

CROSS THE LINE

McCabe determined to bring the Davids in and inform them of the gravity of the situation. McCabe began, "Your daughter has been institutionalized against her will. You already know that. If we're careful, we'll be able to get her out. We will file for a bench ruling. Do you have a family doctor, a pastor or anybody else who could testify for her?"

Abraham David said, "Our doctor is Dr. Stephens. I'm sure he would testify. She has been going to the Campus House at Purdue. Pastor Douglas, who also pastors at Williamsport, will speak for her."

McCabe still looked grim. "There is more. According to the medical charts at the asyl... hospital, a procedure was performed upon Cynthia. She has been sterilized."

Rosa David shrieked and fainted in her chair. Abraham shouted, "I will kill them!"

McCabe cautioned, "I can't imagine the shock and pain you're feeling, but you wouldn't be able to get to these people. They're very prominent and well protected. Please, for your own good and the good of Cynthia, try to keep from getting vengeance. Let us handle this in court."

Stewart and McCabe took time to console and calm the Davids. As the Davids left the office, McCabe assured them he would do all he could to obtain Cynthia's freedom and restore her reputation.

That night, Abraham David was at the Wabash Inn. He was drinking from a flask he carried in his hip pocket. As he was drinking, he was also ranting and raving about Cynthia's story and how wrong it was. The Editor-in-Chief also happened to be in for his supper. He moved Abraham over to a more secluded booth, attempted to calm him and listened. He said, "For your daughter's sake, we need to attack without naming her."

A week later an editorial appeared in the *Watchman*.

PERFECTLY LEGAL?

Last year, in March when the new law was signed, this editor had strong objections to a law that could allow, encourage or force an individual to be sterilized without consent. What could be the motivation behind such a law? Do we have a society where a certain segment should decide whether another segment is "worthy" of reproduction? Criteria for sterilization might include insanity, criminal behavior and even pauperism.

Some argue the law is not intended to punish people for their behavior. Rather, it is designed to ensure the procreation of an "acceptable race and the reduction of unacceptable races." Last year, when this issue was argued in the Indiana Legislature, the matter was academic. It was a bad law to which the paper objected. Now, regretfully, the issue is no longer academic or hypothetical. There is news of a young girl who has been ordered into the custody of the Central State Insane Asylum where she was violated by involuntary sterilization.

The paper will not divulge the particulars of this situation simply to protect the victim. Otherwise, a full scale investigation as to the motives and methods used to perpetuate this heinous action would be forthcoming. How was it determined the individual was worthy of institutionalization? She was ordered to appear in court and upon the testimony of some "witnesses" and others who should have protected her, she was forcibly admitted. Once admitted, two "respected" resident physicians were allowed to offer an opinion affecting the victim's future and violating her person.

The irony of the situation is that rape is one of the justifications for sterilizing a criminal. A rape victim suffers no less violation than this girl. This was all perfectly legal according to the letter of the law. According to the spirit of the law, which is to protect citizens, this is an immoral law. The situation occurred simply because a political leader in a nearby county wanted to protect his son from public disgrace and scandal. Innocent citizens should not be sacrificed upon the altar of the ambitions of the demagogues. Laws should not be written which enable them to do so.

Next to the article was placed a picture of the Shultz family; Congressman, Mrs. Schultz and Frederick, coming down the steps of a church. The caption read, "Congressman Shultz's response to involuntary sterilization law in Indiana: "That is a state law and therefore an issue for the State of Indiana, not a federal issue."

The article was the talk of the town. Three days after being published, the editorial was found on the 'wire' through United Press International and Squibbs. Residents across the state learned about the atrocities that had been committed. Most were in disbelief, and wondered how such a law could have been signed into practice. Although nobody was named, people began speculating who the powerful political family might be. Some, who didn't bother to read carefully, associated the placement of the photograph with the content of the article. Most realized there weren't many families in the adjacent areas that fit the profile.

Stewart filed for a bench ruling to overturn the order for incarceration. The names of the attorney's filing the motion and the name of the judge issuing the order was a matter of public record, once he was able to locate the records. Judge Halstead issued an order for McCabe, Stewart and Richard Douglas Senior to appear in Tippecanoe Superior Court.

After a hearing date was set, Stewart returned to the Central State Asylum to prepare Cynthia for testimony. He met her in the same consultation room as before. Cynthia looked more bedraggled and bewildered than she did upon the first visit. Stewart wondered how anyone could keep their mental condition and emotions together in her situation, and in this place.

He encouraged her and made sure she understood all that he instructed her to do. He said, "When they give you your medications, put them in your mouth until you are away from the nurse. Then simply slip them into your hand. Hold them there until you get to your room and flush them down the toilet."

Cynthia asked, "Why?"

Stewart told her, "Those drugs aren't to help you. They are simply used to manage you. It appears they've increased your dosage since I first met you. If you take them until your hearing, you'll appear dull to the judge and make him think you are in need of institutionalization."

Cynthia mechanically shook her head and said, "I see."

Stewart said, "Something else you need to do."

He waited until Cynthia acknowledged, "Yes."

Stewart advised her, "You will need to refrain from mentioning your pregnancy or your perceptions of 'Jeremiah's Sanctuary.'"

Cynthia broke down sobbing, "They stole him from me! They killed him!"

Stewart comforted her as best he could, "Had you been to a doctor or seen anybody who could confirm that you were with child?"

Cynthia, still sobbing shook her head, "No."

Stewart continued, "We have no proof that you were with child. They would use that claim against you to confirm that you're still delusional and need to be protected from yourself. There would be no legal repercussions for what they've done to you and your child. Unfortunately, they followed the law in what they did. At least they followed the extent of the law to which we can argue."

The day of the hearing, Dr. Stephens and Pastor Richard Douglas were present in Tippecanoe Superior Court. Cynthia was escorted by a Marion County deputy. As she walked into the courtroom, Stewart breathed a sigh of relief. She looked for him at the table and smiled. He could see she had been able to follow his advice and refrain from ingesting the medication. She was wearing civilian clothes, looked fresher and wore modest appearing make-up.

Lawrence Fields of Houser and Fields also appeared to argue against the proposed ruling. Judge Halstead heard arguments for both sides. Dr. Stephens testified that Cynthia seemed to be in good mental and emotional condition prior to her incarceration. Pastor Douglas testified that although the Davids did not attend his church regularly, he knew the family from infrequent visits. Cynthia occasionally attended the Campus House at Purdue. Judge Halstead then turned to the Editor-in-Chief and asked. "How did you find out about this situation?"

Stewart leaned toward Richard and said, "You don't have to answer that."

Judge Halstead said, "Are you retained as council for Mr. Douglas?"

Stewart said, "Your Honor, could I please confer with Mr. Douglas for one minute?"

Judge Halstead said, "Not until you answer my question."

Stewart looked at Richard and nodded. Richard nodded back. Stewart said, "Yes, your Honor, I am representing Mr. Douglas."

Judge Halstead said, "You may confer."

After a brief whispered discussion with the Editor, Stewart said, "My client respectfully refuses to answer the question based upon the First Amendment. He will not reveal the identity of his sources."

Judge Halstead turned red with rage. "Mr. Douglas, you will answer my question or be held in contempt. I need to know whether your attorneys violated attorney-client confidentiality by 'leaking' this story to you."

Richard said, "Your Honor, I can assure you I did not obtain the facts about this situation from Mr. Taylor or Mr. McCabe."

Judge Halstead continued, "Your article, with the juxtaposition of Congressman Shultz tends to incriminate by association."

McCabe answered, "Your Honor, Congressman Shultz's opinion was sought as the view of a respected public official and member of the community."

Judge Halstead said, "On that, I remain dubious, taking his picture of a Sunday morning, coming out of church. I am going to quote an article from the *Harvard Law Review*, written by Samuel D. Warren and Louis Brandeis, published on December fifteenth, eighteen and ninety, 'The right to privacy is the right to keep a domain around us, which includes all those things that are part of us, such as our body, home, property, thoughts, secrets and identity. The right to privacy gives us the ability to choose parts in their domain that can be accessed by others, and to control extent, manner and timing of the use of parts we choose to disclose.'"

McCabe asked, "Your Honor, may I respond?"

Judge Halstead said, "Proceed."

McCabe continued, "In a Democratic society, private citizens should be protected from excess intrusiveness and observation from the government. Elected officials and government, in general, should have the expectation of being monitored by the citizenry. Thomas Jefferson said, 'If given the choice between a government with no free press and a free press with no government, I would choose the latter.'"

Judge Halstead said, "Yes, the public actions and policies of political figures should be analyzed and questioned by the press and the general population. However, the Yellow Press should not use modern technology, such as photography and the telephone to invade the private lives of government officials."

McCabe said, "That is our argument, your Honor. We are asking that the private action of a public figure or a relative of a public figure should not use the law to invade the right to privacy and other rights of a citizen."

Judge Halstead calmed down as if he remembered his initial intentions in disposing of this entire situation, "All right, I have made my decision. This court is ordering the release of Cynthia David from the Indiana Central State Mental Hospital. Mr. Douglas, in the interests of Miss David, you are issued a gag order. You may publish no more articles specific to this particular situation."

Stewart said, "Thank you, your Honor."

On the train back to Williamsport, Richard asked, "Judge Halstead can't order me to refrain from questioning the law, can he?"

McCabe answered, "I'm glad you didn't ask that in court. He might've told you that you were to refrain. We didn't want to poke that bear with a stick any more than we had to."

Richard asked, "Do you think he considered the merit of your argument and realized he shouldn't have ordered Cynthia into custody in the first place?"

McCabe answered, "No, I think he went along with Congressman Shultz and used his power and influence to put a scare into Cynthia. I don't think he ever anticipated the tragic turn of events the law allowed and this situation took. I think your article was effective. They thought they would simply sweep this under the rug, protect young Freddie one more time and use the law to trample the innocent public. I think they might have been shocked by the public outrage and simply wanted this situation to go away."

Two weeks after Cynthia was released, Richard and Daryl were working late to get an edition out. Suddenly, a shot was heard from somewhere in front of the building. They both heard the bullet ricochet off the metal frame of the press and lodge into the ceiling. They ducked down behind the large metal frame. Suddenly, a dull thud was heard on the roof. And flames showered all around the building. Daryl looked out through the darkness and thought he recognized the assailant.

Richard pushed Daryl back a few feet while keeping himself and Daryl in a crouched position. He moved a light-framed crudely built shelving unit used to store miscellaneous items out of the way and revealed a trap door. "Follow me shut this down behind you!"

They crawled several feet through a roughly cut tunnel. They finally came up through the floor into a little storage shed that stood behind the office. From the small window, Richard looked in the direction of the newspaper office. He could see nobody. He watched, hopelessly, as the little office became totally engulfed in flames.

Daryl said, "I always wondered why you didn't have a back door to the building."

Richard smiled and said, "If I had a back door to the office, somebody would have been watching for us to duck out. This way, they figured they would burn us or shoot us. The shed has a back door, though."

He moved a few items away from the back wall and lifted a small trap door inward. He sat down on the dirt floor and pushed away some old galvanized tin that was stacked against the back of the building. Richard led Daryl through a wooded area that led into one of the small canyons that lined the west edge of town and ran perpendicular to the river and parallel to Washington Street.

They wound around and came back out on Washington Street several blocks from the office. They kept stopping to listen to determine if anybody was following them. They came out behind the houses on Fall Street and proceeded in the cover of darkness to Stewart's back door. Fortunately, the solarium door was unlocked and the outside light was not on.

Richard ducked down by the door on the floor and knocked. Eventually, the door was opened and Stewart looked out. "What on earth are you up to?"

Richard and Daryl kept low and moved through the back door. "Let's get inside and I'll explain."

They sat at the kitchen table. Richard looked around the windows to see if he could see anybody moving in the street. "Let's keep the lights off. I don't want somebody passing in the street to see us."

By this time, Victoria came into the kitchen. As she looked around in surprise, she said, "What on earth is all the commotion?"

Richard said, "I can explain."

As Victoria started to brew some coffee, she looked at Daryl and jokingly said, "I should have known, if it was something out of the ordinary, Daryl Dailey was involved."

Richard was quick to defend Daryl, "This one is not his fault. Well, not totally his fault. Actually, we don't know who is after us."

Stewart said, "I would ask if you have offended anybody lately, but might be better to ask you to list those you haven't offended."

Richard relayed the account of the shooting at the office, the fire and their escape. Finally, he said, "This doesn't appear to be the work of Schultz. I think they wanted that situation to go away as bad as Judge Halstead did. Besides, his style is to use his overbearing influence and the law to bully the general public."

Stewart said, "It sounds like an act of cowardice by somebody hired to scare you and probably kill or cripple the Wabash Watchman."

Stewart went upstairs and retrieved his Winchester. He said, "You two will sleep in the guest room tonight."

Stewart inquired, "Are you sure you didn't see anybody?"

Daryl reluctantly said, "I might have seen Jackson Hunter."

Stewart asked, "Why didn't you say so?"

Daryl said, "I wasn't sure. Besides, this guy can be dangerous if he's not caught."

They continued to sit in the dark and drink coffee for about two more hours. As they sat, they constantly listened for footsteps in the yard, dogs barking or any sounds of horses or automobile traffic down Fall Street. They finally heard the fire wagon heading back up town.

Stewart talked to Sheriff Anderson in the morning. Sheriff Anderson assured Stewart he would "shake the bushes" and see what he could find out. Later, Sheriff Anderson, on a hunch went to visit, Jackson Hunter, brother-in-law of Town Marshal, Alfred Graves. He knew Jackson belonged to a secret organization that he did not talk about in public. He saw a can of kerosene and asked him what he was doing the previous evening.

Sheriff Anderson arrested Jackson, who was released on his own recognizance as the evidence was circumstantial. Prior to the arraignment hearing, as Daryl and Stewart were crossing the street between the law office and the court house, Jackson Hunter came around the corner of the courthouse. Stewart glanced and saw Hunter produce a knife. Hunter yelled, "So you are going to testify against me?"

Stewart grabbed for Daryl just as Hunter slashed at him. Sheriff Anderson was approaching on the sidewalk as he saw the situation develop. He ran to assist Stewart and Daryl. Daryl pulled back with an increasingly large blood splotch on his shirt. Stewart and Sheriff Anderson wrestled Jackson to the sidewalk as the sheriff quickly handcuffed him. As a deputy approached to assist Sheriff Anderson, who escorted Jackson to the county jail just behind the courthouse, Stewart assisted Daryl.

Stewart asked, "Are you hurt badly?"

Daryl, still standing, said, "No. luckily, we saw him coming. I think you deflected the knife. He only got me in the side."

Stewart said, "We better get you to the doctor."

Daryl had a slash wound in the abdominal muscle on his right side, just above his waist. He was treated and released. Jackson was held in the county jail without bail. Two days later he was arraigned. The prosecutor allowed him to plea to the lesser charges of assault with a deadly weapon instead of attempted murder. Stewart was not able to examine him as a witness to attempt to determine who he worked for when he burned the office of the Wabash Watchman. His plea resulted in a four year sentence.

On the way back to the office, Stewart asked McCabe, "Do you think he had someone of influence backing him?"

Without taking time to think about his answer, McCabe said, "Absolutely!"

Chapter Twenty-Four

TIME LINE

A little over a year passed since Cynthia Walker was placed into the care of the Central State Asylum and released. She became very active in the church Stewart and Victoria attended. Stewart and Victoria had another boy. They named him Michael. Victoria hired Cynthia as a nanny during the summer and vacations while she worked on her degree to become a teacher.

McCabe asked Cynthia to stop by the office when she was uptown. A little nervous, she stopped by the next day. McCabe said, "Come on in and have a seat. There's nothing to worry about. I just want to tell you that a benefactor has retained me to inform you that your tuition and housing will be paid in full to continue your education."

Cynthia started crying and asked, "Who did this for me?"

McCabe smiled and said, "Sorry, client confidentiality."

Michael bought a Ford from the dealership in Attica two years prior. He was agitated after he bought his new Nineteen O' Seven Tin Lizzy, and Henry Ford sold them new for less to the dealerships each successive year. Whitney reminded him that he did not have to worry about a few hundred dollars. She said, "Ford should be paying you, as much time as you put into tinkering with that thing. At least, we can get into town on a regular basis, every week or so."

Richard wrote his stories and co-opted a deal with the *Fountain County Neighbor* to print and circulate his paper. He chose the *Neighbor* over the *Review Republican* as he thought his views differed too much from those of the *Republican.* He also figured that if he was competing with the other Warren County newspaper, he should get outside assistance. He said, "At my age, it's too late to rebuild and start a publication."

He also discovered that he had more time to write and poke his nose into everybody's business since he spent less time in setting type, selling and proofing ads and preparing photo plates. He discovered the benefits of a division of labor. The *Neighbor* hired another employee to visit Williamsport to obtain copy for advertisements. The *Neighbor* carried a disclaimer, "The views of the Editor of the *Wabash Watchman* are not necessarily those of the *Fountain County Neighbor.*"

The Editor and Michael also teamed-up in a new hobby. Since Michael was more mobile with his new car and he and Richard had more time, they invested money and research into Ham Radio. They each spent a couple of hours most evenings listening to broadcasts and reports intercepted from around the world.

The Christian Church at Pence also found a pastor that would meet on Sunday mornings. His name was Rick Jones. He was a student at Lincoln Bible School in Illinois and came to Pence each weekend, until he graduated. Then, he and his wife moved to Pence. This arrangement allowed Pastor Richard to move his Friday night meetings to Victoria and Stewart's house. Since the meeting was more convenient and not so traditional, the Editor-in-Chief even began attending.

Daryl was working some on the farm and continued to do photography and write articles on a part time basis. He was able to do his own darkroom work and photo composition in Attica. There was less work since Richard had the *Neighbor* crew did every step from the final copy to distribution. Daryl had previously filled-in to do whichever task needed accomplishing.

Whitney and Victoria threw themselves into supporting women's causes and seeking suffrage. They wrote letters and guest editorials, participated in personal lobbying and anything else they could do to support the cause from home. They were able to attend an occasional conference or rally in Indianapolis or Chicago. Cynthia and her family seemed to recover remarkably from the injustice they had endured. Abraham David said, "It was the persecution which has made our people strong."

He was Jewish by heritage, but he and the entire family had converted to Christianity, and were attending the meetings at Stewart and Victoria's house. They benefitted greatly from the teachings about forgiveness and healing. It was difficult, but they also learned to pray for their enemies. Cynthia copied a verse on a card and taped it to her vanity mirror, *"Avenge not yourselves, beloved, but give place unto the wrath of God: for it is written, 'Vengeance is unto me; I will recompense, sayeth the Lord.' (Romans 12:19)"*

She never got over the affection for Frederick. She believed, in her heart that Frederic really loved her and would have done the right thing except for his family's prejudice and interference. She moved on, therefore, she was neither excited nor happy when she read Richard's editorial about Congressman Shultz losing the next election. For her father Abraham, the news brought a little more joy. Neither was happy when they read six months later that the entire Shultz family had been killed when their nineteen hundred and eight, Cadillac Runabout was hit by a train at a crossing in Tippecanoe County near Battleground. Of course, Richard said, "With twenty or so car builders in Indiana, they shouldn't have been driving a car made in Michigan."

Sven and Heidi were still on the English Lake farm. Victoria and Whitney pooled some resources to buy additional acreage and increase the beef and dairy herds and a new steam tractor for each farm. Michael and Stewart visited the farm as often as possible. They had some disagreements over whether they should take the Tin Lizzy or the train. The train won out for about six months of the year.

On one trip, Stewart and Michael took the Editor-in-Chief along for the ride. He told Michael he used to hunt and fish on the Marsh in his younger years. Stewart and Michael knew they would not have to come up with any conversation or attempt to entertain each other on the long ride with Richard. He said, "I stayed at the Pittsburgh Gun Club in English Lake. One time I was there when Lew Wallace was fishing. He used to love to fish there. Some people claimed he even wrote part of *Ben Hur* at the Lodge.

"Wallace fished from his houseboat, which he named the 'White Elephant.' He was there in eighteen eighty when he received a telegram from his publisher in New York that *Ben Hur* would be published. He was reported to have said, 'Of all the rivers I have visited around the world, this is the most beautiful.'

"The draining of the Grand Kankakee Marsh was one of the greatest tragedies of modern invention and progress. It was an action that began prior to the Civil War and was put on hold due to the War. Later, politics and corruption on both sides of the argument slowed the draining process. The land was home to the Potawatomie Indians and thousands of types of wild animals. It was so massive that it was called the 'Everglades of the North.'

"Originally, an estimated five hundred thousand acres of swampland existed between St. Joseph County Indiana and the Illinois state line along the Kankakee river. It was such a popular wilderness paradise that hunters came from all over the United States and Europe. That was how the town near the confluence of the Kankakee and Yellow Rivers became known as English Lake. Hunters claimed that during duck and goose migration the sky was black for miles as the flocks blocked the sun. In eighteen and ninety-three, dredging began. They straightened the two hundred and fifty meandering miles with oxbows and basins of the Kankakee to ninety straight miles. A couple of presidents, including Teddy hunted here."

As they looked around the farm, Richard was visibly shaken. He could not believe the swamp was gone except for a fraction of the original acreage. He said, "Gone, all gone."

After they returned to Williamsport, Richard contacted Daryl. He said, "Get your stuff together. We're going to a field that is about six miles from the northwest of the center of Indianapolis."

Daryl asked, "What's going on?"

Richard told him, "There's a test track called the Speedway. We're going to an air display."

Daryl scrunched his eyebrows and tilted his head slightly forward, "An air display?"

Richard continued, "Yes, the Wright Brothers are bringing several biplanes for a week long exhibition. We will only be there a few days."

Daryl said, "Alright."

On the train, Richard explained the origin of the test track. "There are several motorcar manufacturers in and around Indianapolis. I have a list right here. Let's see, there are Marmon, Cole, National, Marion, Overland and American Underslung. Indianapolis is estimated to be fourth in the country in the number of automobiles produced."

Daryl asked, "Why are they involved in an air display?"

Richard said, "Last year, they held the National Championship for gas-filled balloons. It was the first competition held there. It was held before the racing surface was completed around the track."

Daryl remained glib, "Oh, sounds interesting."

They were able to catch a livery that made constant trips between the depot and the track. When Daryl laid eyes on the track, he was almost overwhelmed. "How big is this oval?"

Richard answered, "It is two and a half miles around."

Daryl watched and photographed the entire time they were there. He was so caught up in watching the planes that Richard had to frequently remind him to take photos. On Friday, June seventeenth, Walter Bookins took one of the Wright Brothers planes up to four thousand and thirty-eight feet, establishing a new world record.

On the way home Daryl said, "I have to go back there. I also have to find out more about flying."

The Friday evening meetings were going very well. Pastor Richard began to come home to Williamsport every Friday and minister at the Campus House every Sunday. He enjoyed concentrating on just two churches and spending more of his time in each. There was not a large group attending, but he noticed the "Sabbath Group" as he affectionately called them wanted to get deeper in the Word of God. He thought back to Pentecost how the early believers met in houses rather than the synagogues or temples and felt a sense of awe.

Another interesting development occurred. Abraham David began relating the details of his Jewish heritage. He knew things about the significance of the Old Testament and Jewish tradition that most traditional Christians did not realize. He even took time, with Richard's encouragement to teach the significance of his newly learned New Testament Christian values with the verbal traditions.

He said, "It has been my life mission to study the Jewish Torah. Torah means teach. As a young man, I contemplated and prepared to be a rabbi. Life got in the way and I married and started my business. We were blessed with Cynthia. Although I did not become a formal teacher of the Torah, I have studied it with the discipline and intensity I would have as a teacher. I knew my efforts would be rewarded and the time would be restored.

"My studies of the Jewish written and verbal traditions compliment my newfound Christianity. My Savior and the Holy Spirit complete my life and fellowship with the Father. The only thing I do not understand is why Jewish people could not accept a Jewish Messiah. I would like to read from Nehemiah, Chapter eight, verses one through four:

> So Ezra the priest brought the law before the assembly, both men and women and all who could hear with understanding, upon the first day of the seventh month. And he read therein before the broad place that was from before the water gate from early morning until midday, in the presence of men, women, and those who could understand; and the ears of all the people were attentive to the book of the law. And Ezra the scribe stood at a wooden pulpit that was made for that purpose.

"I believe my calling is the same as that of Ezra, to read from the law to all who understand. That is my spiritual platform, the place like a pulpit where God elevates me to perform my tasks and to encourage and equip others."

All the believers were enthralled by the combination of Pastor Douglas's extensive knowledge of the scripture and his prophetic vision. They were equally amazed that "Father Abraham" as they called him, had no formal training in the understanding and delivery of the Jewish traditions. He used his own preparation and knowledge gained from personal study to relate the significance of the festivals, the commandments and especially the Sabbath, the Old Testament prophets, and many other Jewish principles.

As Pastor Richard was teaching from the second chapter of Acts one Friday evening, a huge blaze could be seen from in front of the house. Two shots were fired into the upper stories of the Taylor home. Stewart ran out onto the porch and stood boldly, calling, "Come out you cowards and show yourself or shoot me right here."

Stewart could see nobody behind the flames. He expected to be shot dead any second. Michael and the Editor ran to the door and told him to get back inside. Daryl ran upstairs to the top of the spire. From this vantage point, he could see behind the burning cross, the flames clearly illuminated Jackson Hunter.

As Jackson turned to run down the street, he shouted, "Jew lovers!"

The town marshal Alfred Graves conducted an investigation. He made no arrest as he said Jackson had an alibi for that evening. Stewart learned that Jackson had been released from prison for 'good behavior.' Stewart said, "I wish the incident had happened in the county. Maybe Sheriff Anderson would have obtained justice."

Stewart was grateful to be practicing law. After another year and a half, he found himself drifting back into the same pattern he established while he was alone in Wellspring. He loved Victoria, and his sons, Raymond and Michael and played with them, read to them and included them in every activity he could. This was new to him as he had never been around babies or toddlers for any length of time in the past. He also attempted to help around the house, but Victoria was so competent in managing the things that he felt his efforts were mostly symbolic.

While Cynthia was away at Purdue, Victoria hired a local girl to fill in as housekeeper and nanny. Even when Cynthia was home from school, Victoria kept a housekeeper and allowed Cynthia to concentrate on the boys.

They spent almost every other weekend on the farm. Stewart liked to work in the shop on those weekends, making furnishings and other wooden items for gifts and to make the house a home. Stewart began exercising on his contraption longer periods of time in the afternoon. He also spent about fifty hours a week in the office, when McCabe didn't run him out. By contrast, in Wellspring, after everybody moved back to Indiana, he concentrated on the law, his hobby of woodworking and his exercise. The law was his life. It had almost become an idol to him. Now, although he still practiced the law, it did not hold the same amazement and intrigue he experienced in his first two years.

He knew what disillusionment was, and that the newness wears off of everything eventually. This was different, though. He knew there was a haunting feeling that hung over him. He had recurring nightmares about the Central State Asylum. He realized there had to be other cases in which people were incarcerated against their will and with little or no due process. He continued to write letters to everybody he thought might listen and possibly be sympathetic to the situation.

He knew that the governor, even though he had met him in social settings on several occasions, had no interest in repealing or amending the law. He had engaged in an ambitious campaign to write Lieutenant Governor, Thomas Riley Marshall. Finally, Marshall was elected to the governor's office in nineteen hundred and eight. After he took office two years prior, he placed a moratorium on involuntary sterilization. Although the practice was discontinued momentarily, the law remained on the books.

One day Richard showed Daryl a clipping from the Associated Press. David Graham Phillips, the journalist who made such an impact on him in his youth, had been shot on January twentieth, nineteen and eleven. Daryl just stared at the clipping in shock. "What happened?"

Richard said, "Apparently, his muckraking and journalistic crusading got him killed. He was walking up the steps to the Princeton Club in New York City. Fitzhugh Coyle Goldsborough walked up to David and said, 'Here you go' and fired six shots from a thirty-two caliper gun. He turned the gun upon himself and said, 'Here I go." He shot himself in the head. Phillips died the next day at Bellevue Hospital. Phillips must have cast dispersions upon Goldsborough or his family, real or imagined. Did he ever tell you he was from Indiana?"

Daryl, dazed, nodded his head in the affirmative and said, "Yes, Madison. I was hoping to see him again. He was so young. He did so much for me after my parents died."

Richard said, "I'm sorry, son."

In other matters, Michael could see that Stewart had lost his luster and was mechanically aping his way through life. Michael and Richard were definitely concerned with Stewart's wellbeing. By the spring of the year, Michael, Daryl and Richard came up with a plan. Richard saw it as an opportunity to cover and report on an historic event. Daryl knew it was his opportunity to return to Speedway. Daryl also seemed to grow closer to the other men after the news of David Graham Phillips.

Michael prepared all he could by reading everything available on the field of psychology. He was intrigued with increasing his understanding of human nature and maladies suffered by people who had experienced trauma and stress. He also learned about different tendencies people might exhibit in regards to different mental and emotional abnormalities.

Michael also believed prayer and an understanding of Biblical principles was important. In his planning, he spent time with Pastor Douglas every chance he could, picking his brain and putting the study of psychology and Biblical principles into perspective. Richard admonished him, "Yes, you can demonstrate concern and love for an individual, but be cautious of attempting to fix him."

Michael said, "It is worth a try. I had to deal with myself and others as we came back from the war in Cuba. I think I can be direct, yet discreet. Knowing we care should help."

Chapter Twenty-Five

BETWEEN THE LINES

They convinced Stewart to take a camping trip over Memorial Day weekend. He asked, "Will I need to bring the Winchester?"

Michael told him, "No, there are no mountain lions or bears in Indiana."

They arranged to pack the Tin Lizzy and head out on Saturday morning. Richard and Daryl waited at Stewart's so Michael would only have to make one stop. Since the car only had two narrow bench seats, most of the gear was secured to the running boards on both sides. Michael noticed that Stewart also brought his briefcase. Michael asked, "Are you planning to do some work?

"No, I just brought a couple of books and papers I might look at if there's time. We're supposed to relax aren't we? I relax through reading."

Michael affirmed, "Yes, we're supposed to relax. Sometimes, you have to totally get away from your normal routine, even relaxing habits."

Stewart kept asking questions about the trip, "Where's a place to camp in Central Indiana?"

Michael said, "I found a place just west of Indianapolis."

By Saturday afternoon, they arrived at the Speedway. As they approached crowds were concentrating into small entrance areas past ticket booths. People arrived by trains, horse drawn conveyances and on foot. There was even a shuttle system from the downtown hotels by motor coaches. They could hear cars practicing. They drove to the Georgetown Pike and bought a pass into the infield, accessed by crossing the bridge.

They set up camp in a designated campground within sight of the track. The Speedway was so big one could have gotten lost inside the infield. They watched practice for a few hours. As they watched, car number twenty-nine blew a tire on its fifth lap of a practice spin and hurled into the northwest turn just before the home stretch. It appeared the mechanic was thrown from the car before crashing into and ripping out several feet of the retaining wall. The driver jumped out before impact. They watched until they learned nobody had been killed and both team members were taken by ambulances. The car was up righted, and driven to the garage under its own power, and had new tires put on. Saturday practice resumed.

They decided to go back to the campground, which was located behind the pit area across from the grandstands in the middle of the home stretch. The campground had filled with more campers while they had been watching practice. After supper, they were sitting by the campfire, talking about the past, their futures and things in general. Michael asked Stewart, "When were you the happiest in your life?"

Stewart thought and said, "There've been different times. Of course my happiest day was when I married Victoria. Coming to Indiana and our courtship were nice too. I love our sons. They can be a handful."

Michael continued, "What was the longest time you were happy?"

Stewart said, "Up in the cabin. Everything seemed like time was standing still. There were no distractions and stresses. Survival was the only focus, except when we had time to read and discuss the 'Profound Truths' of life."

Michael asked, "Can a person enjoy life down here with all the responsibilities?"

Stewart said, "Yes, I think so. It's just that after seeing what some people do to others, it can be disappointing. It takes some of the wind out of your sails. I've discovered that the entire legal system is not a matter of justice. It's more a matter of resources and staying power. Those who have the most money win over time, so much for the ideals of youth - justice and equality and all that. It's the Golden Rule - He who has the gold rules."

Richard said, "If we live long enough, we will see our ideals fade, crash and burn."

Daryl added, "I guess we just have to keep getting up when life knocks us down."

They talked into the night. The next day Richard found a copy of the *Sunday Indianapolis Star.* He read some of the details from the accident of the previous day. "Apparently, car number twenty-nine was driven by Harold Van Gorder of Pittsburgh. The car was going about eighty miles an hour when it blew the tire."

Daryl asked, "How do they know how fast it was going?"

Richard said, "They're using velocimeters. Van Gorder knew how fast he was going."

Stewart asked, "A velocimeter?"

Richard affirmed, "Yes, it measures their miles per hour. According to the article, the mechanic, Walter Bardel, of Brooklyn knew they were going for the wall. He jumped from the car. He misjudged the juxtaposition of the rear tire and was run over by the car."

Stewart asked, "What was the extent of his injuries?"

Richard continued, "According to the *Star*, he sustained a 'broken left shoulder, ragged scalp, a wound over the left eye that was so ragged it could not be stitched, a wrenched back and bruises on the left side of his head, left hip and arm.'"

Daryl asked, "Could you imagine hitting that brick track at eighty miles an hour?"

Richard said, "And I quote, this is confusing wording, 'Dr. H.P. Allen and Thomas J. Duggan said, 'While injuries were very severe, were not serious unless complications set-in or internal injuries develop. Van Gorder jumped clean and had slight abrasions on the forehead.'

"Finally, C. A. Ernise of the Lozier Company, who is here looking after Lozier interests said, 'While we do not wish to criticize Van Gorder, I do not believe that any man who has not had experience in track racing can hold a high-powered car on a track when a front tire is blown. We are very sorry that a Lozier car should figure in such a smash-up.'"

Stewart asked, "Who would have experience on this track with a tire blowing out at eighty miles an hour? The company is covering their assets."

Richard concluded, "The Ernise quote continues, '…Van Gorder has given us several scares during practice, and arrangements have made whereby he would not be permitted to drive in the race on Tuesday.'"

Stewart was mad by now, "I would like to represent Van Gorder in a liable suit. That was a slanderous statement to make to the public."

Michael, "Easy, they all knew the risks going in."

Stewart concluded, "Yes, but they were shared risks. The company has hung Van Gorder out to dry, publicly."

They finished breakfast and returned to the track to watch some more practice and the conclusion of time trials. There were forty cars preparing for the Tuesday race. At practice, it was not difficult to talk as the cars were limited to a few on the track at a time. Still, conversation was inhibited when two or three rounded the track in a pack.

Richard and Daryl stayed to watch the activity. They had press passes which got them into the pits. Richard was able to talk to car owners, drivers, mechanics and others while they were awaiting their turns on the track. For a few minutes he was even able to talk to James Allison, one of the track owners. Mr. Allison seemed to indicate that he and the other track owners liked the free publicity.

Stewart and Michael made their way back to the campground. As he poked at the fire, Stewart said, "There's something else that has been bothering me. Judge Manly Hall, from Fountain Superior

Court started asking me to join his lodge a little over three years ago, about the time I was representing the David family."

Michael asked, "Didn't he die just after Christmas this year?"

Stewart affirmed, "Yes, he died. A strange thing also happened. His widow brought two books by the office. She asked if I'd be interested in having them. I said, 'Sure, I love books.'

"I don't think she was supposed to give these to somebody outside of the Lodge. I didn't realize that, but she gave them to me fair and simple. I started reading this one during January and February. It was written by Albert Pike in eighteen hundred and seventy-one. The title is *Morals and Dogma*, subtitled, *Supreme Council of the Thirty Third Degree of the Scottish Rite*."

Michael asked, "Did you find it interesting?"

"Yes, to a certain extent. So much of it is written in esoteric language and full of symbolism. He speaks of 'Adepts, the Princes of Masonry, Rose-Croix Illuminati, Ancient Mysteries, Order of the Templars and Arcanum Arcanorum.' I looked the last one up. It's Latin for 'secret of secrets.' They're shrouded in secrecy and require an initiation ritual. It's ironic! We are here at this race to relax and enjoy the entertainment, yet I feel there is another race going on. It's the contest for the human race, staged between God and a shadow remnant of the religions God told the Israelis to eliminate."

Stewart fumbled with the book and looked at some of his page markers. "I want to read some of his quotes to you. Tell me what you think. On page one hundred and four, Pike says, the Order, '... conceals its secrets from all except the Adepts and Sages, or the Elect, and uses false explanations and misinterpretations of its symbols to mislead those who deserve only to be misled; to conceal the Truth, which it calls Light, from them, and draw away from it.'"

"On page eight hundred and nineteen, he states, 'The Blue Degrees are but the outer court or portico of the temple. Part of the symbols are displayed there to the Initiate, but he is intentionally mislead by false interpretations.'"

Michael said, "I don't know much about them, but I know secrecy and initiation rituals differ from the grace of God, which is a free gift and not shrouded in secrecy. I understand that all the 'Temple' emphasis is based upon the temple of Solomon.'"

"Yes, Pike further states, 'It is not intended that he shall understand them; but it is intended that he shall imagine he understands them. Their true explanation is reserved for the Adepts, the Princes of Masonry.'

"Judge Hall claimed the organization was not a spiritual or religious group, yet Pike states on page two hundred and nineteen, 'That Rite raises a corner of the veil, even in the Degree of Apprentice; for it there declares that Masonry is a worship.'

Michael asked, "How can there be worship without a religion or a god?"

Stewart said, "They claim to believe in the Great Architect of the Universe. They claim to honor all religions equally. It gets into astrology and idol worship, attempting to draw power from physical representations made by man. On page eight hundred and forty, Pike states:

> It was the remembrance of this scientific and religious Absolute, of this doctrine that is summed up in a word, of this Word, in fine, alternatively lost and found again, that was transmitted to the Elect of all the ancient Initiations: it was this same remembrance, preserved, or perhaps faned (sic) in the celebrated Order of the Templars, that became from all the secret associations, of the Rose-Croix, of the Illuminati, and of Hermetic Freemasons, the reason of their strange rites, of their signs more or less conventional, and above all, of their mutual devotedness and of the power.

Michael said, "I remember hearing about Pike being a mason. He has a statue in Washington and is buried thirteen blocks from the Capital."

"Yes, he was a thirty-third degree and supposed to be the most knowledgeable in 'the Craft' in his time. I wonder if they mean 'occult' and 'Occult' in the same way we understand the terms. Here he mentions the word 'occult' in another passage and it's capitalized:

The Occult Science of the Ancient Magi was concealed under the shadows of the ancient Mysteries: it was imperfectly revealed or rather disfigured by the Gnostics; it is guessed at under the obscurities that cover the pretended crimes of the Templars; and it is found enveloped in enigmas that seem impenetrable, in the Rites of the Highest Masonry.

"According to Pike, the Masons believe two forces were present in the Garden of Eden. They seem to get the forces confused. On five hundred and sixty-seven, Pike describes the Garden:

...the Prince of Darkness...made Adam, whose soul was of the Divine Light, contributed by the Eons, and his body of matter, so that he belonged to both Empires, that of Light and that of Darkness. To prevent the light from escaping at once, the demons forbade Adam to eat the fruit of "knowledge of good and evil," by which he would have known the Empire of Light and that of Darkness. He obeyed: an Angel of Light induced him to transgress, and he gave him the means of victory; but the Demons created Eve, who seduced him...

Michael looked at Stewart with a wide-eyed expression. "That's the exact opposite of Scripture! He's saying God and the angels are the demons. He says, 'An Angel of Light induced him to transgress.' His words even conflict with themselves. Maybe he was inspired by demons in his writing. Isaiah says, 'Woe to those who call evil good and good evil; who substitute darkness for light and light for darkness.'"

Stewart assured Michael, "I've been feeling some strange impressions from reading this stuff. Mostly, I feel despondency, greater than the type you and I talked about in the cabin. That was a general and natural feeling. This is a type of spiritual oppression. I've never experienced it, so I have trouble describing it. I think visiting the Indiana Central Asylum and attempting to help Cynthia has added to this feeling."

Michael said, "So, this has been building up for three years now?"

Stewart said, "Yes, it has intensified since I read this stuff. Pike gets more direct on page three hundred and twenty-one. He says, 'Lucifer, the Light-bearer! Strange and mysterious name to give to the Spirit of Darkness! The Son of the Morning!'

"He added exclamation marks to the end of those three sentences. He continues, 'Is it he who bears the Light, and with its splendors intolerable blinds feeble, sensual, or selfish Souls? Doubt it not! for traditions are full of divine Revelations and Interpretations...'"

Michael said, "That's enough! What's that other book you brought?"

Stewart picked the other book up and looked at it. "It's by Helena Petrovna Blavatsky. She was one of the founders of the Theosophical Society and New Age Movement. The Masons published *New Age Magazine* since nineteen hundred and four. Even though the Masons don't admit women to their lodges, she was alleged to have been given a certificate of adoption by John Yarker in eighteen and seventy-seven. In her book *The Secret Doctrine,* she stated on page two hundred and forty-three:

> …to view Satan, the serpent of Genesis, as the real creator and benefactor, the Father of spiritual mankind. For it is he who was the 'Harbinger of Light,' bright radiant Lucifer, who opened the eyes of the automation created by Jehovah, as alleged; and he who was the first to whisper: 'in the day ye eat thereof ye shall be as Elohim, knowing good and evil'—can only be regarded in the light of a Saviour…

Michael sat, thinking for a while. "We have always known there were forces fighting for the very human race and the conquest of the world since the Garden. It's amazing to find those who belong to organizations who admit to having the goal of perpetuating this evil – this domination of the world."

Stewart agreed, "Yes, and finally with one more statement, I will rest my case. It's common for Masons to take the Oath of Nimrod."

Michael just sat, as if he were dazed. They were interrupted as Daryl and Richard soon returned from the track. Breaking from his near trance, Michael asked, "Is anybody ready for supper?"

They decided to drive back to a local café they saw on the way in by the Crawfordsville Highway. While they were eating, the talk around them was on the race. Some of the people were placing bets on the number of deaths and injuries that might occur in the race.

A man at the next table asked Richard, "Hey, how many drivers and mechanics do you think will be killed or injured? Some say twenty."

Richard, unable to hide his indignation answered, "None, I hope."

The man said, "What are you, goodie-two-shoes?"

Richard calmly responded, "No, I just take no delight in seeing other people's suffering."

The man, with a surprised and embarrassed expression, turned and talked to the people at his table, ignoring Richard the remainder of the time the four ate. After supper, they returned to camp and sat around the campfire talking until well after midnight. By the light of a kerosene lantern, Richard gave some updates from the paper articles he had been reading and some of the interviews he conducted in the pits.

Chapter Twenty-Six

THE RACE IS ON

Since Richard was working on an article, he introduced various topics about the race to see how the other three reacted to each topic. He figured if Daryl, Stewart and Michael asked questions and engaged in conversation, it might be an interesting topic. If he stated some fact he had discovered, and nobody seemed interested he made a mental note to let that topic go uninvestigated for the article.

He told them, "Ray Harroun is a favorite. He was named 'Most Successful car driver in the United States for nineteen hundred and ten,' by *Motor Age Magazine.* He broke two speed records at Daytona earlier this year."

The time trials were concluded on Saturday and Sunday. Monday was open for practice. Stewart and Michael watched the cars practicing for several hours. Richard and Daryl continued to gather as much information and as many photos as possible for the article.

That night Richard told them, "There were forty-six teams who paid the five hundred dollar entry fee. Of those, forty-four showed up to race. The track mandated that drivers had to qualify at an average speed of seventy-five miles an hour from a running start. For most, that was no problem. Several drivers, over the two days of time trials, reached eighty-eight miles an hour. Four cars failed to qualify."

Daryl said, "I can't wait to see the whole race!"

The race was to begin at ten on Tuesday morning. They made their way out to the track at nine. The crowd was excited, yet orderly. They bought four programs for a nickel a piece. Richard said the owners predicted that one hundred thousand people would be in attendance. While they watched, the cars were brought from the pits and lined-up.

Carl Fisher, one of the track owners decided that a running start should be used. As he was the Indianapolis agent for the Stoddard-Dayton passenger car, he provided one for the race. He also offered to drive the inaugural lap. Through practicing the formation the previous days, he determined that forty miles per hour would be a good rate for the starting lap.

The cars were numbered by their placement in the line-up. The front row included the pace car on the inside. Number one and next to the pace car was Lewis Stanger. Completing the first row and numbered accordingly were, Ralph DePalma, Harry Endicott, and Johnny Aitkin. There were an additional six rows of five cars each with car number forty in the eighth row.

At ten o'clock a bomb was dropped to signal the drivers to start their cars. Carl Fisher led the way as the drivers followed in formation. The cars puffed along, almost concealed by the smoke and dust from burning castor oil and petrol. The track looked like it had snowed as it had been covered with white sand to absorb the castor oil.

As the pack neared the start/finish line after the initial lap, Pop Wagner signaled the start of the race with a red flag. Johnny Aitkin led to the first turn and continued to lead for the first four laps. Spencer Wishart took over at lap five and led until lap fourteen in his imported Mercedes Grand Prix motor car. Fred Belcher took over the lead with a chain driven Knox.

The race was suspended while a fatal accident occurred on lap thirteen when Art Grainer's Amplex turned over and slammed into the wall at eighty-four miles per hour. His mechanic, Sam Dickson, from Chicago was fatally injured. At lap twenty, Ralph de Palma, an Italian driver led for four laps. Ralph had been a dominant leader in the previous two years of racing at the Speedway. Richard discovered that Ralph de Palma believed in a strict regimen of exercise and proper eating to stay in shape for the grueling race circuit.

Harroun plodded along and led ninety out of the last one hundred laps. His objective was to drive at his own pace, regardless of what other drivers did. During the previous year at practice, he had been conducting tire tests. He calculated that driving between seventy-five and eighty miles per hour, he could cut the number of cumbersome tire changes in half. Richard had Daryl watch the pits and attempt to keep track of the number of tire changes Harroun made. Daryl told him Harroun stopped for four tire changes. All of those were the left rear tire. The other three remained intact the entire race.

On the other hand Ralph Mulford ran second or close to second the entire race. The ten laps he led were out of the last one-hundred laps up to one hundred and eighty-one. He was a Sunday school teacher who wore a bow tie and drove from Detroit with his wife in his Lozier, with as many spare tires as they could carry in and on the car. He ended up changing tires fourteen times, with several blowouts. The last blowout caused severe damage to his rim while limping the car around to the pits. Precious time was lost in the attempt to hammer the rim out to change the tire.

Harroun sailed to the finish line, receiving the checkered flag, virtually unchallenged for the last nineteen laps. Only twelve of the forty competing cars finished the race. Mulford protested saying he lapped Harroun when the accident on lap thirteen caused some confusion on the track and in the scorer's booth. It was pointed out that Mulford's lengthy tire repair in the last twenty laps cost him a considerable amount of time.

Michael, Stewart, Daryl and Richard planned to stay one more night to allow the crowd to die down and leisurely drive home on Wednesday. As they were sitting by the fire, Daryl asked, "Where did they ever come up with the idea to pave the track in brick?"

Richard explained, "When the track was first built they used crushed or powdered rock covered with tar for bonding. With use from automobile and motorcycle races coupled with automobile manufacturers' testing their products, the surface broke down, so quickly that a nineteen o' nine, three hundred mile Wheeler-Schebler Trophy contest was flagged short by sixty-five miles from completion.

"They had to consider a more substantial material. The owners arranged for Wabash Clay Company of Veedersburg to supply enough bricks to repave the track. Three million-two hundred thousand bricks, weighing ten pounds each were brought by rail from just east of the Illinois-Indiana line, about seventy-five miles due west. Each brick was laid on its side on a smooth bed of sand. Mortar was brushed into the cracks between the bricks. The entire operation took only sixty-three days."

Stewart said, "That was an engineering marvel!"

They all agreed. That night Stewart had a dream. He dreamed he was watching the race. As he watched he saw the drivers as political leaders. The mechanics and owners were their promoters and handlers. Those running the show were the four track owners. The drivers and car owners were in earnest. They put their savings, their reputations and their very lives into winning the race. They were expendable and replaceable, though.

After he awoke, very rested, he thought about the dream all day long. Positive results came from the race as the auto makers could test their cars so the public could compare performance. They could also find new developments by pushing the limits of man and machine such as finding ways for the automobiles to smoke less and use less fuel. There could even be improvements in aerodynamics and safety, like Harroun's mirror.

The crowd paid to be entertained. No matter how much they cheered or observed and described any cheating or suspicious actions by the contestants, they could not change the outcome of the event. The track owners made the rules and could include or exclude anybody they chose. They could also write their own rules limiting how the drivers could compete. Their goal was to collect the entrance fee. In return, they offered entertainment and competition. There were two gates to enter. Which gate would you choose? But what was the entrance fee? Was this just a car race? What economic, political and spiritual forces vie for the human race?

After Stewart returned home, he took Victoria and the boys for a stroll down Fall Street. They walked to the Williamsport Falls and watched the small stream trickle through the ravine it had been cutting for centuries. Stewart observed, "How long do you think that stream has been cutting through the cliff?"

Victoria answered, "Ever since the glaciers deposited the smooth sand there."

As they walked down East Monroe to the edge of the old quarry, Stewart reflected, "Only a few years ago they were still mining this quarry. The foundations of almost every structure in town are built with it. The stone cuts easily with tools or when exposed to wind and water, but as it sits in a foundation it gains strength and becomes a very resilient and durable building material.

"The sand stone is like us when we're young. We're pliable and easily molded. As we grow older and are arranged in a wall with other stones, we become more durable and are able to withstand the weathering of life's storms. We gain strength and protection from the others placed in our close proximity. Hopefully, we don't become rigid and unusable or unchangeable when we learn new direction, information and inspiration."

Stewart was reading in his study before bed. He read verses from chapter two of Joel, and from Ezekiel thirty-three about the watchmen on the wall. It was clear that the watchmen were called to warn the nations and encourage them to turn from wickedness in the hopes God would relent in His judgment. The watchman was also warned that if he failed to sound a signal and the people perished, he was held accountable. If he sounded the alarm and the people perished, he was absolved of responsibility. He remembered Abraham David's reading from Nehemiah.

That same night he had another dream. In this dream he saw Ezra's platform and other types of work surfaces. He saw an actor upon a stage, a preacher speaking from a pulpit, a watchmen walking upon the flat surface on top of the wall, and the altar Moses was instructed to build from stones that were uncut by human hands. He saw a brick mason laying blocks from the top of a scaffold. Finally, he saw himself sitting upon a porch, simply enjoying his time with Victoria and his boys.

He awoke with a start. The sun was already shining brightly through the curtains. He smelled cinnamon rolls baking and coffee brewing from the kitchen. He hurriedly got ready for work. As he entered the kitchen, Victoria was busily preparing breakfast. He kissed her and said, "I'll only have time for coffee! I'm late."

Victoria said, "Have a seat. I already told McCabe you wouldn't be in until ten this morning."

Stewart asked, "I'm only working two days this week and now it is one full day and a partial day?"

Victoria retorted, "McCabe and the entire legal system will survive."

At first Stewart felt a little perturbed, but he quickly realized Victoria was probably concerned about him. As he sipped coffee, he wandered over to the back window and peered out at the boys playing in the sand box and alternately running to the swing where Cynthia was swinging them. Stewart smiled and said, "That's right. Cynthia is out for the summer. Do you think she's truly happy?"

Victoria smiled pleasantly and responded, "Yes. I honestly believe she's bounding back and letting the past go. She's getting on with her life. It's you I am concerned about."

Stewart did not attempt to put on a brave face and deny he had been suffering. He simply replied, "I know it's been difficult living with me. I believe going to the track was the start of something. Their concern for me was evident. Michel and I were able to get to the bottom of some of my deeper concerns. I have a meeting scheduled with him and Pastor Richard for this Saturday morning. I honestly feel I'm on the edge of a breakthrough."

Victoria stopped her preparations and looked Stewart directly in the eyes and said, "We've all been praying for you. I've been praying for you. I'm hopeful for healing and restoration. I want my husband back."

Stewart told Victoria about the dream from the previous night. He said, "I think it stems from studying the ideas about the watchmen on the walls. I've also been reading Nehemiah. After the Jewish people returned from captivity in Babylon, Nehemiah received word the wall around Jerusalem had been destroyed and lay in ruin. He fasted and prayed and asked for forgiveness for the children of Israel who had sinned against God, both in his and his father's house. He said, 'We have dealt corruptly against Thee, and have not kept Thy commandments.'

"Nehemiah had a vision and a purpose, yet he was depressed over reports of the condition of the wall. He was a cupbearer to King Artaxes. The king asked why his countenance was fallen. He told the king that his city lay in ruin and he wanted to go and rebuild it. The king asked him what he needed. He told the king he needed a letter written to the governors so he could pass through their land and a letter to Asaph keeper of the king's forests for lumber.

"The wall was for blessing and protection. The blessing was the use of the temple inside and receiving God's Word. The protection was from the rulers surrounding Jerusalem. Sanballet and Tobias were attempting to ridicule and threaten the builders to demoralize them. Nehemiah received blessings from the king. The workers held a trowel in one hand and a sword in the other. Eventually, the workers cried out that they were being taxed by the excessive usury or interest charged against them. Nehemiah put a stop to that. All the workers worked together as if they had one mind. The project was completed in fifty-two days.

"Nehemiah and the others had a vision and a purpose. They could focus and concentrate on the task. I believe God has gifted me and given me a calling in the field of law. I also believe He is calling me to a greater purpose. This may sound strange, but I feel like I am supposed to be a Watchman on the wall. I just don't know how that is supposed to work out in practical terms."

Victoria smiled and replied, "We're given a little revelation at a time. When we put into practice that which we've been given, we're shown more. I'm thankful He's showing you His will for your life."

Stewart showed up at the office at ten. McCabe asked, "Did you have a good weekend?"

Stewart reflectively answered, "Yes, it was good."

McCabe said, "We're in court in an hour. Come on in and get caught-up on our brief."

As they walked across the street to the courthouse, Stewart was fully conscious, yet somewhat distracted. He thought it was a mental sluggishness from being away from work and totally relaxing for almost a week. He also recognized all the different ideas that were fighting for resolution in his mind. As they crossed North

Monroe Street to the courthouse, he noticed the new courthouse in a different way. He looked up at the dome and thought about a secular temple attempting to channel justice to earth through human efforts and understanding.

As they were waiting in the galley for their hearing, Stewart was almost in a trance. He recalled another courthouse, where behind the judge's bench was a stained glass window portraying Lady Justice. He knew she was the Roman goddess of Justice. She was also the allegorical personification of Themis and Dike and Isis of Egypt. Stewart recalled his conversation with Michael, how the languages were scattered into roughly seventy different tongues at the Tower of Babylonia, yet most languages kept similar mythical and esoteric images and legends.

He remembered the old courthouse burning down a few years earlier. This was the second courthouse to burn in Williamsport. He wondered if the curse placed on the town by the Indians had worked. He looked at the judge's bench and remembered the dream about platforms. He looked at the defense and prosecution tables and thought of the scales of justice. The dome resembled the national capital and so many statehouse domes. Was this architecture an effort to channel justice to earth and appeal to heaven for wisdom?

Then he had another vision. He saw the natural stone altar Moses was directed to build. He remembered his dream ending with the porch as a platform. He could envision stones quickly plucked up to execute Stephen, no courts and no justice, just swift retribution. Stones that were used for stoning probably had the blood of the martyrs and the prophets on them from previous use. He also realized that God had sent meteors or fragments of stars to earth to stone the enemies of Israel as recorded in the Book of Joshua.

Richard's article about the race came out on Thursday afternoon. Daryl also printed a picture of Ray Harroun and his Marmon Wasp. Stewart read it in the evening:

WISHFUL THINKING AND BRAVADO ARE NO MATCH FOR EXPERIENCE AND INVENTION

The inaugural running of the Indianapolis 500 was held at Indianapolis Motor Speedway this past Memorial Day. By the end of the day, 6 hours and 42 minutes after the start, crowd favorite, Ray Harroun sailed his yellow Marmot "Wasp" across the finish line. His prize money was $14,250, plus $10,000 accessory money for first place. Second place earned $5,000; third place $3,000; on down to $500 through tenth place.

With an event drawing the interest of an estimated 100,000 spectators from all over the nation and the world; 40 drivers; 23 automobile or automobile accessory manufacturers; 4 track owners; and, untold political municipalities and principalities, controversy was inevitable. Ralph Mulford claimed to be the winner. The track owners entertained the controversy for a few days, changing the finishing order several times, but never taking Harroun out of first place. Carl Fisher finally declared the controversy was over and the finish posted by Wednesday evening would stand.

What were some of the other controversies? As this reporter observed and interviewed drivers, mechanics, car owners and track owners, some other concerns surfaced. Marmon built the "Wasp" specifically for the race. Other drivers drove modified family cars to the track and raced them. The Marmon was built like the fuselage of an airplane with a tail protruding out the back. They called this concept "aerodynamics."

Harroun also placed four small metal rods on his car that held a mirror. With his mirror, he did not need a ride along mechanic to watch behind his car. This greatly reduced the weight of the car, allowing it to go further and faster with less fuel. By using the velocimeter (of which all drivers had access), he calculated the speed that would save his tires the greatest amount of wear, thus reducing "pit stops." For the race, the car engines were restricted to 600 cubic inches of displacement. Most of the cars used a 4 cylinder arrangement. Harroun's Marmon "Wasp" used 6 cylinders.

By pushing men and machines to their limits, new advances in industry and invention will develop, thus saving lives and resources. This reporter believes the car is here to stay. We have to learn to live with it. Sure there will be controversies with any new and great event. I hope the race is continued in future years. Finally, let drivers, car owners and fans who disagree with "manufactured" race cars competing with "stock" passenger cars, hold separate speed events or endurance challenges in the future.

That night Stewart dreamed about bricks, blocks or stones that were cast by a manufacturing process, cut stones that were hewn in a quarry and natural stones that were collected from the field to be used for buildings and fences. When he awoke, he had no recollection of this dream, although he still remembered the platform dream from the previous night.

Marmot Victory

Chapter Twenty-Seven

A PROPHECY
AND A PRAYER

Before Stewart left for work on Friday, Victoria reminded him, "Don't forget we have the tent meeting tonight at the fairgrounds. I'm really excited that Richard was able to get the churches together to sponsor Brother Seymour's visit before he heads back to Los Angeles. I know he's on the cutting edge of a revival. Just getting the local churches to work together on a project was a miracle. Please be home in time to get ready, so we can get there by seven."

Stewart said, "I believe in God, but do you really believe in all that stuff?"

Victoria responded, "Well Ephesians says, 'Jesus gave to the church apostles, prophets, evangelists, pastors, and teachers, to equip His people for the work of service and to build up the church.' Why should we believe He gave us evangelists, pastors and teachers, but eliminated apostles and prophets? Joel told of sons and daughters prophesying in the end times. Do you think we have ever been closer to the end times?"

At the meeting, they sang Amazing Grace. Stewart was reminded of the time five years earlier when he first attended the church in Wellspring. They also sang *All Hail the Power of Jesus' Name.* Pastor Richard stood up and offered a prayer for the meeting. Then, before he introduced William Seymour, he said, "It is not often that the local churches get together and agree on a project. It is also rare to have a guest speaker who is on the cutting edge of a great revival. I truly believe the Pentecostal Revival is about to sweep across the United States just as it did in Wales a few years ago.

"If we are willing to allow God to challenge our thinking and our beliefs, we will be part of the revival and part of the solution. If we think we already have what we need and do not need to listen and grow, we will be bypassed. Remember the new wine and the woven threads. They represent the Holy Spirit. Do not attempt to fit the Holy Spirit to your belief system. Let your faith change and grow with the revelation of the Holy Spirit.

"Second Chronicles seven and fourteen says, 'If My people who are called by my name shall humble themselves, and pray and seek my face, and turn from their wicked ways; them and I will hear from heaven and will forgive their sin, and will heal their land.' Ladies and gentlemen, Brother William Seymour."

Brother Seymour stood up. "Thank you for your kind words. I covet only your prayers. There is trouble at the mission. Whenever God moves, the enemy makes a counter move. As the Holy Spirit is poured out on Azusa Street, Los Angeles and the nation, there is trouble. Man attempts to control the Spirit and dish-out the blessing through prescribed and controllable programs, doing things the way they always have, staying within their level of comfort.

"When Jesus was transfigured on the high mountain, Moses and Elijah appeared. Peter, who always offered an answer, even when a question was not asked, offered to build a tent for each of the three. God spoke from heaven and told the disciples to listen to His Son. From fear, the disciples dropped to the ground. Jesus touched them and restored them. That is what we need to do – fear God, listen to the Son, fall on our faces, if necessary, and let Jesus restore and direct us. We do not need to build new buildings and create new programs. We do not need to build new tents in which God will dwell. We are the tabernacle. Let us empty ourselves so He may fill us and empower us.

"I will have to cut my visit short and head back after this meeting. We need your prayers for the Mission, for the nation and for revival in general. I usually don't preach this way. Most of the time, during our meetings, I just sit and pray and get out of the way and let the Holy Ghost work.

"Stephen gave a prophetic account in the seventh chapter of Acts. He was addressing the Sanhedrin, the religious leaders of the day. The account was inspired, as he was not an educated man. He relayed some Biblical history of the promise and the faith of Abraham. He proclaimed the account through the prophets and ended by stating the Jewish leaders had killed the prophets and Jesus. His message brought such conviction of the Holy Ghost; they drug him out then and there to stone him. I have a similar message, yet I hope the results are not the same. I pray for God's conviction to fall on you. I hope you feel no compulsion to drag me out and stone me."

The crowd chuckled at the comment. Stewart glanced at Victoria, who was already looking, hopefully, in his direction. Brother Seymour continued:

> Daniel of old was given the gift of knowledge and wisdom. He might have even taught the Magi the secrets of finding the Messiah through the science of astronomy. He knew the difference between astronomy and astrology. God gave his people the stars for signs and seasons. Astrology and sorcery were used since Nimrod and Egypt in forecasting the fate of nations and individuals through witchcraft. Those nations sacrificed their children to their false gods made visible to them only through demonic manifestations and idols made with human hands.

> Nimrod used bricks to build the tower, a portal to channel spirits between heaven and earth. God confused their language and scattered the builders. The Egyptians

enslaved the Jews and built tombs and crypts for the secret sciences, divinations and witchcraft. Moses, through faith, demonstrated God's power to handle the serpent and part the Red Sea for the deliverance of the people. He struck the rock in the dessert and produced water for the preservation of the people. Moses was told to build an altar of uncut stones to worship. He carried a tablet that he had cut for the law to be written upon by the hand of God.

The Jewish people were blessed by the true God of Abraham, Isaac and Jacob, even though they have been persecuted by the other nations since the beginning of time. Jacob was traveling from Bethel to Haran. He laid his head upon a stone and had a dream. He saw a ladder reaching heaven with angels ascending and descending into and out of heaven. He built a stone monument to God, not to himself or man.

The nations that have blessed the Israeli people have been blessed. The nations that have persecuted them have been reduced from their great and glorious stature. When an invading army attempted to destroy the nation and retreat, they were hit by hailstones from heaven. When the remnant of Israel was threatened with extinction in Persia, Esther and Mordecai were miraculously put into place to preserve them. God even removed Queen Vashti to do so.

Solomon built the temple and the walls for blessing and protection. His kingdom, however, was based upon slavery and usury. He married women of many nations and religions, against God's direct warning. He also turned to other gods. He built a temple to Moloch in which they sacrificed children upon the altar. The nation was torn by civil war. The temple of God was destroyed and the Israelites were carried off into captivity by the Assyrians and Babylonians. Nehemiah rebuilt the wall and the temple for blessing and protection. The builders carried a trowel and a sword.

Daniel interpreted the dreams of his ruler. He saw a mighty statue that represented the kingdoms of the world. The statue was top-heavy as the denser and more precious material of gold was at the top. The statue narrowed toward the base as the materials became less dense and less valuable, yet stronger. The strength of the iron in the base was reduced as the iron was mixed with clay. The iron could represent the faith in God mixed with the clay - pagan religions and the traditions of man. Daniel also prophesied a knowledge explosion toward the end of times.

In Daniel's vision, he saw a stone taken from the mountain, but not with human hands. The stone was cast at the feet of the great statue, representing the kingdoms of the world. The stone became a mighty mountain, taking over the entire world. The stone became the cornerstone which the builders rejected.

The builders were the religious leaders, the rulers of the nations and those who ruled in secret societies and called themselves the "Builders." In man's perception, the significance of the temple became more important than the One worshipped in the temple. The builders later worshipped the secrets of their craft and the secrets of the temple.

There was no need for a temple or a portal to heaven. Jesus told Nathaniel that through Him, they would see angels ascending and descending into and out of heaven. Jesus also said, "Do you see this temple, I will tear it down and rebuild it in three days. He was talking about His resurrection, upon which the church was built. He said, "If you fall upon this stone, you will be broken. If this stone falls upon you, you will be crushed."

He stopped and pointed at Stewart in the fourth row. "Would you come up here, please?"

Stewart wanted to crawl under the seats. He could feel himself blushing and even feeling anger to be embarrassed and called upon. Seymour said, "You do want to receive a prophet's reward?"

Stewart shuffled around the feet of the people who were crammed into the tent with chairs arranged too close together. He finally reached the end of the aisle and made his way to the platform. Brother Seymour placed his hand on Stewart's head. Stewart closed his eyes and bowed his head. Mr. Seymour said:

If you fall upon Him, you will be broken through repentance. He will restore you and place you in the church for blessing and protection. He will guide you into a ministry and offer you a platform. You will be a voice to the nations, calling for repentance, pulling down strongholds, exposing darkness and restoring the breech in the wall.

You will be a watchman upon the wall for warning and deliverance.

The nations you warn, especially your own, which was built upon slavery and usury, sacrifices its unborn children, worships idols and seeks entertainment over wisdom will repent. It will turn back to the Lord and honor the God of Abraham, Isaac and Jacob. It will be broken, but not beyond remedy and return. If this nation does not honor the Lord, but remains proud and the Chief Cornerstone will fall upon it where it will be broken beyond repair.

Stewart stood on the altar visibly crying, unable to speak. Victoria got out of her seat and ran up to join him. She said, "Now, what do you think?"

Stewart just stood there crying and shaking his head, while Victoria hugged him in a sustained, loving and comforting embrace. As they proceeded home, he was speechless. Victoria only smiled.

The next morning Stewart had his meeting with Pastor Richard and Michael. He told them of the previous despondency, countered by the prophecy. He said, "I believe the timing of this meeting and the prophecy of last night are no coincidence."

Michael said, "Coincidence is God doing something great and choosing to remain anonymous. Have you ever heard preaching like that?"

Pastor Richard said, "I believe that was pure prophecy."

Stewart told them about the dream from the track. He also mentioned his discussion with Michael, years earlier, about the nation's capital. He read the passages from Pike and Madame Blavatsky and New Age theosophy. Richard said, "I've heard of some of these things. I had no idea how direct they were. That's probably why they're secretive. I believe bringing this stuff out in the open is part of Daniel's prophecy about the 'Increase in knowledge in the end times.' "

Stewart agreed, "It was only by chance that I came across these books. What am I supposed to do with this discovery?"

Richard said, "I don't claim to be able to interpret dreams, but I believe your dream was revelatory. Most people, like the spectators at the track, want to consider themselves as 'good.' They're happy to watch the drivers and race teams perform. They cheer and maybe protest something they believe to be an unjust ruling, an unfair decision or cheating for advantage by one of the racers or race teams. The track owners determine what will make them the most profit. They make the rules and determine the outcomes in an effort to provide entertainment."

Michael added, "Just like the political process, people cast their vote and leave the remainder of the practice to the politicians. They think voting is the extent of civic duty and patriotism."

Stewart said, "Judge Manley Hall told me his lodge did several benevolent and philanthropic acts for people. I've heard other people say the secret societies couldn't be in league with the devil as they do charitable things."

Richard said, "Since creation, people have had an innate desire to draw close to God. The first lie was the deception that we could eat from the tree of knowledge of good and evil and not die. Lucifer told Adam and Eve, '...You will not die, but will be like God...' Accepting that lie and acting upon it brought sin and death into the world and caused the fallen nature of mankind.

"People want to belong and feel like they are part of something. It partially satisfies the God-given desire for fellowship with Him and others. Do you think people would willingly follow the Deceiver if he came out with his agenda and demonstrated how evil he was until they were completely and hopelessly hooked into his domain? People are in such deception that they justify the evil in which they engage by saying the ends justify the means."

Stewart said, "So people can knowingly and willingly serve the devil or they can do it tacitly and passively, even apathetically?

Richard affirmed, "Jesus said, 'He that is not with Me is against Me; and he that gathers not with Me scatters.'"

Stewart said, "There are deacons, priests, pastors and men and women of God who have allowed themselves to be bound up in the seductive lies of the 'Angel of Light."

Michael interjected, "Where does the fine line between decent and wicked vanish in the foggy mist where iniquity masquerades itself as virtue? Behind which veil of perception does clarity end and deception and illusion begin?"

Richard smiled and said, "Well said."

Michael replied, "Thank you. That's something I've been working on in my writing."

Richard affirmed, "Again, Jesus said, "You cannot serve two masters. You will end up loving the one and hating the other.""

Stewart asked, "What about the oaths of secrecy and swearing by the temple of Solomon, and the curses for violating the secrecy?"

Richard said, "Jesus told us not to swear by the temple or the gold in the temple. It seems the builders of the temple are more interested in the physical structure than the Lord of the temple. James, in chapter five and verse twelve of his book, said, 'But above all things, my brethren, swear not, neither by the heaven, nor by the earth, nor with any other oath: but your yea be yea, and your nay be nay, that you fall not under judgment."

Michael said, "Matthew says, 'Let your yes be yes and your no be no. Anything more is of the devil.'"

Stewart affirmed, "So, if we are not sure, any organization that makes us swear to secrecy and binds it by a curse is of the devil?"

Richard acknowledged, "Yes."

Stewart asked, "So, what now?"

Richard said, "Jesus taught about casting out unclean spirits and demons. He said, "The unclean spirit when it goes out of a man passes through waterless places, seeking rest and finding none determines to return to the home or person it left and finding it clean and well swept resolves to bring back seven other spirits more evil than itself.

"So we have to denounce any involvement you may have had or any attachment you might have experienced through your dealings with Judge Manly Hall or any attachment that may have possessed any of your ancestors or attached itself to any artifact or idol you have wittingly or unwittingly, knowingly or unknowingly brought into your house or upon yourself. If you had willingly taken any of the oaths, there would be a more specific prayer with which to beseech the Lord.

Richard said, "We need to pray that you have received no demonic spiritual attachment and to be delivered from any that might have been attracted to you. We both have to make sure we let other people know of the motives of secret organizations. Even though people crusade for a political point or wrestle and joust for political remedies to world problems, the only answer is to request of the Lord, 'Thy kingdom come, Thy will be done.'"

They had already been in the meeting for almost two hours. Stewart offered Michael and Pastor Richard coffee. As he brought the coffee into the room, he said, "I almost forgot. I had two different dreams on two consecutive nights this week. Do you want to hear them?"

Michael and Richard both said, simultaneously, "Sure!

Stewart relayed the content of the dreams as accurately as he could. Afterward and, with a little more discussion, Richard said, "Repeat after me:

"I denounce any involvement or attachment to any secret societies that involve greed and witchcraft, intended to manipulate, deceive or dominate humanity and my family. I denounce oaths and curses, idolatry, Great Architect of the Universe, New Age Religion, Illuminati, gods and goddesses of Egypt, Baal, Nimrod, mysticism, Gnosticism, occultism, sun worship that attempts to reach God through human effort, the illusion of enlightenment or the god of 'Reason.'

"I ask for deliverance in the name and blood of Jesus and the power of the Holy Spirit, from any spiritual oppression, possession or demonic attachment, unclean spirit, any diminution of the power and claims, mockery or blasphemy of the Name of Jesus, the Father or the Holy Spirit. I denounce any doctrine of Lucifer and proclaim deliverance from any claims of such doctrine against ourselves or our families, whether unwittingly or known activities.

"I accept and serve the Lord, Father God, Jesus Christ, His Son and Savior and the Holy Spirit. I am a servant offering my life to proclaim the mercies and grace of salvation, which requires no secret initiations or curses. I offer my life as a living and dying sacrifice to expose the deception of the devil and educate and inform the world to resist all of the deceiver's efforts to establish a New World Order, a One World Religion, a One World Government and the Mark of the Beast."

The men ended the meeting and agreed to not let things get so far out of hand before meeting again. As history and experiences have demonstrated, life has been famine or feast. Stewart felt most of the pieces of the puzzle were in place. The change did not occur in a day or overnight, but as he looked back, he could see the progress and growth. Stewart made his main goal to discover God's will for his life and reach his full potential through God's inspiration and empowerment.

He sought balance and focus. He attempted to refrain from compulsive activities and to appreciate and watch his young family grow. He focused on his profession of law and attempted to be regular with moderate exercise and reading. He knew he would have to begin writing, either to chronicle his own progress or to develop thoughts as the planks in his personal platform.

He even fasted a day or two a week, most of the day or part. He knew fasting was not to bargain with God to gain his requests. It was to align himself with God's will and discover direction. He read Isaiah fifty-eight, "Is not the fast I have chosen: to loose the bonds of wickedness, to undo the bands of the yoke, to let the oppressed go free and that ye break every yoke? Is it not to deal thy bread with the hungry and bring the homeless and poor into your house; when you see the naked, to cover him, and not to hide yourself from your own flesh?"

Several days later, Stewart was called early in the morning. McCabe had died of a heart attack. Stewart and Victoria were shocked, as McCabe seemed so healthy just that week. The funeral was scheduled and William Jennings Bryant delivered McCabe's eulogy. Bryant was one of the most famous politicians of the era. He had been candidate for president three times.

Cynthia married a young man. Victoria and Stewart helped her adopt two children. Victoria, Stewart, Whitney and Michael also used their time and other resources, coupled with Stewart's legal attainments to assist other couples in adopting children. They also supported the New York Foundling Society with finances, letter writing and placing children from the orphan trains.

Before the year ended, a monument was dedicated at Battleground. Richard and Daryl attended the ceremony on November eleventh, one hundred years after the battle. Former Governor Hanly also attended. Richard handed him a copy of his editorial, "Perfectly Legal" from the eugenics law of previous years.

One year later, Richard and Michael were listening to the Ham radio late one night when they heard an S.O.S from the north Atlantic. Apparently, the Titanic, the unsinkable ship hit an ice berg. It was eerie listening to the desperate signals and for them to go silent at about two twenty-five, Greenwich Mean Time.

Later, Richard and Stewart learned that John Jacob Astor the Fourth was onboard the Titanic and did not survive. He and Michael discussed how even the mighty were not immune to disaster. Michael also remembered the conversations about John Jacob Astor I, and his attainment of wealth, and conspiracy theories regarding Astor's connections to Jefferson. Stewart said, "I read a book, *Futility, or the Wreck of the Titan.* The similarities were eerie. Both ships had only enough lifeboats to satisfy the law yet were inadequate. I have since had a dream in which the ship hit the ice berg and two politicians were arguing over lifeboat placement."

Everybody was so busy, that another year passed. One other development occurred that reaffirmed the need for America to beware of shadow government. Richard's latest editorial:

THE FEDERAL RESERVE ACT PASSES UNDER QUESTIONABLE CIRCUMSTANCES

On December 23rd, 1913, Congress passed the Federal Reserve Act under questionable and nefarious circumstances. Not many articles were published other than simple announcements. One observer had a different view as he was able to connect the dots. This editor has stated before and will state again the words of Thomas Jefferson regarding the press. He said, "If I had to choose between government without newspapers, and newspapers without government, I wouldn't hesitate to choose the latter."

Jefferson said about banks: "If the American people ever allow the banks to control the issuance of their currency, first by inflation and then by deflation, the banks and corporations that grow up around them will deprive the people of all property until their children will wake up homeless on the continent their father occupied. The issuing power of money should be taken from the banks and restored to Congress and the people to whom it belongs. I sincerely believe the banking institutions are more dangerous to liberty than standing armies."

The bill was slipped through Congress on December twenty-third, when most Representatives were home for Christmas. Those voting for the law had little knowledge of the content. It went through committee without Republicans being asked to attend. The law legalizes counterfeiting for the banks in the printing of money. It is also an example of the wolf guarding the sheep or the inmates running the asylum, as the law gives bankers the right to regulate their own industry.

Representative, Charles Lindbergh, with whom this editor corresponds regularly, said, "This Federal Reserve Act establishes the most gigantic trust on earth. When the President signs this bill, the invisible government of the monetary power will be legalized...the worst legislative crime of the ages perpetuated by this banking and currency bill."

He also said, "A radical is one who speaks the truth."

Finally, He said, "The new law will create inflation whenever the trusts want inflation. From now on depressions will be scientifically created."

As we look at and learn from history, J.P. Morgan was probably responsible for creating the bank panic of 1907. This was in preparation to soften the Representatives of the United States to accept this banking trust by the bankers. It also allowed the citizens of the United States to be in bondage to usury and monitory enslavement.

Chapter Twenty-Eight

HOOSIER FLYING SQUADRONS

Another development of national significance also began in Indiana. J. Frank Hanly, former Indiana governor from Williamsport was writing letters. From his home in Lafayette, he wrote to some close personal political, educators and church friends and associates. He was testing the waters to determine if these people were interested in building a coalition. The coalition was to abolish the manufacture, sale and consumption of alcohol through an amendment to the Constitution of the United States of America. Hanly was attacking the liquor issue and comparing it to the abolition of slavery.

Hanly had been successful in passing a local options form of prohibition while governor in Indiana. The law allowed counties in Indiana to determine if they were to be "dry" or "wet." Hanly was proud that eighty-eight out of ninety-six counties chose to go dry or prohibit the sale of alcohol. He looked at the state map and determined that rural counties were more moral since the counties that allowed the production, sales and consumption of alcohol were the larger urban centers.

Apparently, by nineteen fourteen, he figured he had enough interest in the project, as he called a meeting to be held at the Neal House in Columbus, Ohio. In a speech he later recounted the efforts to organize:

> More than a year ago, a year ago last November, I called as many of these men and women as I could reach,-these (sic) men and women whom you have heard here these past three days,-to meet in an upper room, a room which had been once occupied by Lincoln, and there we knelt around a common altar! "What," you say, an altar in an upper room in a hotel?" Yes, my brother, please God, an altar anywhere where a contrite soul bows in supplication to the Father.

> And there in that upper room we dreamed and planned this great campaign, covering every State in the Union, stretching over a period of nearly nine months, requiring the service of more than twenty people, and costing in round numbers more than two hundred thousand dollars. That was the thing we dreamed; and we knew what it meant. We knew some of us would put health upon its altar-and mayhap life itself.

From that meeting, they put together a group of lecturers and scheduled a lecture series to visit two hundred and fifty-five cities, including every state capital and large city. Their message was simple. They published a motto: "We stand for the abolition of the liquor traffic. On this issue we fight."

They expanded their motto into a sort of mission statement which read, "Whenever a politician or an executive officer, or a political party prefers the liquor traffic above the public morals, such men must be set aside and such parties abandoned. To the accomplishment of this high purpose we dedicate ourselves."

They called themselves "The Flying Squadron." The coalition was made up of men and women who had been church leaders, educators and politicians who were concerned about the evil of liquor. They made a schedule and sent two groups out, each group holding three evening meetings in each major city. Their campaign began in Peoria, Illinois on Wednesday, September thirtieth, nineteen hundred and fourteen. It ended in Atlantic City, New Jersey, on Sunday, June sixth, Nineteen hundred and fifteen.

Daryl worked the farm part time and continued to work for the newspaper. It seemed neither interest was enough to challenge him sufficiently. When Michael bought a nineteen and ten Ford, he sold his used machine to Daryl for three hundred dollars on a payment plan. Daryl was able to save one hundred dollars for a down payment and then pay ten dollars a month for twenty-four months. He had his own room in town and always managed to work hard enough to make the car payment, pay rent, and buy food and clothing.

Daryl was unable to focus on anything too long. The newness of the photography and writing articles had worn off. Farming was always regular and he enjoyed working with Michael and sometimes Stewart on weekends. He even went to the English Lake farm when Sven was shorthanded. At the English Lake farm, he found fewer distractions and was, therefore able to work longer hours. He never stayed more than two weeks. He enjoyed driving his Tin Lizzy back and forth in warm weather.

With a car, money and time, Daryl was able to expand his horizons. He found he could get all the alcohol he wanted in Illinois. After all, the back of the farm was the Illinois line. He could go to Hoopeston or Rossville. He knew every back road. He could even get across on farm lanes, if necessary. Once he found a source, he contacted a couple of establishments around the area that would be interested in "providing additional services and comforts" to their patrons.

Daryl figured it was a victimless crime. He was just saving people who could go get their own alcohol the effort and the time. He also figured that anytime someone legislated morality, they created a market by restricting the supply, thereby increasing the value of the commodity.

Besides, if he hauled enough "product" it made his time worthwhile. Another thought that Daryl justified was that he could stand on the back of the farm. The fence was still partially up and partially rusted and rotted out. You could see where the Illinois farmer plowed and planted, leaving a grassy hedgerow between the farms.

There was no distinct line that differentiated Illinois from Indiana. There was only a grassy, weedy hedgerow with no defined edges. If he stepped west two feet, he could legally have a drink. If he stepped back east, he could be arrested for even possessing alcohol.

As he continued his practice, he obtained more boldness as those who practice misdeeds, felonies, misdemeanors and malfeasances often do when they go undetected. He expanded his territory and spent more and more time building his own personal business.

One Friday, he showed up at the farm at eight-thirty A.M. Michael came out to meet him. Daryl handed him the balance of the amount he owed on the Tin Lizzy. Michael said, "The paper must be paying you pretty well. We thought you wouldn't be able to pay the car off for over a year."

Daryl agreed, "Yeah, I've been managing my money pretty well."

Michael said, "That seems strange. I've been noticing fewer articles in the *Watchmen*."

Daryl said, "That's something I need to discuss with you. I need more time to work the other jobs...the other job. I have been doing a lot of other tasks at the paper. I need more time available to cover photos and stories."

Michael agreed, "I'll work with you. We'll give you whatever you can handle."

Daryl thanked him and drove off. He felt guilty, as he knew he had not been honest with Michael. Somehow, the more Michael trusted him, the more guilt he felt. The next day a train wreck occurred over the Wabash between Williamsport and Attica. Daryl was sent out to cover the story and photograph it.

Apparently, a portion of the bridge collapsed, throwing the locomotive and a combination baggage and passenger car into the Wabash. While Daryl was photographing the wreckage, Richard was collecting the facts of the incident. They learned that three people had been killed and several passengers were injured and taken by special train to Lafayette's Saint Elizabeth.

As Daryl was wrapping up, he found Richard talking to Sherriff Anderson, who said, "Daryl, I haven't seen you in a while. You must be doing a lot of farming, driving a nice Tin Lizzy like that.

I've noticed you haven't been publishing as many photographs and stories as you were for a while. Farming must pay well."

Daryl agreed, "Yeah, it's paying well."

Richard asked one more question, "Will there be any jurisdictional problems?"

Sheriff Anderson looking puzzled asked, "What do you mean?"

Richard explained, "Well, you have an accident in Warren County and in Fountain County. Where is the imaginary line between jurisdictions for the coroners?"

Sheriff Anderson smiled and said, "Oh, I see where you're going. Maybe in a big city like the line between Chicago, Illinois and East Chicago, Indiana, there would be problems. Here, we don't split hairs. We just do our jobs and cooperate. Besides, most of the investigation is handled by the Interstate Commerce Commission."

Richard smiled and said, "Just curious."

Sheriff Anderson returned the smile and added, "That's your job."

Although Sheriff Anderson acted very congenial, Daryl felt as if he knew more than he was saying. As Daryl and Richard made their way back to his car, he looked back and saw Sheriff Anderson watching them, with a perplexed look on his face. Daryl felt uneasy, the way he would have felt if he had disappointed his father in some way.

Richard posted his article, dated Tuesday April eighth:

TRAIN WRECK ON WABASH BRIDGE—3 KILLED

This past Saturday, April 5, 1914, the eastbound Wabash Limited, a passenger train traveling across the bridge from Williamsport plunged into the Wabash, killing 3 railroad employees. The three killed, all Indiana men, were: fireman, J.L. Miller of Peru, who was scalded by the blast of the boiler as it hit the cool water of the Wabash River; engineer Timothy P. Hull, Peru, was crushed to death beneath the train; and, express man Harry Thomas, of Huntington, crushed by trunks. About 40 passengers were injured and taken to St. Elizabeth's in Lafayette by special train.

The derailing was the second incident of the day on the bridge. A few hours earlier, the Continental Limited, a freight train, #69, with locomotive #2456, consisting of 49 cars and a caboose, was heading west from Attica to Williamsport. The train eventually traveling to Logansport, encountered difficulties crossing the bridge. The engineer of the Continental Limited noticed the last car of the freight train had derailed on the bridge, dragging the car across the bridge into Warren County. The car was cleared and pushed over onto the river bank. The Continental Limited backed across the bridge to the telegraph office in Attica and notified the Wabash Limited, train #4 to hold in Williamsport.

The bridge was inspected and a switching engine slowly made its way across the bridge. During the inspection, it was noted that a knee joint had been damaged and 17 ties supporting the cross span of the bridge had been dug up by the damaged freight car. Upon successfully crossing in the switching car, the Wabash Limited was instructed to cross slowly. The train left Williamsport at 1:49 P.M.

The accident occurred at 1:58, according to the engineer's watch. As the engine almost reached the Fountain County side, the last section of the bridge collapsed, hurling the engine and the combination baggage car and day coach into the water. The day coach was crowded and one end fell into the river while the other end hung up on the bridge support. The injured passengers were rescued from the day coach with no loss of passenger lives.

As freight gets heavier and people travel further and faster, we will need to insure that safety standards and methods of inspection keep up with manufacturing and invention. The accident occurred in two counties, but the injured and the families of the dead do not care whether they plunged into the Wabash in Fountain County or were brought to safety in Warren County. The workers and passengers only expected a normal travel day and to reach their destinations safely. One can only imagine the terror of helplessly plunging to your death or being injured in a metal tube on rails.

As Stewart read the article, he wondered how the legal profession would be affected by the advent of high speed transportation and other improvements in inventions and industry. Daryl was experiencing a haunting feeling after seeing the wreckage and the bodies being pulled out of the water. He continued his personal enterprises. One factor he had not included in his calculations was the competition. His initial thoughts were simple; buy the "product" and drive it to the customer to receive a profit. It did not occur to him that others enjoying a profit from an illicit activity might not want to share the rewards.

As he was pulling into the dark alley behind one of his customer's establishments, he gasped and slammed the brake as a person stepped out into the alley right in front of him. He could see in his headlights that it was Jackson Hunter. Daryl yelled, as his engine died, "A man could get run over doing a stupid thing like that."

Hunter calmly retorted, "A man could get killed taking somebody else's business."

Daryl said, "It's a free country. I can conduct business as I see fit."

Jackson said, "You might have legal rights and all that under the law. Remember, you're not operating under the law."

Daryl said, "I thought you were in prison."

Jackson said, "Yeah thanks to you I was in prison. I got out after two years of my sentence on good behavior. Let's let bygones be bygones. We've had our trouble in the past. Why don't we find a way that we can be of benefit to each other? You know kind of a division of labor."

Daryl could not see who or if anybody else was concealed in the shadows, and if so whom it might be. He knew that Hunter would not likely confront him so directly unless he had some backup strategically placed. He asked, "What's on your mind?"

Hunter said, "Oh, I was thinking seventy five, twenty five. Seventy five percent of the profits go to me and twenty five percent for you."

Daryl said, "Let me think about it."

Jackson answered, "Don't disappoint me."

After Jackson left, Daryl watched him in his rearview mirror. He could see that another man joined him at the entrance of the alley and they disappeared into the night. He started shaking, partially from the sudden fright he was able to suppress until this moment and partially from the rage he felt from the veiled threats. He knew he could not trust Jackson Hunter to be honorable about the trade. He also knew that Jackson would probably do something more underhanded than another direct confrontation.

The next day Daryl saw Jackson in the street as he was heading out for breakfast on his way to the paper. "Have you thought about my, uhm..., offer?"

Daryl said, "Oh yes, I've thought about it."

That night Daryl realized that Jackson Hunter had probably been watching him for some time and had figured his schedule. Customers wanted their deliveries on schedule so they could make accommodations to receive and store the product. Daryl decided he would deliver the product he had and get out of the business. It was not worth getting his head busted or going to jail. He had saved enough money to get by and he had two jobs for which he was grateful. Besides, somewhere along the way he had begun to grow a conscience.

As soon as he stopped his car and began to lift the carton out of the back seat, he heard a gun hammer click into locked position. A flashlight beamed and a voice said, "Set the box down and slowly raise your hands. It was Town Marshal, Alfred Graves.

Officer Graves cuffed Daryl and took him to the jailhouse. The next morning, Stewart received a message to appear for an arraignment hearing. At the hearing, Judge Raub said, "Bail is denied. Dailey is considered a flight risk. He has business dealings with Illinois, only twenty miles from here. It would be too easy for him to slip over the line and establish a new life of crime over there. By the time we would waste the judicial system's time and money to arrange extradition, he would be gone."

"John J. Hall, Prosecuting Attorney said, "Since this is Mr. Dailey's first offense, in which he has been caught…"

Stewart said, "I object! My client has no prior convictions."

Judge Raub answered, "Sustained. Would prosecution stick to facts and not make inferences and innuendoes?

Mr. Hall replied, "Your honor, we have a conditional plea we would like to offer."

Judge Raub said, "Please approach."

Hall said, "We have knowledge of a special group that has formed to defend our nation. It is called the First Aero Squadron. They are engaged in Texas and other parts of the Southwest. A member of that prestigious group resides right here in Warren County. Vernon Berg, from West Lebanon contacted me just this week asking if I knew a photographer and journalist to publicize the activities of the First Aero Squadron. I told him I did not know of any, but would keep my eyes and ears open. Coincidentally, Mr. Dailey possesses the specific talents and experience sought by the Squadron."

Stewart replied, "Let me consult with my client."

Daryl, able to overhear the conversation, stood and shouted, "I'll do it."

Judge Raub slammed the gavel. "Mr. Taylor, please control your client. I will tolerate no more outbursts."

Stewart talked privately to Daryl, "Take a few days to consider."

Daryl objected, "What, in jail? No thank you. I'm ready for a change!"

Stewart said, "Your honor, my client accepts your kind offer."

Judge Raub said, "Alright. Mr. Daily will be held in Warren County Jail until he is released into the custody of Mr. Berg to accompany him back to Texas. He will serve for two years as a journalist in the United States Army, at which time he may be released or choose to serve at his pleasure. He will be required to enlist and be subject to Federal and military jurisdiction for any infractions, desertion or legal offenses in that two year period."

Pastor Richard visited Daryl in jail and reminded him that he could be forgiven for any offence and to keep his spiritual desires alive. He gave Daryl a Bible and prayed with him. Editor-In-Chief Richard also visited him. He said, "I'll be sad to see you go. You've been like a grandson to me. I guess I'll slow down and just do some writing. We'll have to get someone from Attica to do our photography."

Daryl promised, "I'll send exclusives to you, stuff I don't even send to the Wires. That should create some local interest."

Richard replied, "Thanks, son. Keep your powder dry and your head down. Don't volunteer for anything. Stay safe and come back to us in one piece."

Daryl assured him he would. He shipped out for Texas ten days later with Vernon Berg.

As the war was beginning in Europe, the communications industry was taken over by the United States government. Amateur radio operation is America was virtually outlawed. Editor-in-Chief, Richard and Michael were told at the hardware store they could purchase no more vacuum tubes of other electrical devices associated with Ham radio. On the way out of the hardware stores, Richard was heard mumbling beneath his breath, "Well, we will just have to hope our equipment holds out!"

Chapter Twenty-Nine

WARS AND RUMORS OF WARS

After about thirty hours of travel they finally crossed the Texas border at Texarkana. Daryl thought they would be close to the base. He failed to realize Galveston Bay and Texas City were about another third of the total distance away. After spending ten days in jail and almost two days traveling, he was ready to get started with his new assignment. He missed the farm, the paper and Williamsport. Mostly, he missed the Editor-in-Chief, Pastor Richard, Michael and Stewart. He recalled the trip to Speedway to see the Air Display five years earlier and the race two years later. As always, though, he was ready for new adventure.

Daryl remembered how Pastor Richard knew so much about the Bible and Biblical events as it related to world history and prophecy. He not only knew the history, but could connect the significance for the listener or reader to be fascinated by the topics and see the implications of the intricate details he related.

Michael read and understood his Bible and was willing and able to relate the Bible to human nature and more recent world history. Stewart was a family man with a strong legal mind. Daryl smiled as he remembered how, after reintroduction to him in Wellspring; he thought Stewart might be some kind of a conspiracy nut. Now he began to realize as he experienced more of life and the real world, Stewart's theories were making more sense. Daryl was also grateful for Stewart's legal counsel in the occasions where he got himself into scrapes and relied on Stewart to "bargain" with the authorities for his "freedoms." The bargains always included some type of fair service and provided growth opportunities.

Then, there was the Editor-in-Chief. The day they met on the banks of the Wabash, Richard had already sized him up and determined his character. Richard had one question. The answer would determine if he would give Daryl an assignment and a potential job as a photographer, "Can you take pictures with that Kodak or do you just point and shoot it?"

Richard educated and indoctrinated Daryl every day on the microcosm and macrocosm of the newspaper. He said, "We live in the microcosm. We can be in the middle of a major event and not realize the significance. You might be a soldier, caught up in a war and so preoccupied with survival that you never consider the motives of the leaders and politicians, backed by the globalists and industrialists, or if you were manipulated into being there. You do not see the big picture from the trenches"

He never really appreciated how sophisticated Richard was for a small town editor. Richard told Daryl on a daily basis, "You are not creating the news. You are not discovering some new science or establishing new facts. You are connecting the dots. The dots are out there and people see them. They just fail to realize how interconnected they are and how events cause reactions in other occurrences like a string of dominoes."

Funny, he considered how he failed to realize how immensely these friends affected him when he was with them every day. He missed them greatly. As Daryl thought, he had an epiphany. Was it a coincidence and chance that he and the other men had come into contact, each with a unique and complementary perspective? Or was the meeting of these men and their families Divine Providence? He remembered Pastor Richard saying, "We all see in part and we all know in part."

Oh, howbeit the parts they saw when they put their perspectives together! The Editor-in-Chief would always say, "Yeah, and if we're not closed-minded, we will learn from others, even those with whom we disagree - if we will only listen."

Daryl vowed that if he ever got back together with those four men, he would make the most of the combination of their perspectives and special talents. But, then, what did he contribute to the group? That is what he would dedicate himself to – finding his perspective. He would learn and attempt to understand everything the others had to offer. He would contribute his share, instead of just being an observer and a listener.

Here he was, maneuvering for a war. Europe was at war. There was no war for America. The Mexican Revolution had recently escalated. He thought about the editorial cartoons in the San Francisco Examiner, depicting a Mexican man complete with sombrero, torch, pistol and spurs running on a treadmill toward the setting sun with "Progress" printed on it. The title over the drawing read, "Revolution." The cartoon depicted how fruitless the pursuit of Progress was and how much energy was wasted in the process. It indicated how Mexico would willingly engage in violence as depicted by the pistol and anarchy, in the torch, yet they remained stagnant.

One cartoon from the *Chicago Tribune* entitled "Our Eyes Are on Them," showed a huge shadowy battleship turret with eyes in the ends of the artillery, looking over a primitive Mexico. Smoke was exhausting from mountains like volcanos with citizens trembling at the sight.

He remembered the conversation on the train when Michael, Stewart, Sven and he were talking about the Globalists and the Panama Canal. Unbeknownst to Daryl another conversation was developing among the men he admired so much. The men were enjoying a cook-out on Stewart's back porch in Williamsport. Richard said, "American Industrialists needed the Canal. Columbia was recalcitrant to go along with the project. The people of Panama wanted to secede from Columbia since eighteen thirty-one. An advisor told Roosevelt a revolt was needed in the Republic of Columbia. The revolt resulted in the Thousand Day's War between the Conservative Party and the Liberal Party.

"The war precipitated from claims of fraudulent elections against the Conservative Party. It was aggravated by the economic crisis brought on by falling coffee prices. The war lasted from eighteen eighty-nine until nineteen hundred and two."

Michael added, "When the first treaty negotiated between Panama and Columbia failed due to Columbia's refusal to ratify, Roosevelt dispatched the United States Navy to pressure and threatened a naval blockade on Columbia. The papers called Roosevelt's actions "Gunboat Diplomacy." The railroad, which claimed neutrality, yet favored Panama's claims was reluctant to ship goods to Columbia. The rebels seceded without much further opposition.

"By this time, the Panama Canal was nearing completion, although Columbia continued making claims to the rights and voicing grievances about the United States Intervention. The current Mexican Revolution was similar to the Panama situation. American industrialists held over one quarter of the Mexican land. They became nervous and asked William Howard Taft to intervene."

Stewart said, "I told Daryl that with the revolution and the threat of revolution, the United States Ambassador helped plot the February, nineteen and thirteen coup d'état in Mexico. Taft did not intervene, but President-elect Woodrow Wilson did after he was horrified by the murder of ousted President Madero. He made it a priority to stabilize the regime."

Richard said, "Globalists have always been ready to overthrow stable monarchies and dictatorships. They acted overtly and subversively by creating a revolution and disguising the effort as a human rights or a national sovereignty battle. They used the masses to do the fighting for the globalists and industrialists."

Pastor Richard said "Read Matthew twenty-four. Verse six says, 'You will hear of wars and rumors of wars, but see to it that you are not alarmed. Such things must happen, but the end is still to come. Nation will rise against nation, and kingdom will rise against kingdom."

Michael told Daryl, several times in the past, to read another verse out of Matthew twenty-four. He said, "Verse twenty-eight says, 'Where the carcass lies, there the eagles will gather.'"

Daryl looked around. Everything he could see that was American had the symbol of the eagle on it. Where the globalists needed control and security, a monarch was killed. There the eagles gathered.

At first, Daryl was thrilled to fly. The first time he got into the cockpit and heard the engine roar, thrusting wind into his face from the propeller he felt exhilarated. As they taxied down the runway and headed into the slight wind, Berge pulled on the throttle until they reached forty miles per hour and lifted off. He remembered how the bumpy runway was left behind as they lifted into a smooth airstream, suspended above the ground. They ascended to three thousand feet where roads became tan or gray threads, houses, cars and people appeared to be children's toys, laid out on a huge patchwork quilt. As they ascended, Daryl realized he would gain a wider perspective from up here.

He was amazed and grateful he was assigned to the Squadron rather than serving time. The other planes had a pilot and an assistant pilot. Daryl was the only "embedded" photographer assigned to the unit. Therefore, he was under stricter military supervision than any of the photographers who worked for regional news outlets or submitted their work to the Associated Press and the United Press Associations.

Daryl had a working knowledge of the mechanisms and the history of the "wire services" from his newspaper experience and from Richard's daily lesson and lectures. He understood how some of Richard's stories, like the train wreck, went out over the wire to any other news subscriber outlets. He knew Richard could print any stories from the wires.

Daryl reflected back on one of his lectures by the Editor-in-Chief, "The Associated Press grew out of the New York Associated Press and then it was revealed that the two organizations had entered into a secret agreement to share news and profits from selling the news. Melvin Stone who founded *Chicago Daily News* in eighteen seventy-five served as Associated Press General Manager. Stone had a reputation for accuracy, impartiality and integrity.

"The Western Associated Press was an Illinois Corporation when an Illinois Supreme Court decision in nineteen hundred stated that Associated Press was 'a public utility and operating in restraint of trade.' This ruling resulted in Associated Press's move from Chicago to New York where corporation laws were more favorable to the formations and operation of cooperatives."

Over supper, Daryl asked Berge, "How did the Squadron get to Texas?"

Berge said, "Back in nineteen and ten, First Lieutenant Benjamin D. Foulois spent a year learning to fly at Fort Sam Houston outside of San Antonio, Texas. He learned by writing letters to the Wright Brothers and claimed to be the only pilot who learned through correspondence. In March the War Department deployed nearly thirty thousand troops in response to the Mexican Revolution. Coincidentally, in the same month, the United States Congress appropriated one hundred and twenty-five thousand dollars as the first funds for military aviation. The funds were used to purchase five planes for the Signal Corps.

"Ideally, the squadron would have had twenty or thirty matching planes, with the standardized engines, gas tanks, and controls. That was not the case as the army had no idea how to budget for a flying squadron. Therefore, planes had to be ordered when the budget would allow. That meant two planes at a time for a total of only eight. The Squadron spent its time experimenting. They flew out over the Texas prairie and back, each time testing how far they could fly under varying conditions. The conditions did not vary much during the spring of nineteen and thirteen.

"The Signal Corp spent the next few weeks supporting the Maneuver Division until May tenth, when a fatal plane crash took the life of Lieutenant George E. M. Kelly. The post commander put a stop to flying at Sam Houston. The border clash had quieted, so the Maneuver Division had been dispersed until earlier this year, when border violence was renewed."

After a few weeks of taking off and flying over the same terrain, returning back to the base, recording results, processing photographs, writing articles and making adjustments, then taking off again, the flying became routine. During a warm May afternoon flight, Daryl found himself dozing off to the drone of the engine and the gentle swaying of the airplane.

When he awoke with a start, he was reminded of his dream the night he and Richard spent at Battleground. In the dream he dropped his camera. As he recovered the camera, he saw himself behind his camera, flying through the air. Until this moment, he did not remember the dream since a few days after returning from Battleground.

When they landed, he told Berge about the dream. "I think the dream when I dropped the camera and retrieved it was a premonition or harbinger. It gave me a glimpse of becoming a photographer and losing the privilege, then picking it back up before too much loss."

Vernon said, "Wow! Maybe God has His hand on us."

Daryl said, "I sure hope so!"

In June, the Squadron was transferred to San Diego, California, to form the Signal Corps Aviation School. During his time in San Diego, Darryl learned about three recent developments. Everybody, especially those in the armed forces, was talking about the European War being declared over the assassination of Archduke Franz Ferdinand of Austria-Hungary. He learned the Panama Canal had officially opened. He also learned of the development of a recent industrial advancement in the technology of electronic communications.

The teletypewriter was introduced in nineteen fourteen. It allowed typed messages to be sent to another place over wires or radio or radio waves. Although wire photos were primitive, using a photocell, it allowed photographs to be sent by wire so affiliates could finally print photographs from any place in the nation or world. A teletypewriter had a keyboard, a printer and a transmitter. As Daryl thought about the teletypewriter, he remembered Daniel's prophecy of a knowledge explosion Pastor Richard and Michael had talked about so many times.

Foulois worked to secure standardized supply trucks, equipment and supplies to make the unit mobile. The trucks were converted four wheel drive chassis for which the men built special bodies designed to transport them, along with equipment and supplies needed in the field. They converted one of the Jeffrey "Quad" one and one-half ton trucks to be a mobile machine shop that could make repairs in the field. He also purchased several hangar tents. His goal was to obtain a plane that could travel a minimum of forty miles per hour and achieve duration of four hours of flight.

They chose the Curtis Jay En-Two because it was streamlined, had frictionless controls, a positive fuel pump as opposed to gravity fed pump and a tachometer—the device that could measure the number of times the propellers revolved per minute of operation. The Corp moved around from Fort Sills, Oklahoma, and Fort Sam Houston in San Antonio, Texas. During this time, the Squadron experienced shortages in parts and equipment. Foulois had an ongoing battle with the Curtis Aeroplane Company over engines and crankshafts. He refused to accept some orders of parts until the problems were worked-out to his satisfaction.

Wilson campaigned in nineteen and twelve, vowing to keep the United States out of the European War, should it develop. Now that one was full blown "over there" Churchill and others wanted the United States to intervene. Germany did not want the United States involved.

Daryl was reading a copy of the *Watchman* sent by Richard. In a letter, Richard told Daryl that most of the newspapers were printing anti-German propaganda. He said most of the major media that was controlled by the Rockefeller-Morgan interests had gotten together and determined what the papers would print. He published a small statement that was sent out over the wire, but most papers refused to print it. Of the fifty newspapers slated to carry the notice, only the *Des Moines Register* and the *Wabash Watchman* ran it. The ad read:

NOTICE! TRAVELERS intending to embark on the Atlantic voyage are reminded that a state of war exists between Germany and her allies and Great Britain and her allies; that the zone of war includes the waters adjacent to the British Isles; that in accordance with formal notice given by the Imperial Government, vessels flying the flag of Great Britain, or any of her allies, are liable to destruction in those waters and that travelers sailing in the war zone on ships of Great Britain or her allies do so at their own risk.

Richard ran another story, part of which read:

On May 7, 1914, a German U-boat commander torpedoed the British liner Lusitania. The ship was en route from New York to Liverpool, England. Among the 1,950 passengers, 1,198 died. 128 Americans lost their lives.

There was also a controversy about a second explosion. The Germans claimed the torpedo did not sink the ship. Rather, the ship sank from a second explosion, which they attributed to the ship being used to transport war materials including explosives and ammunition. When the press requested the manifest of the ship, attorneys for Cunard Company argued the records were a matter of proprietary rights. No Congressional investigation was ever launched.

Conspiracy theorists were buzzing that the Lusitania was registered as an armed auxiliary by the British Admiralty. They also claimed that the Cunard Company was J.P. Morgan's closest competitor in the international shipping trust, which included two of Germany's largest shipping

lines and Britain's White Star Line, the owners of the
Titanic. Rumor had it that Morgan attempted to take over
the Cunard Company in 1902, but was blocked by British
Admiralty, as they wanted to keep Cunard out of foreign
control, in case her ships could be pressed into military
service in times of war. As always, follow the money.
When J.P. Morgan is involved, whatever the outcome, he
stands to profit.

Americans still did not want a war. Brigadier General John "Black
Jack" Pershing was willing to get American troops on the ground
and in the air in Europe as soon as possible. Until that might happen,
he wanted to build his aero squadron into the soundest flying unit
it could be. The problem was, there had never been a flying combat
unit in the United States. Developments were being made for the
European and Canadian flying squadrons while fighting a war.

Much to Wilson's dismay, Poncho Villa was already receiving
notoriety as a modern day Robin Hood. He was popular in the
newspapers. There had already been a documentary in nineteen and
twelve, named *Life of Villa*. A legend circulated about an incident
that occurred while filming a battle scene between rebel forces and
federal troop near Ojinaga. Allegedly, cameraman Charles Rosher
was captured by government troops. They brought Rosher before
the commanding general, claiming he was an escaped spy.

Rosher was sure he was about to be executed when the Mexican
general noticed Rosher's Masonic pin on his lapel. The general gave

a Masonic greeting, to which Rosher responded. The general was also a Mason and treated Rosher like a guest until he was later released after a deal was negotiated with the Mexican government for American troops to cross the border to pursue Villa.

On March ninth, nineteen and sixteen, Villa snuck across the border to Columbus, New Mexico and attacked the town and the Thirteenth Calvary Regiment. Before he retreated eight United States soldiers and ten residents of Columbus were killed. Wilson responded by Dispatching Pershing and ten thousand troops to pursue Villa.

On March twelfth, the Aero Squadron flew to Fort Sam Houston. The planes were dismantled and placed in crates. The squadron equipment, supplies and parts were also loaded onto flat cars. Foulois posted ten men with rifles on a flat car at the front of the train and ten men with pistols in the sleeping cars. He stated he was as just concerned about Americans interfering as he was about Mexican obstruction. The train was also accompanied by an infantry company with several boxcars of ammunition.

Pershing moved his troops forward. They moved quickly without encumbrances such as supply wagons. The Aero Squadron caught up with Pershing by flying short sorties of about twenty miles each. They were instructed not to engage in combat unless fired upon and then to use diversionary tactics as much as possible.

The men began to believe they were required to chase Villa, not to catch him. They were able to offer valuable reconnaissance advice as the columns were moving into unfamiliar territory, not quite sure which direction the rebel might have taken. The activity was constructive in refining the aircraft, chasing the rebel deep back into Mexico and providing realistic practical maneuvers for the Aero Squadron and troops. Preparation was always done in the eventuality that America would have the opportunity to fight in the European Theatre.

One situation occurred when Daryl accompanied Lieutenant Herbert A. Dargue on a reconnaissance flight which was forced down near Chihuahua City. While Dargue was making a few minor repairs, local residents began stoning the plane. Daryl jumped out and began taking pictures. He and the pilot noticed that the hostile crowd had calmed and quit throwing rocks when being photographed. Daryl continued to pose and click his camera long after he was out of film. Finally, the minor repairs were made and the two took off amidst a shower of rocks.

Daryl learned another lesson about the power of the press shortly after this. On April third, nineteen and sixteen, an article appeared in the *New York World*. The article claimed that officers were complaining about the problems with the Signal Corp. The problems involved deficiencies with the airplanes and in notifying officers of the Signal Corps who controlled army aviation. A quote included, "The aviators, mechanics, and assistants were more like family than any organization of the entire army."

From the War Department, General Scott wired Pershing to determine if any of his men had leaked the information. Daryl was called in to resolve whether he had written the article. He read it and admitted he had sent a letter home mentioning some of these problems, but had not written a formal article. Pershing, who backed his flyers, did not press the issue.

Pershing also knew that airing the problems of the Signal Corps would place pressure on Congress to release more funds to make improvements in America's military aviation program. Daryl did not mention the possibility that Richard might have written the article and sent it out over the wires. At least, he provided Richard with the exclusive he promised.

Daryl received a package from home. The label was written in Victoria's handwriting and the return address was from her and Stewart's home address. When he opened it, he found some chocolates, books, letters from Pastor Richard, Michael and Whitney and Stewart and Victoria and some copies of the *Wabash Watchman*. He looked through the *Watchman* for one of Richard's articles. This one was dated July seventh, nineteen sixteen, from the previous summer.

FINE LINE

Last week the circus came to town. Several of our readers were there. Of course, not all of our readers could attend as it was only a three day event and fell during the middle of the week. We had a triple dose of all that is American as we also celebrated Indiana's Centennial and Independence Day during the week. There were clowns, elephants, aerialists, performing animal acts and big cats.

Combining the circus parade with Indian's Centennial and Fourth of July parade was a great idea. This editor believes the combined events drew a larger crowd than each event would have individually. Possibly, the European War and the constant threat of our ever-increasing possibilities of becoming involved bring out a sense of patriotism. Perhaps the circus provided the same entertainment, distraction and excitement—the excitement of children seeing it for the first time; the nostalgic sense of adults revisiting the excitement they experienced as children. Even though this editor has been to the circus several times in his many years, there was still something new to see.

Personally speaking, I possibly had an epiphany while watching the young woman walk upon the wire. She exhibited beauty and grace. As I watched, I realized she existed between two worlds as she was suspended between the ground below and the big top above. She performed without the security of the safety net. Her focus was on the wire and on maintaining balance as she seemed unconcerned about the reality of the ground below. It was as if she was suspended only a foot above it.

I reflected back to the teachings and readings of my many years. The wire was the fine line we each walk. Some of us trudge along on the ground giving to the dictates of terrain, obstacles and pitfalls. I have had the privilege of observing those who seem to walk the wire. They live in this world, but seem to operate upon a different plane. A spiritual plane, if you will, bound to earth's gravity, but a little closer to heaven. Of course, unseen forces work to knock them off the wire, but they focus on balance, not the dangers, real or imagined.

I have not been what you might call a religious man, but I have recently examined my ways and realized we are all mortals. The fine line is defined by the Lord Jesus. He said, "The way is wide that leads to destruction, but the path that leads to life is narrow."

Daryl read the article and was quiet for a long time. He had a feeling that Richard knew something and was saying more than his words indicated.

Dog Fight

Chapter Thirty

FINISH LINE

Daryl realized he had completed his sentence and would be free to go whenever the Aero Squadron returned to the states. He could also go to war with some of the other men if he chose. Unless the United States entered the war, other men in the unit were considering how they would be going to Europe. Right now, he could not even think of a future. They began crossing the border to return to the United States on February sixth, nineteen hundred and seventeen.

Daryl decided to go to France. Until the American forces were sent, there were two ways to get to France. Daryl could go to Canada and enlist with the Royal Air Force or he could go to Boston and join the French Foreign Legion. On his way to Boston, he scheduled a stop in Williamsport for a weekend. He wrote ahead to tell Richard he had completed his task in Mexico.

When his train pulled into the depot, he was given a hero's welcome. There were American flags hanging on poles. There was a banner across the front of the building that said, "Welcome home, Daryl."

He saw Stewart and Victoria and their boys, appearing to be about half grown, Michael and Whitney, the Editor-in-Chief and Pastor Richard. Then he looked to the side and saw Sven and Heidi with their son and daughter, Stan and Katie. As he stepped out of the coach, everybody swarmed him and gave him hugs and handshakes. The smaller boys walked up and tugged on the coat tails of his uniform and stared at the insignias and epilates.

They told him a reception was scheduled at Mudlavia. As they drove out to the resort, he rode in Michael's car with Whitney and Richard. Stewart had a nineteen eleven Ford. He truly looked like a family man. Daryl realized how much he missed these people and this area. When they arrived at the resort, it seemed not as grand as it had in the earlier days. The buildings were still there and in good repair, yet there were not as many people as he remembered in the past. Instead of horse drawn carriages and buggies, the front lot was filled with cars.

Michael noticed that Daryl looked a little disappointed. He said, "Kramer claims doctors and the automobile have ruined Mudlavia."

Daryl smiled in acknowledgement. They all checked into their rooms. Stewart and Michael both argued over who would pay for the returning hero's room. They ended up splitting the bill. They instructed Daryl to check into his room and then go down to the basement to take a mud bath. They said they would meet for dinner. After his mud bath, shower and alcohol rubdown, Daryl went to his room and took a nap.

As he met his party for supper, he walked past a man in a wheelchair, who looked vaguely familiar. The man was hunched over and what hair remained was gray. Daryl recognized the voice from the baritone nasal twang. As Daryl walked past him, the man noticed his uniform and said, "A true patriot! Thank you for your service."

Daryl turned and faced the man directly and said, "Sir, you seem to be a little more cordial toward me in uniform than the last time we met."

The old man looked confused, almost shocked. He said. "Son, I'm not from around here. You must have me confused with somebody else."

Daryl said, "Mr. Lynchbaughm, the last time I saw you, you had me arrested and shipped from New York City during the Newsboys' strike. I was the Newsboy who sold you your paper every day."

Lynchbaughm looked down and mumbled, "Oh, oh, I can't seem to recall your perceptions of the scene."

Daryl moved on and joined the others at their table. At supper, he spent a great deal of time relaying the stories and adventures from the days with the Aero Squadron. Michael said, "Now Daryl, you've done more than your duty already in serving your country. If you just stay home, nobody will think less of you."

Stewart added, "Remember, Daryl, your sentence was only two years. You've already been in service over three years."

Daryl smiled. He said, "I'm grateful that you're watching out for me. I want to go to serve my country in France. I've come to realize how close you become as a unit. Sure, I got close to all of you when I lived in town. Richard has become like a grandfather to me. Michael, you have been like a father. Stewart and Pastor Richard are like older brothers. You all have your families and your livelihoods. I always felt like I was just hovering in and out of your lives.

"Being in a unit with the Aero Squadron was the first time I realized the focus and singularity of living in a group, fighting and working for a common cause. We were ensuring each other's survival."

Michael said, "I know the feeling. I still feel like some of the Rough Riders are my lifelong friends. You know the Germans are not going to be throwing rocks at you. They'll be shooting real artillery and bullets. They're playing for keeps."

They had a great feast, coffee and dessert. Daryl enjoyed the two full days at the resort and then shipped out. He ended up in the French Foreign Legion Lafayette Escadrille. They told him he could be a pilot, but that would take possibly four months of training. If he chose to use his skills as an aerial photographer, which they badly needed, he could begin immediately.

Although the corporate propaganda machine cranked on, the United States still refused to engage in another world police action. Ironically, the straw that broke the camel's back originated in Mexico, the country Pershing was policing. Daryl remembered what Michael told him, "Facts are negotiable, perceptions are not."

The element that added authenticity to the document was that it was allegedly intercepted as a communication and decoded. Arthur Zimmerman was acting German foreign secretary to Mexico in nineteen fourteen when he helped start the war by drafting a telegram that announced Germany's decision to support Austria-Hungary against Serbia, following the assassination of Archduke Ferdinand. The action so enraged Russia that it precipitated the war.

Daryl's newspaper instincts caused him to wonder why an acting foreign secretary in Mexico was announcing official German international policy. He also wondered why an individual's personal opinion was accepted as Germany's official policy on international affairs.

In a recent telegram, Zimmerman allegedly advised Mexican President Venustino Carranza that Germany was about to resume unrestricted submarine warfare. He also promised that in the event that the United States entered the war, Germany would assist Mexico "to regain by conquest her lost territory in Texas, Arizona, and New Mexico."

Antagonists claimed this telegram fit the profile of usual wartime diplomatic maneuvering. The fact that the telegram was an electronic transmission, not a legally signed document and was allegedly intercepted by British cryptographers created skepticism. They spent days deciphering the document before forwarding it to the American ambassador on February twenty-fifth. When it was released to the public on March first it was greeted with great skepticism.

Zimmerman was offered a chance to deny the authenticity of the document. On March third, at a Berlin news conference, a Hearst correspondent asked Zimmerman, "Of course Your Excellency will deny this story?"

Zimmerman inexplicably announced, "I cannot deny it. It is true."

If Zimmerman was attempting to draw the United States into the war, he gained his purpose, but what was his motive? Was he attempting to engage Mexico on our southern border? The "Hun" was denounced in the American newspapers. Wilson was forced to declare war on April sixth. On April fourteenth, passage of the War Loan Act authorized **ONE BILLION DOLLARS** in credit to the drained banks of the countries of the Allied Forces.

The members of the Flying Squadron learned that no American planes would be sent to Europe. The United States committed Black Jack Pershing and one hundred thousand infantry. Since America did not show much interest in flying, the Wright brothers had been selling their planes in Europe since nineteen and eight. The French were, therefore, far advanced in the field of aviation. Although attitudes and perceptions changed greatly during the three years of war, Americans viewed the aeroplane as a means of reconnaissance and communication more than a fighting machine.

As Daryl came to the table he overheard some of the pilots talking. "Tommy, reconnaissance fliers have a fifty percent chance of surviving the war."

Tommy said, "I know, but I can beat the odds."

One of them looked up and noticed Daryl. He attempted to alert Tommy to stop talking. "Tommy, I think this is somebody wanting to meet you."

Daryl said, "I'm looking for Tommy Hitchcock. I'm assigned to be his photographer."

The other men around the table had various reactions. One attempted to hide a smirk. He said, "I'm sorry."

Daryl repeated more loudly, "I'm looking for Tommy Hitchcock."

He said, "I heard you. I said, 'I'm sorry.'"

Another glanced at Daryl and then back at Tommy. Daryl stood there looking as if he was anticipating a serious response. Tommy, smiling his charming and disarming smile, said, "I'm Tommy Hitchcock."

Tommy told Daryl to sit down and have some food. As they talked, Daryl learned that Tommy played football, hockey and was a member of the crew team at St. Paul's School. He left school to join the Lafayette Esquadrille. Tommy and Daryl hit it off from the beginning. Tommy asked, "Do you have your equipment? I am heading up this afternoon."

Daryl was to use a fixed camera that was mounted over the side of the plane and operated from his seat. Since he had vast experience as a photographer, he also used his hand held camera to capture scenes other than grid patterns, troop placement and movement. They mounted his camera and stowed his equipment. Tommy told Daryl to go put his flight suit on and come back to the airstrip.

They taxied down the runway and were quickly airborne. Tommy and Daryl flew day after day from about six a.m. to eleven and then from two p.m. until about a half hour before dark. Tommy kept them just above the anti-aircraft barrages that were shot up. Both watched for fighter planes. They got into several close scrapes. After

Daryl was there for six weeks, he received his first package from home. There were some books, canned food items and copies of the *Watchman*. A handwritten note on top of the top paper, from April seventh, nineteen hundred and seventeen, said, "Daryl, I don't know how to tell you this. I will let Richard tell you himself:

THE END OF SELF

I have lived most of my life for myself. I have followed my inclinations and passions, marched to the tune of my own drum, and have never backed down from a good argument. I can honestly say I bear no malice toward any. I have publically admitted that I do not have many enemies, but my friends don't like me much either.

I have not been a religious man although I have believed in God most of my life. My greatest doubt came when my father faced his greatest disbelief after seeing the horrors people can impose upon other people. I only hope he regained his faith before meeting his Maker.

Believing in God and attempting to live right is not enough. The Lord says, "Unless a grain of wheat falls into the ground and dies, it is good for nothing. When it falls into the ground and sprouts, it produces ten, twenty even one hundred times its own self."

We all wish for immortality, but that is a form of self-aggrandizement. I truly hope I have influenced people throughout my life with my writing and eccentric living, at least by revealing that different perspectives to every situation are refreshing and may be enlightening.

Not many people would want to write their own obituary. Who else would do it but me? I only ask that you remember my final words and seek to make your life right with your Maker, the Lord God Jehovah, Jesus Christ and the Holy Spirit. Then my life will have mattered. If you are reading this now, understand that I have gone on to the great beyond with no fears and no regrets.

Daryl thought Richard would live forever. He at least thought he would see him again on this side of heaven. Richard had felt more like family than anybody since he could remember. The others were friends, to be sure, but he realized that he viewed Richard like a grandfather. Being in active duty afforded no time or opportunity to mourn adequately. One had to focus on daily tasks and staying alive. Being with strangers in a distant land did not help. The first inclination a person usually had was to attempt to get home. That was not possible in these circumstances.

One afternoon, as Tommy and Daryl were returning to the base, Tommy flew low over a village that stood, or most of which used to stand, between the base and the front line. There was some time left before dark so Tommy flew low and circled the town. As Daryl watched he saw small brick buildings that were close together. The buildings were three and four story homes or stores with apartments over them. Buildings in Europe were placed close together and stacked vertically to save the limited space. Each building had various degrees of destruction from large holes blown out by bombs and rockets to walls and roofs crumbling, leaving only vertical columns of brick that had once been a corner. He remembered his dream from Battleground and now understood the meaning.

When families have a member in a war, or communities have many young men serving overseas, life somehow goes on. Michael said, "The act of war is so uncivilized and strange to our way of thinking that we have to maintain a semblance of civilization at all cost. Man, in his limited capacity, regardless of political maneuvering or machinations, is unable to refrain from sacrificing their youth in wars. It seems those most in favor of war are those who have the least to lose personally and the most to gain politically and economically."

Three weeks later, a telegram arrived. The telegram simply stated:

> *"We regret to inform you that Daryl Daily, flying reconnaissance over France as a photographer has been reported shot down and missing over Germany. Mr. Daily served his country and the Allied Forces bravely."*
>
> *Georges Thenault, Commander Lafayette Escadrille.*

Stewart, Victoria, Michael, Whitney and Pastor Richard did the best they could, attempting to recover from Richard's death, and now this news about Daryl. They went on about their daily lives, always feeling the extreme sense of loss.

One Saturday afternoon, about six weeks later, a soldier in uniform stepped from the train in Williamsport. He walked the half mile to the house on Fall Street. He knocked on the door. Raymond, now in his early teens answered the door. "It's Uncle Daryl!"

Victoria came into the living room, already scolding Raymond, "I told you not to pretend you saw Daryl. He is…"

As she looked on the porch, she could see Daryl standing there smiling. She fainted. As Stewart, Michael and Whitney came into the living room to see what the commotion was, they all saw Daryl. Stewart assisted Victoria to her feet. They all embraced him simultaneously. They sat in the living room and sipped lemonade and iced tea.

Daryl spent hours and days describing his capture and escape. "Even though the boys fought valiantly, and attempted to draw enemy fire off of us, after the dog fight, our engine started smoking. Tommy signaled to me we were going down. He was able to glide into an open field surrounded by Germans who saw us coming down. They held us in temporary facilities for a few days and placed us on a train to a concentration camp.

"We jumped from the train behind German lines and walked for eight days to Switzerland. We had to hide during the day and move at night. I was thankful that Tommy was a good pilot and familiar with the terrain from the sky. That made recognition of land marks easier from the ground. Once you get an elevated perspective, finding your way is less difficult.

"As we were nearing Switzerland, I encountered an American soldier. He was obviously battle weary and shell-shocked. He was sitting in the trench hanging his head. He said, 'I came because I heard of the atrocities of the Huns, but they didn't bayonet babies and rape women. They were as human and civilized as we were.'"

With little support, or understanding from friends and family, soldiers attempted to return to civilian life as well as they could. Daryl knew that Michael understood the horrors of war. Daryl told Michael, "I still have night terrors. Sometimes I flinch or duck for cover when I hear familiar sounds, such as a backfire of a car or a plane flying overhead."

Michael agreed, "Sometimes, I still have those feelings."

Daryl said, "There is still the feeling of wondering whether my actions, directly or indirectly resulted in the death of another human being."

He still flew when possible. He took photographs for the paper and wrote stories. One day, on March first, nineteen and twenty, he was told to go to the resort. As he stood on Lovers leap, he looked down at the smoldering remains of Mudlavia. He realized the meaning of his other dream with the brick and smoldering wood corner constructions of three and four stories and charred chimneys. Mudlavia was lost. He wrote a small caption to his photograph:

LEAP OF FAITH

The Native American placed spiritual significance upon the convergence of rivers. The white settlers were burned out of their villages on the landing near the confluence of Pine Creek and the Wabash. The Indians allegedly cursed the settlers. Portions of the town and court house have burned on several occasions.

If confluences of rivers have spiritual significance, how much more do the causes of rivers have. Lovers Leap was formed by the convergence of three glaciers: the Prairie Glacier from Judyville; the Northern Glacier forming Pine Creek and the Northwestern Glacier from Lafayette; forming the Wabash River Valley. How ironic that Mudlavia poised right in front of Lovers Leap should burn on February twenty-ninth, Leap Day.

Daryl was also asked to chronicle his experience in the war. After talking to Michael for so many years and enjoying the company of being veterans of foreign wars, he could understand Michael's perspective a little better. He knew what it was to risk his life for his country and the quiet confidence that he did what he had to do. He also realized that those who glorified war were not the individuals who put their life on the line.

Daryl thought back on his persistent training provided by Richard. Although Richard attempted to encourage and train Daryl to be an independent and free thinker, Daryl constantly found himself wondering if Richard would share his perspective and opinions on different topics, or even if the Editor-in-Chief would be proud of him. Richard left a huge and continuing impact and legacy upon Daryl.

The Eighteenth Amendment passed in January, nineteen and eighteen and went into effect one year later. The law resulted in making the production, transportation, consumption or sale of alcohol illegal. Daryl knew firsthand that changing the law did not change people's beliefs and the enforcement of the law was going to be difficult, if not impossible. Frank Hanley died on August first, of nineteen and twenty, when his car was struck by a train. Daryl thought how much of a legend Governor Hanley had been in the little town of Williamsport and how he sought grander and more ambitious impact upon the state and nation. Daryl thought how Hanley left and only returned sporadically. He was brought to Hillside Cemetery, overlooking the Wabash, for his final resting place.

There was a cookout about three months later, over Memorial Day weekend. Victoria and Whitney decided to celebrate the ratification of the Nineteenth Amendment, even though it had passed Congress over a year earlier. Victoria said, "The founding fathers fought for life, liberty and the pursuit of happiness as all men were created equally. Yet, even as they passed this legislation, they owned slaves and viewed their women as property. The struggle is far from being over."

Whitney added, "Even though the Fourteenth Amendment was adopted in Eighteen Sixty Eight, Jim Crow laws, poll taxes and other forms of discrimination have kept people who were slaves or decedents of slaves from enjoying equal rights."

Daryl added, "I know firsthand that laws do not change people's morals or perspectives. We have had prohibition in Indiana for years, yet it did not deter me or others when there was a buck to be made. I am only glad I didn't get killed or jailed for a lengthy sentence. As it worked-out, getting into trouble with the law opened opportunities for me."

Pastor Richard said, "Daryl, getting into trouble got your attention. Repenting of your crimes, and turning to Jesus opened doors for you."

Sven said, "I do not know about dis changing auf people's perspectives. I only know dis country has allowed Heidi and me chances ve vould haf never known."

Daryl told Pastor Richard about the time they took the train up to Discovery. "A man who was offended by our conversation stated that he was a conservative and believed our founding fathers were Christian. Michael asked the man what he meant by being a Conservative. After he stormed out, we talked about the Pharisees killing Jesus and the prophets to maintain their earthly empires. We discussed the Islamic example from Dostoevsky and how a father in the Middle East could kill family members to keep them from converting to Christianity."

Whitney said, "I think sending missionaries to other countries would have a greater impact upon the women there if American women did not have to fight so hard for equality in our country. They would see that our faith matches our actions."

Stewart added, "The First Amendment of the Constitution states that it does not promote nor restrict any religion. We have freedom of religion, not freedom from religion."

Michael said, "So, there is no proof the founding fathers were Christian. Some of the monuments in Washington honor pagan traditions, religions, occult and mythology."

Richard said, "The need to believe the founding fathers were Christian is tantamount to stating, 'I am saved because my father attended church.'"

Stewart said, "The nation should be influenced by the prophets and the church rather than the other way around. I firmly believe if America had embraced the Azusa Street Revival and the move of the Holy Spirit, we might not have had to engage in the War to End all Wars."

Richard said, "It boils down to faith and acting upon your faith. Nobody is totally good or totally evil. Everybody is flawed and human. Even the good in people is not enough to get them into heaven. Depending upon the government for your faith is like seeking a sign. Those who seek a sign will not be given one. Jesus said:

> "An evil and adulterous generation seeketh after a sign; and there shall no sign be given it but the sign of Jonah the prophet: for as Jonah was three days and nights in the belly of the whale; so shall the Son of man be three days and nights in the heart of the earth. Then men of Nineveh shall stand up in judgment with this generation and shall condemn if: for they repented at the preaching of Jonah; and behold, a greater than Jonah is here. The queen of the south shall rise up in judgment with this generation, and shall condemn it: for she came from the ends of the earth to hear the wisdom of Solomon; and behold one greater than Solomon is here."

Pastor Richard said, "There is a fine line and a thin veil between what is said and what is done, what is professed and what is acted upon in belief. People either purpose to ask for the Lord's will and His kingdom to come or they directly or tacitly work to perpetuate the other kingdom."

There was a long reflective pause as each friend pondered these words and marveled at the many life experiences that fused them together. They realized how they shared a common belief that made the bond between them even stronger.

Victoria broke the silence asking Stewart, "How's the meat coming along?"

He replied, "Let's eat now, rather than offer a burnt sacrifice!"

ABOUT THE AUTHOR

uthor of *Woodcutter's Revival,* and the sequel, *Fine Line,* Jerry Slauter is a retired school teacher. He graduated from Ball State University with a Master of Arts degree in Education. Jerry has been very active in various political and educational groups. He has established, administered and taught in an alternative school in Knox, known as the ACE Program (Alternative and Continuing Education).

He completed administrative training and certification and advocated for fair treatment and voluntary professional development for teachers. His major focus has been on education, both in formal school settings and in chronicling the life lessons learned from living every day. He has owned and operated small businesses and managed or supervised in manufacturing and retail sales.

Jerry is a husband, father and grandfather. He loves to travel, write and work in his wood, metal and leather shops at home. He has become a certified gunsmith and built and uses a wood fired pizza oven.

If you would like for Jerry to visit and speak at your school, church or other organization, contact him at: jerrysworldsavings@me.com.

Jerry Slauter

ABOUT THE ILLUSTRATOR

Scott "Doc" Wiley has been illustrating since the age of three. He has always loved to hike in the Shenandoah Mountains and take photos of the splendor of nature.

Retired from the Army, Scott served as a tank commander and combat correspondent in Viet Nam. Scott also earned a Doctorate in Art Education from Ball State University. Scott illustrated portraits of Washington and Lincoln that hang in Tippecanoe County Courthouse in Lafayette, Indiana.

More recently, Scott has served three deployments to Afghanistan. He illustrated a portrait of Patton that hangs in the Army Chief Chaplain's Office in the Pentagon. It survived the attack of 9/11. "Scott...has a passion for American History and produces detailed realistic 'etched graphite' illustrations from historical photographs. Research precedes execution."

His current projects include History of Defense Warning/ "As You Were – Life in the Field of the 11th ACRVVC." He has recently completed illustrating *The Woodcutter's Revival* for long-time friend and author, Jerry Slauter. Scott spent over 360 hours of research, planning and drawing. He also spent several hours writing narratives for each illustration. The efforts are obvious as they are on display at http://wileystudio.smugmug.com

Scott "Doc" Wiley

PROMOTE
FINE LINE

If the *Fine Line* touched you or if you believe it might be of benefit to others, please share it.

You might already have ideas how to promote concepts on the Internet, such as FaceBook or Twitter. If you are enthusiastic about it, share your enthusiasm.

- Give the book as a gift.

- Write a book review for your local newspaper, magazines or web sites. Amazon reviews are particularly effective.

- Talk about the book in small groups at church, work or other social, professional or service groups.

- Give the book to church, educational, political or service organizational leaders.

- Offer several copies to women's shelter, prisons, rehabilitations homes, libraries, or any place people might enjoy a message of hope and healing.

- Post blogs in which you share part of the book that touched you the most, without giving away too much of the story. Leave a little of the intrigue so the reader can find their own experience with the woodcutter's Revival.

- If you own a business, store or shop, place a display of the books on the counter or display table to resell to customers. Books can be purchased in discounted, wholesale volumes.

- Send emails to your entire list with links to:

www.WoodCuttersRevival.com
http://wileystudio.smugmug.com

If you would like to contact the author to schedule a visit to your church or organization, go to:

www.WoodcuttersRevival.com

or email:

jerrysworldsavings@me.com